PRAISE FOR /

SEA CASTLE

"The plot comes together like the proverbial puzzle, each juicy piece adding a bit to a disturbing big picture. A savvy police procedural that executes a familiar formula with panache."

—*Kirkus Reviews*

"Mayne combines a brilliant, innovative female lead with a plausibly twisty plot. Kinsey Millhone fans will love McPherson."

—*Publishers Weekly* (starred review)

"Mayne creates a world that blends the crime writing of Michael Connelly with high-tech oceanography in his Underwater Investigation Unit series . . . The series never ceases to be fascinating, making characters sink or swim as lives are on the line and the story veers in unexpected directions. Required reading for any suspense fan."

—*Library Journal*

THE FINAL EQUINOX

"Science fiction fans will want to check this one out."

—*Publishers Weekly*

"A lively genre-hopping thriller written with panache."

—*Kirkus Reviews*

"This mix of science, thrills, and intrigue calls to mind the work of James Rollins and Michael Crichton. *The Final Equinox* has it all and shows why Mayne is one of the brightest talents working in the thriller field today."

—Bookreporter

MASTERMIND

"A passionate and thorough storyteller . . . Thriller fans will be well rewarded."

—*Publishers Weekly*

SEA STORM

"The fast-paced plot is filled to the brim with fascinating characters, and the locale is exceptional—both above and below the waterline. One doesn't have to be a nautical adventure fan to enjoy this nail-biter."

—*Publishers Weekly* (starred review)

"Strong pacing, lean prose, and maritime knowledge converge in this crackerjack thriller."

—*Kirkus Reviews*

"Fans of the Underwater Investigation Unit [series] will enjoy this installment, and those who love thrillers will like this too."

—*Library Journal*

BLACK CORAL

"A relentless nail-biter whether below or above the waterline. Even the setbacks are suspenseful."

—*Kirkus Reviews* (starred review)

"Mayne's portrayal of the Everglades ecosystem and its inhabitants serves as a fascinating backdrop for the detective work. Readers will hope the spunky Sloan returns soon."

—*Publishers Weekly*

"Andrew Mayne has more than a few tricks up his sleeve—he's an accomplished magician, deep-sea diver, and consultant, not to mention skilled in computer coding, developing educational tools, and of course, writing award-nominated bestselling fiction. They are impressive skills on their own, but when they combine? Abracadabra! It's magic . . . Such is the case in Mayne's latest series featuring Sloan McPherson, a Florida police diver with the Underwater Investigation Unit."

—*The Big Thrill*

"Andrew Mayne has dazzled readers across the globe with his thrillers featuring lead characters with fascinating backgrounds in crime forensics. The plots are complex, with meticulous attention to scientific and investigative detail—a tribute to the level of research and study Mayne puts into every novel. A world-renowned illusionist with thousands of passionate fans (who call themselves 'Mayniacs'), Mayne applies his skill with sleight of hand and visual distraction to his storytelling, thereby creating shocking twists and stunning denouements."

—Authorlink

"As I said before, a solid follow-up with thrilling action, especially the undersea scenes and the threat of Big Bill. Here's to more underwater adventures with the UIU."

—Red Carpet Crash

"As with the series debut, this book moved along well and never lost its momentum. With a great plot and strong narrative, Mayne pulls the reader in from the opening pages and never lets up. He develops the plot well with his strong dialogue and uses shorter chapters to keep the flow throughout. While I know little about diving, Mayne bridged that gap effectively for me and kept things easy to comprehend for the layperson. I am eager to see what is to come, as the third novel in the series was just announced. It's sure to be just as captivating as this one!"

—*Mystery & Suspense Magazine*

"Mayne creates a thrilling plot with likable yet flawed characters . . . Fans of detective series will enjoy seeing where the next episodes take us."

—Bookreporter

"Former illusionist and now bestselling author Andrew Mayne used to have a cable series entitled *Don't Trust Andrew Mayne*. If you take that same recommendation and apply it to his writing, you will have some idea of the games you are in for with his latest novel, titled *Black Coral*. Just when you think you might have things figured out, Andrew Mayne pulls the rug out from under you and leaves you reeling in fits of delight."

—Criminal Element

"The pages are packed with colorful characters . . . its shenanigans, dark humor, and low view of human foibles should appeal to fans of Carl Hiaasen and John D. MacDonald."

—*Star News*

THE GIRL BENEATH THE SEA

"Distinctive characters and a genuinely thrilling finale . . . Readers will look forward to Sloan's further adventures."

—*Publishers Weekly*

"Mayne writes with a clipped narrative style that gives the story rapid-fire propulsion, and he populates the narrative with a rogue's gallery of engaging characters . . . [A] winning new series with a complicated female protagonist that combines police procedural with adventure story and mixes the styles of Lee Child and Clive Cussler."

—*Library Journal*

"Sloan McPherson is a great, gutsy, and resourceful character."

—Authorlink

"Sloan McPherson is one heck of a woman . . . *The Girl Beneath the Sea* is an action-packed mystery that takes you all over Florida in search of answers."

—Long and Short Reviews

"The female lead is a resourceful, powerful woman, and we're already looking forward to hearing more about her in the future Underwater Investigation Unit novels."

—Yahoo!

"*The Girl Beneath the Sea* continuously dives deeper and deeper until you no longer know whom Sloan can trust. This is a terrific entry in a new and unique series."

—Criminal Element

THE NATURALIST

"[A] smoothly written suspense novel from Thriller Award finalist Mayne . . . The action builds to [an] . . . exciting confrontation between Cray and his foe, and scientific detail lends verisimilitude."

—*Publishers Weekly*

NIGHT
OWL

Other Titles by Andrew Mayne

Underwater Investigation Unit Series

Sea Castle
Sea Storm
Black Coral
The Girl Beneath the Sea

Theo Cray and Jessica Blackwood Series

The Final Equinox
Mastermind

Theo Cray Series

Dark Pattern
Murder Theory
Looking Glass
The Naturalist

Jessica Blackwood Series

Black Fall
Name of the Devil
Angel Killer

The Chronological Man Series

The Monster in the Mist
The Martian Emperor

NIGHT OWL

A TRASKER THRILLER

ANDREW MAYNE

THOMAS & MERCER

Text copyright © 2023 by Andrew Mayne
All rights reserved.

No part of this book may be reproduced, or stored in a retrieval system, or transmitted in any form or by any means, electronic, mechanical, photocopying, recording, or otherwise, without express written permission of the publisher.

Published by Thomas & Mercer, Seattle

www.apub.com

Amazon, the Amazon logo, and Thomas & Mercer are trademarks of Amazon.com, Inc., or its affiliates.

ISBN-13: 9781662506437 (paperback)
ISBN-13: 9781662506444 (digital)

Cover design by Shasti O'Leary Soudant
Cover image: © DougLemke / Getty; © Irin Fierce / Shutterstock

Printed in the United States of America

NIGHT
OWL

PROLOGUE

Her smile was made sincere by her remarkable restraint. From the curl of her lips to the flush remaining in her cheeks, she had been experiencing perfect joy at the moment the projectile went through her forehead.

Unfortunately, the smile posed a small inconvenience for Adrik. He set his phone down with the camera still running in a patch of dirt that hadn't been stained by the woman's blood or that of her boyfriend, the young lieutenant lying next to her.

He tried to push the cheek muscles down and mold the face into a more natural expression. He'd done it before but still marveled at the way morticians could turn even the most traumatic grimace into the very image of serenity.

"What the hell are you doing?" asked Luka as he climbed down from the fire escape with his rifle slung over his shoulder.

"Fixing her face. She looks happy," Adrik told him.

Luka looked out into the small industrial area surrounding the building. "We should all be so lucky. Take the photo and let's go."

"You know the man only gave us five hundred euros for the last one, and she was smiling too. I tell you he's doing it intentionally."

"She was an old woman. We probably did her family a favor."

Adrik continued to work on the face, then sat back in satisfaction. "See?"

Luka squatted by Adrik and glanced at the head. "She looks like she's trying to say something."

"Exactly. Serious expression equals more money next time."

He took her photo, then uploaded it in an application with green-on-black text and the logo of a crimson skull in the corner. A moment later, a notification popped up.

He held the phone up for Luka. "See? Nine hundred for the woman. Five thousand for the drone pilot. I told you. Presentation is everything."

Luka stood. "Two thousand here, five hundred there. Smiles or no smiles, I'm tired of these shit bounties."

"We could always go back to Uncle Volo," said Adrik.

"And throw more old men out of hospital windows?" Luka tapped the weapon slung over his shoulder and pointed at the phone. "This is the future. Put a notice up. Raise our price. Tell them we'll work anywhere."

"Just like that? You think it's that easy? Every scum from here to Kamchatka is offering himself up for hire," said Adrik.

"Put her photo up. Put his. Put all of them. Even the photos from Chechnya. Advertise."

"Advertise?" Adrik laughed. "Like we're some internet company selling old aircraft parts?"

"An ad's an ad. Someone sees it, presses a button. We do something. They pay us. What's the difference if we responded to their listing or put one up ourselves?"

"Advertise . . . ?" Adrik asked again.

"Advertise," said his cousin.

BETWEEN THE LINES

If you spend too much time being professionally suspicious and cataloging away every significant detail in a mental filing cabinet, it becomes hard to not do that in your personal life as well. Like how I'm at a party right now and can't help noticing that the two men standing at the table to my left are on their phones texting and occasionally grinning at one another. Presumably they're chatting with a third party—or else they're even more socially awkward than the other scientists and engineers that make up half the people in this hangar.

My hand touches the tattered copy of H. G. Wells's *The Time Machine* in my jacket pocket, and I mentally place the two men and a third person—in hologram form, with masks over their faces—in the Time Traveller's study, which is a room in my personal memory palace. I put them away from the door, to the right of the fireplace. Since I don't know how many more items I'll be adding, I shrink them down to almost mouse size, tucked in the corner, still chatting away.

On the other side of my imaginary room's fireplace, I erect a tiny bar with a mouse bartender serving another mouse. The second mouse has tattoos on its arms, like the man standing at the bar right now, next to the older couple that appears to be bickering in hushed tones. I add two cartoon mice to represent them and insert a dialogue bubble full of angry symbols.

I shake my head at my memory work—actually, I don't shake it. Those tells were trained out of me a long time ago. Instead, I give a mental shrug.

I've been retired—truly retired and not just retired "officially"—for almost a year, and it's still hard to let things go and be a normal person, enjoying things . . . normally.

Part of the problem is that my little tricks are deeply ingrained. And tricks are what they are. I have a terrible memory. I have no choice but to use books and other mental devices to keep track of things.

Memory palaces constructed from imaginary architecture are of no use to me. I need a real place, or a map, in which to file memories away. I could forget the entire east wing of a memory palace that I conjured up as easily as the reason why I walked into the kitchen. Books, maps, and places I've been are real and not so easy to forget.

Ten years from now, if I open a copy of *The Time Machine*, it will begin, as ever, in the Time Traveller's study, and my mind will begin to roam around the room (starting with the corners), and I'll remember all the things I stashed away as clearly as I do now.

Rebecca, the woman in the black dress with the clipboard who is still standing by the entrance of the hangar, also stands at the doorway to the Time Traveller's study. When I noticed another side entrance that caterers and staff were walking in and out of, I added a small door on the study's wall to the left, between the bookcases.

The DJ, playing techno music loud enough to keep the energy going but not so loud as to prevent conversation, perches in miniature on top of the mantel above the fireplace.

And so on . . . everything and everyone stored as I notice them.

When I'm done using the book, it'll go on a shelf in my office along with several hundred others, most full of useless details, others containing professional secrets never to be told.

For example, inside Jules Verne's *Journey to the Center of the Earth*, I once squirreled away a memory in Lidenbrock's study, next to the runic map: a bowl of kimchi with an iPhone and an Android phone. This visualization described the South Korean trade representative I met at a consulate party in Berlin who made a show of using his Samsung phone but would slink off to a corner to text on an iPhone. This little detail led to the discovery that the South Koreans believed they'd been hacked by the Chinese but were too embarrassed to tell US intelligence. At least 99.99999 percent of the memories I store end up being useless. But the .00001 that aren't make all the difference.

Tonight, my pockets contain items left behind by people, which I've casually gathered—a matchbook from the Sea Breeze Resort, a business card for J. S. Kleinfellow, who describes himself as an angel investor in the Bay Area but has a Santa Fe area code, and a ballpoint pen with the words AXWELL AVIONICS printed on the side.

If I were on assignment, these items would be put into a plastic bag and shoved into a file box. Since I'm not, I'll throw them in the trash when I get home and then sit in the dark and drink a beer and think about my son.

Jason is the reason I'm here.

When people die in movies, the filmmakers gloss over little details, like trying to decide when the funeral will be or how to cancel the deceased's cell phone bill.

Kathy and I thought we'd had all those details covered, but then we got a call from the security office at Southwestern Technical, Jason's college.

They informed us that Jason's truck was still parked on campus and needed to be moved.

He'd died in a car accident in someone else's vehicle, so the disposition of my son's vehicle was the furthest thing from my mind. I'd barely registered that he even had a truck—one of many details of his life that I was oblivious to.

I have a cordial relationship with Kathy, Jason's mother and my ex-wife, and she's kept me informed about many things that Jason didn't share with me. But despite her updates, I missed out on a lot.

Jason was never cold or distant with me. He was simply quiet. He'd patiently listen to me talk about something, but he never saw my pauses as an invitation to add to the conversation.

If I asked about girlfriends, he'd openly tell me about the latest girl he was seeing, her family, and other biographical details. It wasn't that he was withholding; he just wasn't forthcoming.

I noticed this when he was young: Jason would be talkative with Kathy, but when I came around, he tended to go quiet.

When I asked Kathy about it, she explained that Jason simply liked to listen to me. I didn't know what that meant. My relationship with my own father was basically nonexistent. I was the by-product of a tryst with my mother while he was married to someone else. When I was a teenager, I spent a few summers at his house in the Hamptons with my half siblings. They were accepting and treated me like a cousin—of which they had dozens—but my father was awkward around me. I could fit all our meaningful conversations into the margins of the first five pages of *The Time Machine*.

I never understood the relationship he had with my mother. But then again, Mom is like few other mothers, complicated and mysterious in ways I still can't fathom. Still, we talk far more than Jason and I ever did.

I think that's what makes it hard to accept that Jason is gone. When I retired, I was hoping to spend more time with him. We had a trip to Europe planned, and I was going to make regular visits to his college. I planned to make up for all the lost time—until I got the call from Kathy and found out there was no time left.

When we learned about the truck, I decided to drive it back from New Mexico to my house in California, then decide what to do.

For some reason, I expected that driving his truck would somehow be cathartic.

It wasn't.

In the strange way that life works, it led me here—to this loud party in an airplane hangar in Mojave that my new acquaintance, Kylie Connor, insisted I attend.

I knew who Kylie Connor was when I first met her, but I didn't realize the young woman who offered to help me change the flat tire on Jason's truck *was* Kylie Connor.

Connor's name pops up in the news feeds I follow relating to certain tech industries. She was a media-shy entrepreneur who created a business-to-business platform for industrial equipment, then pivoted to aerospace—her original course of study—and created a mysterious start-up that there's next to no information about.

Publicly she's described as a brilliant young billionaire.

I know her only as a young woman who made a simple but kind gesture while I was wrestling with my grief and in need.

I don't know how long she saw me struggle with the tire. I can normally fix a flat in a few minutes, but Jason's truck didn't have a spare, and removing the tire—interrupted by random moments of guilt—made me lose my balance as I squatted, forcing me to sit on my ass until I felt strong enough to wrestle the next lug nut free.

Kylie drove me to Walmart in her '72 Camaro so I could pick up a tire repair kit. On the way, I learned that she was visiting the college because she was an alumna and made regular drop-ins to the engineering program to take questions and scout for talent.

I only offered that I was visiting from out of state. I couldn't bring myself to explain the circumstances. I was vague about what I did professionally—something I'm practiced at doing—and she didn't pry.

It was a casual conversation. There was nothing profound about it. But still, watching the way Kylie thought over everything before responding and treated even the most trivial questions with seriousness, I could tell there was something special about that woman.

When I got the email invite from Kylie, I was a little surprised. I was fairly certain I hadn't given her my email address. When I got the call from her assistant, I was even more taken aback. It was an unlisted number. Only a handful of people had it.

How she got it was a mystery to me.

What really stood out was what her assistant Michael said on the phone. While Kylie's email was polite and brief, Michael's pitch was more determined.

"You would be doing Kylie a *tremendous* favor if you came," he said.

If that didn't carry enough weight, the offer to fly me on a chartered jet the hundred miles from Pasadena to Mojave did.

Kylie's email had been enough to get me here. The insistence from her assistant had me questioning her motive.

She's ten years older than my son was, and I don't think their paths would have crossed—as far as I know. Beyond that, I have no reason as to why she requested my presence.

I turn around at the sound of cheering and applause and see Kylie enter through that side service door. She's dressed in a black bomber jacket with a logo on the side that matches the one on the hangar—a cloud with an arrow bursting through it.

She scans the room and spots me. Then heads straight my way.

As she strides in my direction, she nods at the many people trying to get her attention. They pull away when they see she's on a mission. A slightly tipsy man in an untucked shirt holding a beer steps in her path to say something; she dodges him sideways and keeps coming.

I've seen such purposeful strides before. Something is up. Something serious.

"Mr. Trasker, thank you for coming," she says as she offers me her hand.

Her grip is deceptively strong. Kylie stands only a few inches over five feet and is built like a gymnast.

A man in a black shirt with an earpiece comes up and whispers something to her. I catch the words ". . . fueling starts in eight minutes . . ."

She checks her watch, then looks at me. "Can we talk?"

THREAT RISK

Kylie leads me to a large office in the rear of the hangar. I place the room in the hallway near the Time Traveller's study. In it, Kylie has her back to a whiteboard with a bunch of equations that I can't even begin to understand.

"Trasker, this is Martin. He's head of systems," says Kylie.

Martin, a young man in his early thirties wearing a blue zippered hoodie, nods to me.

Kylie indicates a woman in her early forties wearing an elegant dark-gray dress. "This is Morena. She's our legal adviser."

Morena gives me a small grin.

"Over there, Bianca. She heads comms," explains Kylie.

A tall woman in another classy dress glances up from her phone.

"And this is Wayne. He's head of propulsion." Kylie waves to the last person I haven't met.

Wayne, older, but not quite as old as me, gives me a nod.

"You heard about Trasker," Kylie tells the group by way of introduction.

I nod, wanting to ask what they've heard, but the group keeps quiet.

Kylie checks her watch. "We have five minutes to decide. Go or no go?"

"Go," says Wayne.

"Let's do it," says Bianca. "The live stream is over five hundred thousand viewers. We have the *Journal* and *Post* here. If you want to make a splash, this is the time."

Kylie looks at Martin. "What do you say?"

Martin crosses his arms and stares at the floor as if he's trying to see the answer beneath it with X-ray vision.

"I don't like it," he says after a long moment.

"What don't you like?" asks Wayne, a bit aggressively.

"Just a feeling. Things don't feel right," Martin responds.

"A feeling? Are you fucking serious?" Wayne holds his fingers an inch apart. "We're this close to a technical revolution. Tell me what bothers you. My engines?"

"Well, they're not *your* engines," says Martin.

"Now is not the time to be pedantic. We've been over this for weeks. What is it?"

During this exchange, I watch Kylie. She in turn watches the two men argue, then observes me.

I have no idea what the hell I have walked into here.

There's a knock at the door and a man enters, pulling a woman by the arm.

He's in his midsixties. She appears to be a little younger. He's wearing a suit and she a formal dress.

"I thought I'd knock first. Your mother and I wanted to wish you luck," says the man. "Hey, Wayne! Hey, Martin!"

"Thank you, Evan," says Kylie. "Mr. Trasker, this is my mother, Trisha. This is her husband, Evan Fimley."

I can tell Kylie isn't happy with the intrusion, but she handles it so smoothly that I don't think anyone else notices.

"A pleasure to meet you," I reply.

"Are you a VC?" Fimley asks me.

I'm dressed in a sweater and have reading glasses hanging around my neck. In this mostly young crowd, I could see how my formally casual attire and gray temples might make me look like a venture capitalist.

In political circles I blend in to the background when I'm dressed like this. The reading glasses are an affectation I started using in my thirties when I observed that we assign unusually high amounts of trust to people with reading glasses around their necks.

I try to choose my words in a way that will have the least impact.

"I'm just a friend," I reply.

"Oh. Well, good to meet you," says Evan. "You'll have to give me your card when you have a chance. Things are moving so fast. I wish I was still an engineer."

"Hey, guys," Kylie tells them, "we gotta go over a few things. I'll talk to you after."

"Sorry to bother you," replies Trisha.

"I'm here if you need me," says Evan before being escorted out the door by Kylie's mom.

I catch the eye roll from Wayne at the edge of my sight line. I put him in the corner of the Time Traveller's foyer with a large animated eye-roll emoji on his chest.

"Why not put your stepdad in it?" asks Wayne. "I'm sure he'd love to."

Kylie shakes her head. "Don't tempt me. Anyway. Mr. Trasker . . . ?"

"Brad, please," I reply. I respect her formality, but I prefer using my first name. It makes me harder to find. For one, "Brad" isn't even my legal name. I chose it to add another layer of obscurity so that people like me have trouble finding out about me.

"Go? No go?" she asks.

"I have no idea what we're talking about here," I reply.

"Really?" She seems surprised. "I thought you'd have dug around when you got the invite."

"You overestimated my resourcefulness."

"I doubt that," she says.

If I were on a job or something adjacent, I would have done my homework and talked to people in my network. Since this was a casual encounter and I'm trying very hard to behave like a civilian, I didn't approach this with professional scrutiny.

Had I been more suspicious than curious, I would have called Ben Khartoum and asked him to look into it. He would have called back an hour later with everything from the guest list to the 23andMe genetic profile of the chef who made the salmon crackers.

Not a joke.

"Okay, here's the TLDR: We've built a hydrogen-powered jet. You may have seen the solar panels in the desert? That powers the hydrogen-cracking plant that produced the hydrogen," she tells me.

"At a much greater energy expenditure than using a natural-gas plant," says Wayne, sounding frustrated.

"It's part of the plan, Wayne. But that's not the point. The key part here is the engine. We think we can scale it to production for less than it would cost to produce a conventional engine," she explains.

"Not to mention the containment systems," adds Martin. "They're pretty key too."

"Right. Hydrogen is a pain in the ass to store. We have some new technology that makes that a lot easier. It's what I studied in college. Anyway, we built the engines and the plane. Also, the plane is completely automated. But that's not a big deal, because that's been done for forty years."

"That's great," I reply. "So what do you want from me?"

"We think it would be awesome if Kylie flew on the inaugural flight," says Bianca.

"Fly on an experimental plane?" I ask.

"We've secretly tested the plane on more than one hundred flights," says Wayne. "We've had an FAA experimental rating for the last ten flights but declined to put anyone on it."

"Why not a test pilot?" I ask.

"There's no pilot required," replies Kylie. "A monkey could fly it."

"Why not a monkey?" I ask.

"Mm. Bad optics," replies Bianca.

Am I an observer or a participant? Time to decide.

Kylie is studying me. She wants me to decide. Although nobody would look at her and say she looks worried, her actions tell me otherwise.

"I was joking about the monkey. Anyway, if I understand, you all are trying to figure out if you should put the head of your company, the person who signs your checks and the brains behind all of this, into an experimental aircraft."

"Basically," says Wayne.

I think back to when Kylie saw me hunched over the tire, struggling with lug nuts. Internally dealing with what it meant to lose Jason.

"Are you out of your goddamn minds?"

"Somebody has to be first," says Kylie.

"Not today. The mere fact that we're having the discussion should be enough to tell you that," I argue.

Wayne makes an audible sigh. "Every project has its little quirks, and we have our own gremlin. One time I was in Boca Chica and—"

I cut him off. "Gremlin?"

"An expression. Just the normal stuff that gets you spooked if you make too much out of nothing," says Wayne.

"Kylie, can you elaborate?"

"One of our engineers is missing, and we have some other issues," she explains.

"Hell no," I say after placing a gremlin on the table under an over-turned glass in the Time Traveller's study and creating an empty circle with a spotlight illuminating the place where Kylie's missing engineer should be standing.

"Remind me who the fuck you are?" asks Wayne.

13

"Seriously," adds Bianca. "Why is he here? Other than the fact he looks like Kevin Costner."

"He's a friend," says Kylie, as if that's all there is to be said.

I don't follow up with my résumé—although it's now clear to me that Kylie has some idea of who I am.

"Putting anyone on this plane when there's this much hesitation is a bad idea." I point to Martin. "Listen to your systems guy. It's not his job to explain every detail. It's to see if everything feels right. Does it?"

"No, no it doesn't," he replies.

"What about the rollout and flight with no passenger?" asks Wayne. "We've done that a lot."

"With Watkins gone, I'm not sure," says Martin.

"He's covered," replies Wayne. "Come on, Kylie."

"We gotta show 'em *something*," says Bianca.

"Fine," says Kylie. "Let's do it."

I'm about to say something but keep my mouth shut when I see the determination on her face.

I've kept my mouth shut in moments like this before.

I've almost always regretted it.

AIR SHOW

The Sparrow, a sleek silver plane that looks like something out of a science fiction movie, is rolled out of the night and into the glow of the floodlights in front of the hangar.

The crowd goes wild and pushes up against the guardrails separating the party in the hangar from the tarmac. There's at least three hundred feet between the craft and the crowd, but the lighting and the other vintage airplanes at the facility create the illusion of it being much closer. Venting steam caught in the light makes the plane look like a mechanical dragon belching smoke.

I'm in a roped-off section to the right of the hangar in a small crowd with a few other people whose names I don't know. Two of the men are dressed similarly to me; I take them for investors.

On the opposite side of the hangar door is another section with a group of folks who look like they all work at Kylie's company, Wind Aerospace.

I take a photo of the crowd but make it look like I'm snapping a selfie.

"You in aerospace?" asks Evan Fimley, Kylie's stepfather, who appeared out of nowhere.

"No, nothing exciting like that."

Fimley seems friendly enough, despite his impulse to dig up more about me.

Clearly, Kylie didn't share everything about me with him. I shouldn't be surprised. It's not like my entire career's buried under some government office in Virginia. People talk.

Which leads me to believe that Kylie has people who talk to people in the know. It makes sense, now that I have a fuller picture of what she's up to out here. She would have to be in contact with US defense and intelligence agencies, because another term for a fully autonomous jet-powered craft is "cruise missile."

You don't go building something like the Sparrow without a lot of oversight from three-initial agencies and the Pentagon.

I've already spotted four people I'm sure are in the air force, despite their civilian clothes. I put them on the far-right corner of the table where the Time Traveller has set the time machine.

The Time Traveller's study is becoming a bit crowded, but I still have space on the bookshelves and in the chairs and fireplace that I can fill before I need to move into his workshop.

Kylie, who sits inside the replica of the time machine in my literary construct, is walking toward a spot midway between the crowd and the Sparrow.

Cameras flash and a documentary crew moves in closer.

"Thank you for coming," she begins, speaking on a public-address system. "For many of you this is a complete mystery—but I think our location may have clued you in. What you see before you is the result of the hard work of our team and something that I hope will make aviation globally accessible." She pauses. "I hate speeches. So I'll put it like this: I worked on a well project when I was in high school, and it took me to places where people didn't have clean water, let alone the ability to travel halfway around the world like I could. Over five billion people have never been on an airplane. The cost of what we consider a cheap ticket is a year's salary for many.

"When I got my pilot's license, I realized how much flying makes the world smaller in all the best ways. I want everyone to have that.

"And to make that happen, we have to rethink the environmental impact of aviation. We can't tell the rest of the world that this is something only people in the developed world get to do.

"And that's why we're here. We want to make that a reality. One step at a time," she explains.

The crowd applauds and cheers. I clap along too, but I'm a little more cynical. I've been to countless events where ambitious people have laid out their visions for how to make the world better. Politicians talking about clean energy. Industrialists explaining how they'll transform society. Some were even sincere, but almost all were idealists without a chance of making their dream happen.

I don't doubt Kylie or her capabilities. It's the world I have questions about.

Kylie walks to the Sparrow, continuing her address.

"You may have noticed the venting. That's the boil-off from the hydrogen and liquid oxygen. When the thrusters burn, you'll see a clean flame completely free of CO_2.

"Hydrogen jet engines are nothing new. What we think makes this special is the materials and the way we've been able to—" Kylie's words are cut off.

First there's a loud ping, then a hiss.

Next comes a fireball.

I watch Kylie's body turn into a silhouette as she's engulfed in a blazing wall of fire.

The fireball doesn't reach the crowd, but the boom and the concussion slap everyone in the front rows like a thunderclap.

Most of the people around me are knocked off balance, but I was already in a sideways stance and kept my footing.

The blast of hot air feels like an oven door has been thrown open. People are screaming and running. I am too—well, I'm running. Running to where I last saw Kylie.

Burning pieces of the aircraft litter the tarmac. I weave my way through them.

In the distance, the fuselage is still on fire.

"Kylie!" I shout over the ringing in my ears.

I run past something, then realize it's Kylie, crumpled into a ball.

The satin on her jacket is singed and smoking.

"Are you okay?" I yell.

Kylie untucks from her curled-up position. There are scratches across her face, and her eyes look dazed.

"We need to get you to—" I never make it to "hospital."

Kylie's on her feet, her daze gone.

"My mom?" she asks.

"She was back by the bar," I recall from my last glance into the hangar. They were bickering again in the same spot as when I'd first noticed them at the party.

Kylie glances at one of the fire trucks that had been on the tarmac as a precaution. The fire crew is frantically unspooling hoses.

She turns to her team and begins shouting orders. "Make sure the Mojave fire station is sending all their trucks and EMTs! Then call the hospital and tell them what's coming! Also notify Edwards and see how many medical helicopters they can get here! Got it?" She doesn't ask. She tells.

"Affirmative," I shout over the ringing and sounds of sirens.

Kylie runs into the crowd and starts checking people, clasping shoulders, making eye contact, and seeing who needs attention.

I don't see any physical injuries, only the shell-shocked look in the attendees' eyes. We were pretty far away from the blast, although it didn't feel like it.

I suspect there will be a few sprained ankles from people running and tripping as they tried to get away.

The only person in real danger was Kylie.

The fact that she survived is a miracle.

I think back to the moment I saw the fireball—which now sits conveniently in the fireplace in the Time Traveller's study . . .

Kylie's silhouette started to turn the moment I heard the pinging sound.

That was her warning. The engineering part of her brain knew that sound was out of the ordinary and completed the calculation in the blink of an eye.

Kylie was turning and ducking before the fireball even began. She knew—or at least her subconscious detected—what was coming next.

BLAST RADIUS

Kylie has her head down on the conference room table. It's the first time I've seen her stop to take a mental break in the ten hours since the Sparrow exploded. She's been on the phone with everyone from the FAA to the family of one of her employees who was almost as close to the explosion as she was.

Red Quanto, a Wind Aerospace technician who was setting up observation equipment at the edge of the danger zone, was blasted across the tarmac. His overalls were still smoking when we reached him. Fortunately, his burns were relatively minor, and he was the only one who required an overnight stay at the hospital.

Still, Kylie waited until she was certain he was okay before leaving him at the hospital. From the hallway, I heard Quanto joking with her about there being easier ways to fire him.

She laughed and kept up a lighthearted demeanor until she was on the other side of the door. She knew it was dumb luck that she wasn't helping his family make funeral arrangements.

I don't know if she realizes how much that dumb luck extended her way. She could have been in a hospital bed like his or worse.

We'd driven to the hospital, chasing after the ambulance in her yellow-and-black Camaro, the same one she drove me in to pick up a tire repair kit for Jason's truck.

Kylie and her car have a lot in common, though the full story wasn't apparent from the inside. When I'd mentioned how quiet the car was, she pointed out the noise-canceling insulation that allowed you to feel the muscle car's vibrations while not suffering its racket.

"I know I'm a hypocrite for driving a gas-powered car," she'd told me. "I use an electric for my daily commute, but on long drives, this helps me think."

It was a twelve-hour drive from Mojave to my son's college. I can't imagine many other billionaires—especially billionaire pilots—having the patience for that.

Kylie's phone buzzes, and she lifts her head from the table to check it. Wayne and Bianca are seated at the other end of the conference table, busy on their own phones.

Martin is presumably out on the tarmac, helping document the wreckage and taking photographs for analysis later on. While we were at the hospital, the guests dispersed as more investigators arrived on the scene.

"We've got Scott Lander coming in from our firm in DC," says Morena. "He'll be able to deal with the FAA and everyone else. I'll draft a formal letter, and we should also send an email to all the guests reminding them of their NDAs."

"Are you kidding me?" Kylie sets her phone down.

"We're already trending on Twitter," adds Bianca. "I think you need to acknowledge it with a tweet that says something like 'Whoops.'"

"Whoops?" Kylie raises an eyebrow.

"Nobody was killed. If we play it off like it's just part of the process of testing cutting-edge technology, maybe they'll cut us some slack."

"There are already memes with me in the fireball. We're enough of a joke as it is. And I'm not sure we deserve any slack."

I took a look at the news and social media while at the hospital. Much of it was wrong or misleading; none of it was good.

"Fair point," says Bianca.

"No fault for trying. I don't think anyone was prepared for this." Kylie turns to me. "I'm glad you're still here. Ever seen anything like this?"

"Hell no," I reply. "But I've seen much worse."

"Thank heaven nobody died."

Bianca shows her phone screen to Kylie. "Don't be so sure."

"What the hell?" Kylie groans before sliding the phone to me.

It's a retweet of a headline on a tech news website claiming that Kylie was killed—or so badly injured in the blast that she's on life support.

"We could milk this for a while," says Bianca. "Have them focused on you and your condition. Make you a victim and take away attention from the explosion." She quickly adds, "Just a thought."

"We'll be fielding lawsuits from some of the people who were here," warns Morena. "Maybe best to spin it in our favor sooner than later."

"They have a right to sue," Kylie says with a sigh.

"Not if you read the terms and conditions of accepting our invitation," replies Morena.

"Like that will hold," Kylie shoots back. "And I wouldn't try to push that anyway. If this is our fault, then we have to deal with it."

"Who else's would it be?" asks Bianca.

Kylie shrugs. "The gremlin that's been plaguing us? I don't know. This never happened in the simulation. We won't know anything until we look at the data. Any word on that, by the way?"

"I'll check with Martin," says Wayne.

"He's got his hands full. There're a dozen people under him that should be able to pull it up. Go ask Abram," she tells him.

"On it," says Wayne as he gets up and leaves the room.

"I'm going to go through the guest list and reach out to anyone who might be a problem and remind them that it wouldn't be in their best interest," says Morena.

"Can you be less mafioso about that?" asks Kylie.

"I'll ask gently and get Cardwell and his partners to make a few calls," Morena replies.

Cardwell is a super-connected venture capitalist who even I know about. I assume he's one of Kylie's investors. I place a Black AmEx credit card with an image of a wishing well on it in one of the seats in the Time Traveller's study.

"That's good. He has a light touch," Kylie observes.

"And I don't?" Morena says, mocking indignation.

"You're more of a death touch."

"I'm going to check on all the reporters we had here," says Bianca.

"Oh man. I forgot about them," says Kylie, covering her head.

"The good news is that all of them managed to file their stories," replies Bianca.

"How is that good?"

Morena answers: "If they're well enough to report on this fiasco, then it will be harder later to claim any lasting damage."

"This is not the way I want to be doing things." Kylie sighs again and glances at me. "You're not exactly seeing me at my best."

On the contrary: I've been in worse situations and watched people who should have been capable of handling them collapse under the pressure.

I once witnessed a drunk diplomat who got into an accident when his chauffeur—equally drunk—ran into the corner of a bank. While his driver was bleeding from the head and slumped over the steering wheel, the diplomat was yelling into his phone at his assistant, making sure that when it was in the papers it would be clear that the driver was at fault. He hadn't even called an ambulance.

Since I was covertly tailing him, I couldn't exactly break cover and render assistance. Instead, I messaged our dispatcher and had an anonymous phone call made by someone who spoke the language natively. I then took photos and video so we could try to turn the driver into an asset later on by showing him what a bastard his boss was—which makes me a bastard, too, I guess, but only professionally. Well, technically, I am a bastard in the literal sense as well.

I wait for Morena and Bianca to leave us alone, then ask Kylie, "Why did you want me to come? I suspect it was more than a gut check on if you should have been flying that thing."

She sits back in the chair and stares at the ceiling for a moment. "It was more of an instinct after I heard about you."

"*Heard* about me?"

"Don't act surprised. I'm sure you check out everyone you meet. After we spoke, I was curious. I looked you up." She shrugs.

I don't respond. I'm not sure what she could have found that was real.

"And then I found your LinkedIn page and other details," she continues. "All bullshit, of course. A friend of the family once explained to me how spies create boring cover stories and social-media evidence trails. I had a hunch and made a few calls."

"And?"

"You're the real deal. They told me some pretty horrific stuff. Terrorist attacks you helped thwart. Spies you found. Hell of a résumé."

Now that I'm retired, the fact that I spent over three decades in counterintelligence isn't the biggest secret anymore. My best method of concealment is that nobody really cares. Maybe a producer for CNN looking to have a talking head come on, or a book publisher who wants a memoir, but other than that, my career—my history—is old news.

I glance around the Time Traveller's study and see the gremlin under the glass flipping me the bird.

"Tell me about your gremlin."

"Just a phrase. Old World War II pilots used to jokingly blame any odd mechanical problem on gremlins. We've got a poster in one of the work bays from back then with a bunch of gremlins tearing up a Spitfire midflight."

"Do *you* think you have a gremlin problem?"

"If gremlins are real, then we have a much worse crisis on our hands. If you're asking me if there's been a series of unusual events or bad luck, then yes, I think we have a problem," she admits.

"What kind of events?"

"Working backwards from today? Well, the Sparrow exploding was one. All of our data getting wiped from our on-site servers is another. Timothy Watkins, one of our engineers, going missing is another. Douglas Gallar, a seed investor, getting killed in a car accident. Lots of other little things."

"Is this more than usual?" I ask while setting a black box in front of the Time Traveller's fireplace. Inside it, I place a blue-handled screwdriver for the missing engineer, Watkins, and a burned hundred-dollar bill for the late investor, Gallar.

"Much more than in my software companies. Even more than when I used to run the lab at my college. We worked on space-probe hardware with *no* money and had way fewer bad-luck incidents."

"And what do you want from me?"

"I want you to help us. I'll hire you, whatever. Name a number."

"You don't know me. I don't even think you understand what it is that I really used to do."

"The people I talked to spoke very highly of you. They said that you got things done. That's enough for me."

"In my world, 'getting things done' can have a very different meaning," I reply, trying to make my meaning clear.

"I'm not trying to hire a hit man, for crying out loud. I need someone who's an expert on dirty tricks. If I'm being professionally fucked with, I want a professional who's an expert on how to fuck with people," she says, using expletives I haven't heard her use before.

"How about I stick around for a little while," I offer. "No charge. I just give you my thoughts and help you find the people you may need. I've still got friends in the FBI and other places. We can reach out to them."

"Fine. Excellent. Whatever it takes to rid us of our gremlins."

I'm not ready to commit to anything, but the kid's sincere and in a real bind. Plus, there is the fact that I've dealt with more than a few gremlins in my career.

THE CRY

The US consulate in the second-largest city of a country that we'll call "Nolombia" is no longer there. Once upon a time, when the War on Drugs was a bigger priority than the War on Terror, that consulate served as a nexus for joint law-enforcement actions against the cartels that controlled much of the country.

The US embassy in the capital was too compromised with native employees and career diplomats who had uncomfortable social connections to the people they were supposed to be going after.

The consulate was restaffed and rebuilt to provide a coordination center between trusted (well, semi-trusted) local law enforcement and US agencies. The FBI and the DEA had offices there.

In the past, coordination had been done through secret centers in fake satellite offices of foreign companies. This worked well enough until the cartels realized they could bomb the local AT&T office and have the newspapers claim it was a political attack by terrorists—and not a direct attack on US and local law enforcement.

An embassy bombing would be out of the question. If they hit a secret command center, we couldn't acknowledge it—fair play in a dirty game.

For the first six months, things were going fine at the consulate. Then they went to hell.

First came the disappearance of a high-ranking military commander who had helped us plan multiple raids. He'd been working with us anonymously and never even came to the consulate. We took every effort to protect his identity, but one day he failed to show up at a meet and was never seen again.

We (when I say "we," I mean the consulate before and after I got there) chalked that up as the bad luck of being an official in a narco-controlled country.

The next week a translator vanished from her apartment. Her neighbors said they saw and heard nothing. She was simply gone.

Because she worked in the building, this had everyone on edge—more so because she was dating one of the American law-enforcement agents. A bigger deal would have been made of this, but he was still married to a wife back in the United States. The poor girl's disappearance was downplayed because it would have made us look bad.

While her vanishing was bad enough, it was the other thing that was causing people to lose their minds.

The locals called it *el llanto*, or "the cry" in English.

An electrician was the first one to tell the consulate manager that he'd heard the sound of someone crying at night. When he checked the other offices, they were empty.

A cleaning woman was the second person to hear the sound. A suggestion was made that there might be a stray cat in the building or the air vents, so cat food was placed in different locations.

There were no takers.

The American staff dismissed it as the locals' superstitions. Then a visiting DEA agent who was sleeping on a couch at the consulate heard the cry. He described it as an unearthly sound that wasn't animal and wasn't human.

A rumor began to circulate that during one of our joint raids an innocent woman had been killed in the middle of doing penance. Now she was haunting us.

It was a silly rumor—until you heard the cry.

Several tape recorders were left running all night at the consulate, and they captured the sound.

By the time I showed up (I wasn't an official fixer but was sent in as a favor), they had several recordings of the cry.

While I would certainly describe it as spooky, I don't know if I'd call it "unearthly."

J. Smith (we'll call him) was the head of the joint task force. After he played the tape for me, he asked me what I thought.

"Have you done a bug sweep?" I asked.

"Twice a week. Monday and Thursday. We also monitor radio bands nonstop," he explained.

"Anything?"

He shrugged it off. "Not really."

"Not really?"

"I can have them play the audio for you. But we think it's just some stray radio signal."

A half hour later I was in the communication center with a set of headphones over my ears listening to one of the random signals they'd picked up within the vicinity of the compound on the previous Wednesday:

. . . [static] . . . *despierta . . . despierta*

About ten minutes later the voice spoke again:

. . . *no olvides usar el baño mañana* . . .

"Wake up" and "don't forget to use the bathroom tomorrow" weren't exactly "redrum" on the scale of ghostly messages, but the soothing voice and the sheer randomness did make the radio intercept disturbing.

"Spooky, isn't it?" asked Smith.

"I can understand why people are concerned," I replied. "Can I get a list of personnel, the blueprints of the building, and a look at your schedules for all the workers?"

"Sure. But we've checked those already," he explained.

"Did you look at the schedules, the time cards, or security camera footage of when they arrived and left?"

A schedule shows you when someone is supposed to be there. A time card shows you when they made a record of being there. Security camera footage shows you when they actually came and went.

❦

I went through the footage and all the other information Smith could provide me. Aware that the building might be bugged, I walked into Smith's office the next Wednesday and placed a note on his desk.

I'm staying overnight. Don't tell anyone.

Smith wrote under it:

I'll stay too.

We both went through the motions of leaving for the night for the benefit of any potential spies in the staff, then made our way back to Smith's office.

He slept on the couch while I went over the schedules and blueprints.

At 5:45 a.m., I awakened Smith and motioned for him to follow me.

We went down a darkened upstairs hallway that passed the secure rooms where planning took place. I brought us to a stop where the hallway formed a T with another hallway.

I pointed to my ear so Smith would know to listen.

The sound was faint at first, a small squeaking noise. Then it got louder. There was the sound of a door opening, and the squeaking went inside.

A minute later the door opened and the squeaking returned and began heading toward us.

"Long night?" I asked Smith in a loud voice.

The squeaking stopped.

I pulled his elbow and we rounded the corner.

There in the middle of the hallway was the cleaning woman.

Smith let out a laugh, his hand to his heart. "Holy crap, I was expecting . . . I don't know what. Hey, María," he said to the woman.

"Good morning," she said in English.

"Now what?" Smith asked me.

"This," I said, locking eyes with María.

She had been looking at me suspiciously since we'd stopped her.

"María? Her credentials are clean. We're thorough," Smith explained.

"Maybe so. You don't have much protection against identity theft, though, do you? She could be María Marisol or someone using that name," I replied.

"I don't understand," said María. "Can I go home now?"

She started to push the cart away. I grabbed the side and held it still. Besides the cleaning supplies, there was a huge bag of trash filled with newspapers.

"Trasker?" asked Smith.

María made a split-second decision and started to run. She was at the stairs by the time I grabbed her arm. The downstairs guards, hearing the commotion, came running up to us.

"Hold her," I said.

I walked back to Smith, who was still standing by the cart.

"What the hell's going on?"

The answer was obvious: They weren't being haunted by some angry spirit. They were the target of a surveillance operation.

The clues were in all the details they were ignoring.

"You should read up on your espionage history," I told him. "This happened in Budapest in the 1950s. A trade consulate kept having information leaked. They did bug sweeps, searched for wires, investigated the buildings around the block."

"And?"

"They had a problem with hot water and finally knocked out a wet wall to get to the plumbing. That's when they found a small hammock and a ladder leading to the sewer. There was someone in the walls, listening," I explained.

"We check our sewers and all of that," said Smith.

"Same idea, different method." I pointed to an air vent. "You don't have an oversized wet wall, but you do have those."

The air vent was a little over eighteen inches wide and about a foot tall.

"Nobody could fit in there," said Smith.

"I could. You could . . . when you were a lot younger," I replied.

Smith thought it over for a moment. His eyes widened as he looked down at the garbage bag in the cleaning woman's cart.

I pointed to a date on a crumpled newspaper at the top.

It was that day's date. If there were any old newspapers to gather, they would have been from the prior day, or earlier.

I knelt by the side of the cart and said in my best Spanish, *"Está bien. Puedes salir ahora. Estamos comprando helado."*

There was a moment of silence, then a child's voice said from inside: *"Helado?"*

Smith pulled out the newspapers, and I lifted the small child from the garbage bag.

Around his neck hung a plastic bag filled with tape cassettes.

From his facial features, I could tell that he was malnourished and probably a few years older than he looked. God only knew what kind of life he'd lived up to that point.

"Somewhere inside the vents I'm sure we'll find a tape recorder and a radio," I explained. "In the meantime, let's get this little guy to the hospital and have him checked out."

The consulate's gremlin turned out to be a little boy kidnapped by the cartel to spy on us.

DANGER ZONE

There are no signs of gremlins on the tarmac, only thousands of pieces of the Sparrow scattered at random. I left my motel before sunrise to get here early, but there are already officials from the FAA, NTSB, and state agencies taking photographs.

Kylie is standing next to the biggest part of the Sparrow—the front section with a landing wheel propping it up so the razor-thin nose aims at the sky.

"It still doesn't make any sense," she says as I walk up.

"I'm sure we'll get a clearer picture."

I notice a woman in an ATF jacket swabbing pieces of the wreckage and putting them into plastic bags. She's collecting them so they can do a trace for explosives. If this was something other than a mechanical malfunction, then the evidence could be right here.

Although it didn't sound like there was another initial detonation that caused the plane to explode. I think I'd have smelled it as well.

I've been to many bomb blasts after the fact and gotten a sense for chemical explosives. Nothing I'd bet my life on, but a hunch.

"Tell me about your missing engineer." This feels like the most critical question right now.

"Watkins? He's a bit of an eccentric guy. He took some time off for a few weeks, and we haven't heard from him."

"How unusual is this?"

"Watkins is known to disconnect. He'll go off with friends or by himself to Mexico and do ayahuasca."

"One of those," I reply before realizing that Kylie herself could be a Gen Z type that goes searching for themselves in strange places.

"We've got a few of them around here. With Watkins, it's hard to know if he just doesn't want to be found or something happened to him."

"You hired a private investigator?"

"No. My head of security says he's looking into it."

I look around the wreckage and the facility beyond. "You have a head of security? Where is he?"

"His name's Ruskin. I spoke to him this morning. I think he's in Los Angeles. His team is here. Well, three of them, at least," she says.

"Who was doing security here last night?"

"We had two of them and then some local security guys from a firm," she explains.

"And your head of security wasn't here?"

"No. He was monitoring things from there."

"I see. But this seems like the kind of thing that should be monitored up close."

"He's rarely onsite. Martin says that since it was likely a systems problem, Ruskin wouldn't be much use anyway. That piece belongs to Martin and his team."

"Huh. And that makes sense to you?"

"I try to lean into other people's expertise," she explains.

"What if they're idiots?"

"Well, there is that. Security's way outside of my expertise," she admits.

I finally get it. Kylie can determine if a software developer or engineer is capable within a few minutes. That's her talent. Security specialists . . . well, they're *my* talent.

I notice a metal tube with a chunk of foam around it by my feet and realize I have no clue what it is. What any of this is. Talk about being outside one's area of expertise . . .

"Let's assume for a moment that this was sabotage. Who would want to do that?" I ask her.

"We have cameras in all the work bays. Nobody could get close without us knowing."

"That's not the question. Let's look at motives. That can give us an idea about their level of sophistication."

"Can you elaborate?" she asks. This is the engineer part of her that occasionally surfaces.

"If I found a person that had been working as an intelligence asset dead of a heart attack, my first question would be, Who wants him dead? If it's the Russian Mafia, then I suspect that it might be death by natural causes instead. If on the other hand it's the head of a Russian intelligence agency, then I suspect he may have been murdered because they have access to poisons that can do that. Motive implies resources. Not always, but it's a helpful place to start," I explain.

"Okay. Everyone from the Chinese government to the guy on Twitter who keeps creating accounts and putting up images with my eyes cut out. Does that narrow it down?"

I can tell that Kylie's on edge. It's understandable. Few people can handle this kind of pressure.

"I wouldn't say 'narrow it down' as much as 'expand the range of possibilities.' Why the Chinese government?"

"I don't know. This has military applications, and there's been some talk in defense circles about building a next-generation autonomous fleet to handle supply operations. But the Chinese trying to sabotage something so early on doesn't make any sense. The ramifications would be huge, and it's not their style. They're into stealing technology, then underpricing you, more than anything else."

"Competitors?"

"We have a couple. Peter Strausman's X-Lifter is doing something a little similar, but they're way behind and he's a really good guy."

She'd be amazed by what "good" people are capable of, but I keep that thought to myself.

"Let's put it another way: Who benefited the most from this explosion?"

"If we can't get any flight approvals and the FAA starts to clamp down on us, X-Lifter, for sure. But as I said, Strausman's not that kind of guy. None of them are. We loan each other gear and help with navigating regulations. We're competitors, to be sure. But we all want to make sure this industry succeeds. So we help each other out."

There are five hangars grouped together on this part of the runway.

"How many of these are yours?" I ask, pointing to the hangars.

"All of them. We bought the runway and property when everyone else was setting up shop at the Spaceport. It's more out of the way, but there's plenty of room."

"How long will it take you to build another Sparrow?"

"Assuming there's no major design flaw? Four months, if we do the normal amount of testing."

"How much is waiting that long going to hurt you?"

"Can you keep a secret?" she asks me.

"All of them."

"We don't have to wait four months." Kylie points to a hangar at the far end of the compound. "I've got three more Sparrows sitting in there."

"Aren't prototypes generally one-offs?"

"This is aviation. Things break. And if you can't build more than one, you're not going to be able to build a thousand of them."

"So the only delay here is what?"

"Finding out what happened so the FAA will let us fly again. That's what could take the most time. If we can't find out what happened, then it could be years."

"Damn."

"I know."

"Yes, but what I mean is that if someone wants to sabotage your development, then they're going to be highly invested in keeping this a mystery for as long as possible. And that implies some kind of method triggering the explosion that our friends at the FBI and ATF won't be able to find. Something unconventional."

"Now you see why I wanted you for the job?"

"I think I do. If I were to accept, I'd need two things from you."

"Anything," she says.

"The first is easy. I need complete control of your security, the ability to bring in anyone I need, and to fire anyone involved with security."

"Complete control? Is that all?" She laughs.

"I'll be honest with you. Your greatest danger involves getting back on track quickly. If that happens, they may come at you again, even harder. And since I don't think you're the kind to back down, that means I have to get your security into shape for when they come again."

"Okay. What's the second ask?"

"I will respect your need to keep certain secrets, but if I ask you about something, you have to tell me the truth. No matter what."

"That's a tall order."

"Early in my career, I was tasked with looking out for a diplomat. I asked him if there was anything that could be a vulnerability that I should know about. He insisted there wasn't. In the middle of trade negotiations, he began to act erratically and started insulting the other party. The negotiation failed, and we lost out on a major supply of a certain commodity that was strategically important.

"The diplomat was about to be sent home, and I confronted him in his hotel room. There was something he'd held back from me. Had I known, I could have saved the negotiation and his reputation."

"And what was that?" asks Kylie.

"He was on Adderall and Prozac and didn't want anyone at the embassy to know about it. So instead of using the embassy pharmacy, he was going to a local one to have it filled.

"I pulled a pill bottle from the hotel trash and had it tested. We found traces of a psychedelic. Another party had been tampering with his medications."

"Jesus," says Kylie. "That's some low-down, nasty conniving. Did they get away with it?"

"In the short term, yes. In the long term, no. Their actions let us know it was time to take the gloves off."

"I've heard about counterintelligence operatives whose sole job is to wreak havoc with enemies—make them regret ever playing dirty," says Kylie.

"The goal is dissuasion, not escalation. Most people can't walk that line. And in many cases, it would never get that far if people were honest to begin with. Do you understand?"

"Loud and clear. I'll have Morena prepare an agreement to make it official. When do you want to start?"

I check my watch. "Right now."

She shakes my hand. "Consider yourself hired. What's first?"

"I need to bring in someone I trust to replace your head of security."

"Hmm. I thought that would be you."

"Not officially. Not yet. If there is somebody on the other side of this, the longer they're unaware that I'm working with you, the better."

"Are you worried they might be scared off?" asks Kylie.

"No. I'm worried they might bring in someone like me to their side. Assuming they haven't already."

FIRING LINE

Ten men and four women have gathered around tables in the kitchen of the Wind Aerospace operations building. They're all part of the security team that was supposed to be in charge of protecting the Sparrow project and Kylie.

There's a separate group of three dozen security guards that handles the physical security of the base. They're part of a so-called elite team from Black Jack Protection, a Los Angeles–based firm that handles security for rock stars and actors.

Right off the bat, that's a horrible fit. Celebrities deal with an entirely different kind of threat than a CEO of a tech company. Ninety percent of Black Jack's experience is keeping autograph seekers from getting too close and occasionally issuing a stern warning to a stalker.

Kylie's security needs to worry whether Vladimir Putin has decided she's an enemy or the Chinese have hacked her phone.

"Thank you for getting here on short notice," I address the group. "My name is Brad Trasker. You can call me Brad. There are going to be some changes made in light of what happened last night."

"Changes? We didn't build the thing," says Omar Lopez, a heavyset man with tattooed arms.

I've read his file. I read all their files. Some of them might be salvageable.

"Mr. Lopez, do you know what caused the aircraft to explode?" I ask.

"I'm not an engineer," he replies.

"Thankfully you are not. The simple answer is you don't know. None of us do. It could have been an accident. It could have been sabotage. Where was Ms. Connor when the Sparrow exploded?"

"Too damn close," he replies.

"You were one of two people assigned to her personal security last night. Where were you?"

"I was in the hangar. Like most of us here."

I open up the pages of *The Time Machine* in my mind and imagine the study and everyone and everything that I placed there.

"The last place *I* saw you was at the back of the hangar at the bar," I recall. "That was quite a distance away from Ms. Connor."

"I kept her in view. I don't need anyone lecturing me on how to do my job," Lopez growls.

"Since I was the first person to her side, I have to disagree." I raise a hand to tell him to drop it—the same gesture I used with the German shepherds at the agency compound.

"No disrespect, *Brad*," says Brenda Antolí, a woman with her hair pulled back in a tight ponytail. She looks like a former police officer. "Why the hell are you here?"

"Ms. Connor asked me to oversee her security. And you may have noticed that your head of security isn't here right now."

"This motherfucker," mumbles Geoff Savoy from the side.

"Mr. Savoy? You have something to say?"

"I don't know who the fuck you are. You could just be any asshole that walked in off the street for all I know."

"Fair enough. Let's assume I was able to just walk off the street and into what's supposed to be a secure facility. What does that say about the job you're doing? If I remember correctly, you're supposed to vet the visitors list."

"I get updates. I know who's here."

"Then you know who I am and why I'm here," I respond, knowing full well he doesn't.

"So what's your point? Is this something you need to take up with Ruskin?" asks Brenda Antolí.

"I need to figure out who should stay and who should go. My gut tells me all of you need to go."

"All of us?" asks Savoy.

"On September 17, Ms. Connor was at a party in Bel Air. There were six people assigned to her security detail that night. Yet I have a bill from a restaurant called Katana in West Hollywood at the same time.

"The check was signed by you." I point to a redheaded woman named Faye Spencer. "Is this correct?"

"It was expensable," she replies.

"The check says there were six people seated at the table. If you all were there, who was with Ms. Connor at the time?" I ask.

A moment of silence, then Savoy speaks up. "We accompanied Kylie to the event and made sure they had adequate security. Doorway to doorway, she was under our supervision."

"Doorway to doorway? What about what's on the other side of the doorway? Whose house was the party at?"

"Peter Zhulovsky," says Savoy. "He's a movie producer and one of the backers of Kylie's boyfriend's films."

I can tell he feels proud for coming up with that information.

"Correct. Almost. Peter Zhulovsky is the brother of Anton Zhulovsky, a Russian mobster. Their father owned ten percent of the Moscow utility company. Anton now is involved with Vladimir Putin's business inner circle and is directly responsible for at least two people being thrown out of hospital windows.

"Anton is the actual owner of the house. Peter is just a way to wash money. And the security detail that you entrusted Ms. Connor's safety to? Three former Russian Federal Security Service members and two

Russian special forces members. Both of whom had rape and assault charges filed against them. At least one of the former FSS members is suspected of the torture and killing of a Ukrainian diplomat. This is the doorway you delivered Ms. Connor to."

The implications of this are settling in for most of them. Most . . .

"We can't tell her who to date or where to go," says Savoy.

"Correct. But you can tell her who she's with where she's going."

"She was with her boyfriend, Chris Alstead," says Spencer. "He's a good guy."

"He's a movie director. He's not a security specialist, and I doubt he has a clue who Peter Zhulovsky actually is. If he did, and he brought Ms. Connor there anyway, I need to have a conversation with him."

"What the hell is this about?" says Ruskin as he bursts into the room.

He must have driven at twice the speed limit to make it here this quickly. Credit to him for moving fast when he's motivated. Unfortunately, I'm going to have to make an example of him if I want to salvage what I can here.

"I was about to explain who is fired and who isn't," I tell Ruskin.

"The fuck you are," he says as he gets in my face.

I weigh about two hundred and stand just over six feet tall. I keep in shape but wear loose clothes to hide that fact. Few things are more suspicious than a physically fit person posing as a nebbish policy wonk.

Ruskin has fifty pounds on me, most of it muscle. He's a little shorter but looks like he's spent some time inside either a boxing or MMA ring. We're almost nose to nose. "I think you need to leave," he says in a calm but firm voice as he points toward the door.

It's the same voice he uses with paparazzi and overexcited fans.

I'm neither.

If we were in the marine barracks and he wasn't a commanding officer, I'd punch him and get to the inevitable fight more quickly.

If he were an accountant being dismissed for irregularities, I'd have two security guards waiting to take him away.

If he were a drunken diplomat making an ass of himself and trying to start a fight, I'd have men dressed in tuxedos help him to a car.

This is none of those situations. How I handle Ruskin now will determine the relationship I have with the security team going forward.

I choose to ignore him.

I turn back to the team and continue speaking. "I want to see logs of everyone who has been in contact with Ms. Connor. I want event reports for anything unusual. I need this by the end of the day. If you don't think you can provide me with—"

Ruskin steps around in front of me. His nostrils are flaring. He does not like being ignored.

"Excuse me, Mr. Ruskin, but I was addressing the team here. Would you mind stepping aside?" I ask firmly.

He's not used to being the one initiating the aggression. His tactics are intended for belligerent drunks and crazies making sloppy mistakes.

"Savoy and Piker, would you escort this asshole out of here while I go speak to Kylie," says Ruskin.

I glance at Savoy and then Piker, a tall bald man in the far corner. I give them a small shake of the head.

It's all mind games now.

Who do they want to follow? The raving jerk who's probably about to be fired? Or the relatively calm man who isn't fazed or threatened?

Savoy leans forward as if he's about to get up. Spencer puts a hand on his arm and he sits back down.

Ruskin realizes nobody is coming to pull me away, so he turns his ire on them.

"You ungrateful motherfuckers! You don't even work for him. We're contractors, you dumbasses. Let's just goddamn go."

43

"Please feel free to leave if you're inclined. You'll be doing the rest of us a favor," I tell him and the room.

Nobody moves.

Ruskin stares down Savoy. "*You*, Geoff?"

"You have to admit you're pretty shitty at your job," says Savoy.

Ruskin starts to march toward Savoy, but he doesn't remember how close I am to him already. I grab his belt and shove down hard on the back of his neck.

He lands face-first on the concrete floor. While he's still stunned, I secure his wrists with a plastic zip tie I grabbed from a parts shelf earlier.

"Spencer, call an ambulance. Lopez and Savoy, help him to the lobby."

Savoy huffs but gets up and does it anyway.

"Ms. Antolí, would you be kind enough to write this event up. Please be specific," I remind her.

"Why the hell not," she says. "Things are going to get interesting around here."

I'm afraid she's right.

I didn't want this confrontation to turn out the way it did, but I didn't have a lot of options. I don't have time to build a new team. I have to work with what I have. And that meant creating a bit of a shock so they'd adapt more quickly.

Laying out Ruskin during our first meeting was necessary. I just had to wait for the right moment. Not when he was attacking me—but one of their own.

And that's what they'll remember. Ruskin went for Savoy and that's when I flattened him.

Minutes ago, Savoy and I were snarling at each other, but I've made it clear: Back talk and bickering are fine. Threatening someone else with physical violence is where I draw the line.

Put another way: *I'll let you get in my face, but if you do the same to any of my people, that's something else.*

Despite the shocked looks on the faces of the security team, this was mild.

I've gone much further to make a point.

I just hope I went far enough here. If my worst-case-scenario suspicions are correct, Kylie is going to need everyone in the room ready to protect her with their lives.

AUTOPSY

Two days later, pieces of the Sparrow have been laid out on a hangar floor like the parts of a jigsaw puzzle—*if* the puzzle were burned, melted, and ripped apart by an angry adolescent.

I mostly left Kylie and her team to pick up the literal pieces while I went through all the security protocols. Most of her original security detail was willing to work—they simply needed some guidance from a capable adult.

I also called in a favor with a couple of acquaintances, Sophia Elad and Tyler Sennet. I'd first met Sophia when she was in her twenties working for the Mossad. Originally from Miami, she went to Israel on a right-of-return as a teenager, ended up joining the military and then went into Israeli intelligence, and finally came back to the United States to be closer to family and had two girls. Both now in college.

Tyler is an independent research analyst I've used in the past when I run into dead ends. He's an eccentric and a bit of an itinerant traveler. Eccentricities or not, all I had to do to get him to come was offer him a plane ticket.

Strangely enough, I learned some time ago that our paths crossed when we were much younger.

During one summer when my mother sent me to stay with my father and his family in the Hamptons, Tyler was with his family in the summerhouse next door.

Like my father, Tyler comes from a long line of blue bloods. The State Department and intelligences services are filled with people from white, entitled backgrounds. It explains a lot when you think about it.

Despite my father's lineage, I was my mother's son and raised firmly middle-class. I chose the marines as a way to pay my way through college. I didn't expect to find myself in the espionage field, despite my mother's background. It just worked out that way.

Looking at the mysterious pieces of the Sparrow, I wished I had a better understanding of engineering. You could have told me this was an alien spacecraft that blew up over the desert and I wouldn't be able to argue otherwise.

"Think you'll be able to put it back together?" I ask Kylie as she walks toward me.

"Hilarious," she says flatly. "I have good news and bad news."

"Bad first."

"Actually, it's the same news. I just can't tell if it's good or bad. We got a preliminary report back on the chemical analysis. There was no sign of any kind of explosive like PETN or anything else. It was actually easy to rule out because the Sparrow burns hydrogen and there weren't that many complex hydrocarbons in the mix. We've got chemical spectroscopy on all of the components, so it would be pretty easy to tell if there was any from a foreign material."

"So, no bomb," I reply.

"But that doesn't rule out some other clever form of sabotage. Still, the odds seem more than likely I screwed up somewhere," Kylie says with a shrug.

"Or someone who works for you," I suggest.

"I'm the chief engineer. The buck stops here. Which makes it extra frustrating. I don't have a clue how this could have happened. At least with a bomb I'd have an explanation."

"That and somebody out to stop you by any means necessary," I add.

"Is it weird for me to say I'd find that easier to live with than some huge design flaw I didn't catch?"

"NASA had its mistakes," I reply.

"Yes, but they usually knew the reason the moment it happened. We're still in the dark here," she says, exasperated.

"Hey, K," calls out Martin from a table at the far corner of the hangar.

I've noticed that people in her inner circle tend to call her just "K." It's also her name on the company email: k@windaerospace.com.

I follow her over to a white table covered with different pieces of metal and graphite composite. Martin, head of systems, is sitting on a stool looking at something through a lens on a table mount. He's been working since the accident and has only taken naps on a couch in the break room. He's taking it every bit as personally as Kylie.

"Hey, Trasker," says Martin as he notices me when moving out of the way so Kylie can examine the specimen.

"What's all this?" I ask.

"Valves and pieces of the shell from the hydrogen tank. We think this was ground zero for the explosion. From the warping and where they were found, it looks like this is where it started."

"Huh," says Kylie as she looks at the piece under the magnifying glass. "Brad, you want to take a look at this?"

I sit down to see for myself.

I'm looking at a white piece of plastic with a one-centimeter slit cut through it—like a tiny coin slot.

"That slot's not supposed to be there?" I ask.

Martin shakes his head.

"Shrapnel?" Kylie asks him.

"Maybe. But the puncture's coming from the wrong direction. If it was a piece that hit the tarmac and bounced up, we'd see traces of gravel. This is clean."

"It could have hit another piece that was already detached and bounced back," she suggests.

"And the odds of that . . . ?"

"Ridiculously high. But still nonzero."

"It'd be like trying to kill an armored great white shark by shooting a bullet backwards and ricocheting it at a precise angle through the armor to nail it in the gills," says Martin.

"What do you think?" Kylie asks me.

"I'm out of my league here. I've seen plenty of bullet holes and shrapnel. This looks nothing like those. This is very clean. Almost like it was machined."

"We have cameras," Kylie says. "We can see it happening. Or at least we should."

"Can we look at the footage?" I ask. "Start backwards from when the Sparrow exploded and see if there's anything out of the ordinary?"

"You think we'll see a saboteur with a black hat sneak up and place a bomb on the Sparrow?"

"Probably not. But I wouldn't be surprised if we saw something other than what we know already."

FREEZE FRAME

We're seated in a conference room with a large-screen television at the far end. Along with Kylie, Martin, and myself is Nick Tomo, head of facilities for Wind Aerospace—the one accountable for all the buildings and equipment.

Tomo has his laptop hooked up to the AV system and is scrubbing through the different camera angles of the explosion.

In addition to the cameras trained on the Sparrow at the time of the incident, several of the hundreds of cameras around the facility were able to capture some part of the explosion.

"What are we looking for?" asks Tomo. "Mustache-twirling villains with cartoon dynamite?"

Martin gives him the eye. He made almost the same joke a little earlier, but there might be some kind of boundary here.

"If you got that on camera, then let's start there. Otherwise, start with the moment it exploded and roll backwards," Kylie tells him.

Tomo shows us an overhead view of the Sparrow from a camera mounted on top of the hangar. Kylie is standing fifty feet away from the Sparrow.

She turns her head and starts to crouch. This is followed by a white flash that overloads the camera sensor. It fades, and spots of fire cause white glows on the display.

I catch myself on camera running toward Kylie.

"Damn, man. You're spry," says Tomo.

"Isn't it better to run away from an explosive in case there's a second charge hidden to get first responders?" Kylie asks me.

"Normally, yes. But I figured the source was the plane, and there was only one of those. Second, it's my policy to get the wounded away from the scene as quickly as possible," I explain. "If this had been a café bombing in Tel Aviv, I'd *still* be running away from it."

"What other views do you have?" Kylie asks Tomo.

I can't tell if she's professionally curious or needs to revisit the moment she almost died in order to process what happened.

"I got lots. Even thermal," says Tomo.

The image switches to a camera at ground level looking at the Sparrow and the desert beyond. Parts of the Sparrow glow brightly; others are completely black.

I take the black parts to be where the liquid oxygen and hydrogen lower the temperature of the airframe.

The lights on the edge of the tarmac glow white, and Kylie resembles a fluorescent vampire as she walks toward the craft.

A moment later, a white burst engulfs everything and the screen is filled with pale flames and misty, gray-white smoke hot enough to be picked up by the thermal imager.

"Can we go back further?" I ask.

"Sure," says Tomo.

He scrolls the footage back to when the Sparrow is first rolled into position. I notice something at the edge of the desert—a small white glow before it's obscured by the plane.

"Can you go back a few more?" I ask.

"Sure, but the Sparrow won't be in it," says Tomo.

"That's okay."

The Sparrow backs out of frame. A fuel truck drives by and several people walk by, setting up blocks and equipment.

In the distance I can still see the small white glow.

"Go to a few minutes after the explosion," I ask.

Tomo forwards the video to when the fires are getting smaller. The white glow is gone.

"Back," I tell him.

Tomo brings the footage back to right before the Sparrow came into frame.

"What do you see?" asks Kylie.

I point to the white glow. "What's that?"

"That should be one of our roving security teams. We had them out there in case reporters or lurkers decided to sneak across the desert for a closer look," explains Tomo.

"How come they're not out there after the explosion?"

"They were on the tarmac just a few minutes after," he replies.

"Yes, but *immediately after*, they're gone. The timing is . . ."

"Suspicious?" Kylie says, finishing my thought.

"They were so far away already it wouldn't make a difference," says Martin.

The team responsible for perimeter security is a different one than the internal team I lit into a couple of days ago. This was the private firm from LA used as an outer layer of security.

"Call whoever was out there and find out why they left," I tell Tomo.

"I'll do that," he says.

"Now, Mr. Tomo. Time isn't on our side."

"Got it."

Tomo pulls up a number on his computer, then dials his phone.

"Hey, Hal, I have a question for you. We're looking through the footage and notice your security truck wasn't in position at the time of the explosion," Tomo says into the phone. He waits and listens for a time, then, "Aha," he says. "Okay. That checks out. Thank you."

Tomo puts his phone back in his pocket. "He said they got a report about the pressure sensors going off on the east side of the facility. It turns out some wild dogs were sniffing around."

"Wild dogs?" says Kylie.

"That's what he said. They spotted them but hurried back when they heard the explosion."

"But they saw the dogs?" I ask.

"Yes. He says they were able to get pretty close to them," says Tomo.

"Not to be difficult, but does he have any proof?"

"He says he went back with Karputh, and they were able to get the dogs into a truck and take them to the shelter."

"Wild dogs . . ." says Martin.

"You said we'd see something we didn't expect," Kylie replies. "Wild dogs certainly fits that description."

"I have questions," I tell them.

"I can have Hal come here," offers Tomo.

"I'll want to speak to him. But first, I have questions for those dogs."

THE POUND

The Animal Society is a well-kept concrete building at the edge of town. A colorful mural of dogs and cats fills the entire wall facing the parking lot.

"You interrogate many animals?" asks Kylie as we get out of my SUV.

Spencer and Savoy are in the SUV behind us and park by the entrance. I've made sure that at least two people follow Kylie anytime she's not in the compound. And when she is, two people need to be within six seconds' distance of her.

"Why six seconds?" Lopez had asked.

"That's how much time you have to shove your finger into a femoral artery before a victim goes into cardiac arrest from a gunshot," I explained.

I have no idea if that number is accurate, but when someone first told it to me, I understood the real meaning—I have to be ready to put my life on the line at any moment.

I walk ahead of Kylie to make sure the shelter entrance is clear. I would have preferred it if she'd stayed behind, but next to me is probably the safest place for her until we get the rest of the security in place.

"Hi there!" says a friendly woman with gray hair down to her shoulders. "Are you Brad?" she asks as she opens the door to let us in.

I'd called ahead to tell her I was coming. I didn't mention Kylie, but I can tell the woman recognizes her.

"I'm Cassie," she says, shaking Kylie's hand first.

She opens the door wider so we can pass but keeps her body close to it.

The behavior looks suspicious until I realize there are dogs running around and yapping at each other in the lobby.

"It's pretty hot out there so I let them run around here," says Cassie. "Down, Brutus," the woman admonishes a dog that jumped up on Kylie.

She doesn't seem to mind and crouches down to scratch the dog behind the ears.

I glance down as a mutt sniffs at my shoes and looks up at me with pleading eyes.

"I don't have anything for you," I say.

"I think Angie just wants some attention," says Cassie.

I bend down and give the dog a pat. It decides to take a nap at my feet.

"I called to ask you about the dogs that were brought in," I explain.

"Yes. Unfortunately, I can't let you adopt them. But we have others that you can," says Cassie.

"Actually, I just want to see them," I explain.

"The dogs?" she asks.

"Yes," I reply.

She points to the dogs circling Kylie and me. "These are the dogs."

I look down at Angie as she lets out a yawn. "These are the wild dogs?"

"A little rowdy, but definitely not wild. They've all been chipped and their owners contacted," she explains.

"Wait—these are people's pets?" asks Kylie.

"Yes. Well, only two are chipped, but the other one clearly belongs to someone. You can tell by the fact that they've been neutered and groomed and fed. Not to mention they all understand commands."

"Where are they from?" I ask.

"Brutus is from Bakersfield. Angie from Barstow," she replies.

"Those are both along Highway 58," says Kylie, a step ahead of me. "Did they get lost?"

"Only if they were following the Oscar Mayer Wienermobile and it was going really slow."

"Then how did these dogs end up on the edge of our facility?" Kylie asks.

"They were dognapped. Maybe some teenagers out to play a prank. Maybe a sicko. But these dogs only went missing two days ago."

The day of the explosion.

Kylie shakes her head in disbelief and looks at me.

I call Hal, the security guard who found them.

"Hal, this is Trasker," I say when he answers.

"I just saw the Slack update from Ms. Connor about you. How can I help you?"

"We're looking at the dogs, and they don't seem to be that wild. Could you describe the ones you picked up?"

Hal proceeds to describe the three canines at our feet.

"You said they were wild."

"Well, they didn't have any collars, and they were pretty riled up. But they did hop into the truck without me having to ask," he admits.

I suspect that "wild dogs" sounded more impressive than "stray dogs." You always have to parse people's words carefully. Especially witnesses. Even the word "normal" is open to interpretation based on the context.

"Was there anything else unusual when you found them?" I ask.

"They'd been chowing down on the bones of some roadkill. That's why I thought they were wild at first."

"Roadkill. You didn't take a photo, did you?" I ask.

"No. But I can show you the spot if you like."

Kylie and I get out of the SUV and walk over to where Hal is standing. At six foot six, Hal and his bronzed features are hard to miss. He grew up near the reservation and can apparently trace his family history here back several hundred years.

"This is what they were gnawing on," says Hal.

I squat down to get a closer look at the bones. They're rib bones with almost all the flesh gone.

I point to the end and look up at Hal. "Roadkill?"

He makes a painful groan. "I'm an idiot."

"What is it?" asks Kylie as she walks over.

"See the clean edge on the bone? This came from a butcher. This isn't some wild animal that got gnawed apart."

"Have you ever been called out here because of the sensors?" I ask Hal.

"Lots of times," he says.

"Ever find dogs?"

"No. A few coyotes—although it's not supposed to be that sensitive—some hikers, and guys on motorcycles twice."

"Did you get a look at their faces?"

"No. They drove off."

"When was the last time you saw someone on a motorcycle?"

"A week ago, I'd guess."

"Logbook, Hal. Logbook. These details are critical," I admonish him. I make my own mental note and put two toy motorcycles on the edge of the chessboard in the Time Traveller's study.

"Understood."

"Domestic dogs? Butchered meat? Where is this going?" Kylie asks.

"I don't know. But I think we want to have a look over there." I point back toward the base. "Hal, can you take us to the exact spot you were at when you got the call about the sensors?"

DESERT

I can still see the tire tracks from when Hal and his partner were parked out here during the Sparrow launch. About a hundred feet from my right toe is a red flag marking the farthest spot that any of the pieces of the Sparrow were found.

Investigators may have made it out this far, but it would have been a quick search. The farther from the explosion, the larger the search radius. Trying to search this far out would have required a lot more people—not that there was any reason to, since the closest fragment was a hundred feet away.

I walk around staring at the ground a few inches in front of my feet. I try not to look as much as *feel* with my eyes.

It's a weird way to describe it, but I'm not as concerned with colors as I am with textures.

I start from where the truck was parked and walk toward the tarmac.

I can see Kylie's shadow to my right. She's searching the ground as well.

We finally reach the outermost flag, and I turn around and walk toward the truck's location, but a few feet to the right. Kylie does the same.

I come to a stop near the tire tracks.

"Anything?" asks Kylie.

"Scrub brush and dry dirt."

"Any idea what we could be looking for?"

"Nope. We once had an informer go missing from their apartment. We turned the place upside down looking for anything. We found nothing. No blood. No sign of a struggle. We even searched the apartments around there when nobody was in. Still nothing."

"Something tells me you didn't give up."

"No. I went for a walk, trying to figure out what could have happened. I stopped by a trash can at the far end of the street near an alley blocked off with a locked gate. Out of curiosity, I reached inside the trash and found a shoe. Same kind as my informer wore. This told us they may have been taken in this direction. We were able to pull security camera footage from a building the next block over."

"Sure enough, in the middle of the night when they went missing, an ambulance rolled out of that alley and went two blocks before turning its lights on," I explain.

"Did you ever find him?" asks Kylie.

"No. And it was a her," I reply. "Someone with enough pull in that country to arrange for that sophisticated an abduction wasn't going to leave anyone around after they got what they wanted."

"Remind me never to become an informant for the CIA," says Kylie.

"It wasn't the CIA and it wasn't our government she was informing for. Someone sold us her contact information—and apparently sold it to someone else as well. Anyway, that's not the point. I don't really know the point. Hal, do you ever see drones out here?"

"This is restricted airspace," he replies. He's standing next to his truck with his arms folded, watching us.

"Yes, but did you ever see any?"

"No. I may have heard one buzzing around once."

"Do you remember when?"

"No. I know what you're going to say next. *Logbook.* Next time I'll put it in," he says, tapping his head.

"Do me a favor and see if you can remember. Have a seat and make a note of everything that came before and after."

"I really don't remember when," says Hal.

Impatient, I ask, "Was it before today and after Christmas?"

"Well, yeah," he replies.

"Then that's a start. We've already narrowed it down to ten months," I explain.

I catch Kylie smiling out of the corner of my eye. I suspect that most of the people she works with are on the same wavelength.

Hal may be a profound and deep thinker, but I don't know if he has a wavelength.

I turn to Kylie. "Why release a bunch of mutts at the other end of the complex?"

"To distract security," she answers.

"Why?" I ask.

"So they don't see something."

"What didn't they want them to see?"

"How they did it? Who did it? Assuming it's even connected to the dogs and there *was* somebody here."

"For now, we'll assume there was somebody here. Why?" I ask.

"To pull it off. They needed to be close enough."

"Which in today's world doesn't mean radio transmitter. They could have triggered an explosive from halfway around the world while watching the live stream. Why else *be* here?"

"They had to be in physical proximity. If we're thinking a sniper, remember, there wasn't a bullet hole, and the thermal sensors didn't see anyone out here," she points out.

"The first snipers used spears. Then bows and arrows. Snipers with rifles are a new concept. Let's not let the absence of method make us discount anything."

"Or they could have been waiting for the explosion to grab a chunk of it," she speculates.

"How special are the parts?"

"We've got some very special trade secrets, like the coating we use. The pieces with that are in another room under lock and key."

"Did you find all of them?"

"No. But the material is fragile. Some of it could have been pulverized. No way to know," she says with a shrug.

I look at how much ground there is to cover and make a small sigh when I realize my mistake. "We're doing this all wrong."

"How so?"

"Do you have a ladder and a laser?"

"How many milliwatts do you want?" she says with a smile.

"I don't know." Lasers aren't my thing.

"Do you just want to be able to see it, or do you want it to be able to cut a tank in half?"

"Just the kind you can see when it hits the ground." I stare at the hangars and wonder what else she has hidden in there besides lasers that could cut a tank in half.

"No problem. Why the laser, though?"

"We're going to punch a shark in the gills."

SPOTTER

Martin is a small point out on the tarmac, standing on a ladder with a laser mounted to an armature. He's got a laptop strapped to the top rung so he can keep the angle precise.

While the Sparrow was parked on the tarmac pre-explosion, it was sending back telemetry data to a computer in the hangar. Among this data was millimeter-precise position coordinates created by triangulating transponders on the ground. This was even more accurate than GPS and pinpointed exactly where the Sparrow stood before it blew up.

While staring at the scrub out on the perimeter, adding the latest case details to the Time Traveller's chessboard, I came across a fishbowl with an armored shark and a spear stuck in its side. I hadn't consciously added the shark—sometimes my brain does that on its own. This is probably because my mother started teaching me visual mnemonics before I could even read.

Our assumptions are (1) the Sparrow was destroyed in an act of sabotage, and (2) the saboteur was physically present to commit the act.

This implies that the saboteur had a clear line of sight to the Sparrow and a way to damage it that would cause an explosion.

According to Kylie and Martin, the fuel tanks on the Sparrow are so heavily protected that a rifle bullet couldn't puncture them from almost any angle.

Almost . . . any . . . angle.

"If someone couldn't hit this randomly, they'd have to know exactly where?" I'd asked Martin back in the hangar while we were waiting for the laser and a few other pieces of equipment.

"Yeah, but that information isn't available to anyone."

"What if they had the plans?"

"It would still take years to figure it out."

"No, it wouldn't," Kylie interrupted. "I'm such an idiot." She grabbed the laptop from Martin's fingers and started tapping. A minute later, she showed us a 3D rendering of the Sparrow with two red lines sticking out of its sides.

"Watch what happens when I zoom in." She pushed her finger across the track pad, moving along the axis of one of the lines.

The aircraft zoomed quickly, then grew so huge we could pass through an outer layer and into its interior.

Where the red line ended was a piece of hardware that looked exactly like the one on the bench with the odd slot cut into it.

"What did you do?" asked Martin.

"Ray tracer. I made the nonarmored pieces transparent," said Kylie.

"Ray tracer?" I asked.

"In computer animation, you only calculate the photons that would reach the camera. You ignore everything else; otherwise the computation would be too much," she explained.

"Thank you, Alvy Ray Smith," said Martin. "Or rather, screw you."

"Pixar cofounder?" I asked.

"Same guy," said Kylie.

Thanks to Dr. Smith, we had an idea of exactly where a projectile would have to hit in order to wreak the damage it did.

Our goal is to find the origin point of whatever object hit the Sparrow. We'll do this by aiming a laser from the precise point of impact *outward*—more or less backtracking to the location where the projectile originated. Martin's job on the ladder is to train the laser at the precise angle suggested by the computer simulation, then light up the area where the projectile came from.

"How's it looking?" Kylie asks on her phone.

"I think we're set," Martin replies over the speakerphone.

Kylie squints. "Is it on?"

"Yes. I can't see where it's hitting because of the scrub. But it should be about twenty meters to your left." Martin waves his hand and points in the direction we should look.

Kylie gets there first and stares at the ground. She gives me a shrug.

I walk to where she's standing.

"How do we lose the destination point of a deterministic system?" she asks aloud.

"Maybe it's one of those mystery voids people claim are in the desert," Martin replies.

Kylie kneels, then glances up at me. "Well, this is embarrassing." She grabs a fistful of dirt and throws it in the air.

At first, I think she's having a bit of a fit; then I realize she's made a dust cloud.

As the cloud drifts through the desert air, a bright green line suddenly pierces it like a science-fiction death ray.

She throws another cloud of dust and follows the beam to where it terminates.

There's no bright green dot—only a large dried-out bush and a few rocks.

Martin's harebrained joke about mystery voids is starting to appeal to me.

"Trasker . . . am I losing my mind?" asks Kylie. "It should be right here."

It should . . .

"Get back!" I yell.

She jumps backward. "What's going on?"

I throw my arms out and back up with her behind me. "We need to call the sheriff and have them send the bomb squad."

"Bomb squad?"

I point to where she was kneeling. "Want to know why we couldn't see where the beam hit the ground? It's because it's going through a gap and hitting something *underground*."

I draw my gun and aim it at the suspect bush.

The Kern County Sheriff's Department has us backed all the way onto the tarmac while their bomb-disposal team works.

They've got two men on the scene dressed like beetles next to their armored truck. Ahead of them is their robot—a mechanical arm on tracks slowly moving toward the bush.

I'm sure this is overkill, but I need to be careful. I still haven't forgiven myself for letting Kylie walk out there. That was just plain stupid on my part. Especially after her comment about first responders getting hit by a second blast.

Jack Douglas, the undersheriff, is back here with Kylie and me on the tarmac. He's got a monitor on the hood of his truck showing us what the robot's camera can see.

Right now, it's just a bunch of dry dirt and weeds.

We moved the laser beam a few millimeters lower so it would hit the ground in front of the origination site. That's the marker the bomb techs are looking for.

A few yards more and the location comes into view on our screen.

The camera's viewpoint is much lower than our own, almost eye level with the top of the bush—which now looks suspiciously desiccated compared to the other foliage around it.

There's a perfect rectangular shape in the dirt that looks about two feet wide. It's about half an inch thick—like a sheet of plywood that has dirt and brush glued to one side. It seems to cover a hole in the ground.

Martin's measurements were so precise that his laser pointed to the exact gap in the wooden platform through which our theoretical saboteur must have targeted the Sparrow.

"We're going to lift the lid," says a bomb tech over the radio.

The claw on the end of the robot pushes into the dirt below the lid and moves forward until it's in the gap. The tech handling the controller slowly lifts the lid a few inches.

"Waiting," says the voice on the radio.

A few minutes pass.

"Going over with the scope," says the radio voice.

One of the armored men walks to the hole and kneels. On the screen showing the robot's camera feed, we can see a narrow tube snake across the ground and into the gap.

"No wires. No boxes. Just . . ." says the voice on the radio.

We're all on pins and needles waiting for his next words.

"Just a piece of metal. I'm going to flip open the lid," he declares.

This seems rather hasty to me, but I'll let them do their job.

From here I can see him lift the cover, along with the entire bush, and set it aside.

Kylie's fists whiten as she clenches them.

I know the feeling.

"We'll need to probe the ground inside. But it looks clear," says the bomb tech over the radio.

Thirty minutes later I'm peering over the edge of the hole. Kylie is by the truck, waiting for me to tell her it's safe to come over. Trusting that there are no hidden surprises the bomb techs couldn't find, I give her the thumbs-up.

"Well, that's . . . underwhelming," she says, staring down into the hole.

It's actually more of a trench, two feet wide, three feet deep, and five feet long. The only thing unusual about it is a long metal rail leaning against the dirt wall.

"Gun rest?" asks Kylie.

"That would be my guess," I reply.

"How do you think they dug it without us knowing?"

"When our security guards were out chasing someone on a motorcycle, someone else dressed like a ninja could have been here, digging it out."

LONG SHOT

Tyler Sennet is sitting in his suit and tie at a table in the back of the California City public library, running his finger across a page of text. He's got a stack of books in front of him with such titles embossed metallically on the spines as *Early History of Mojave* and *A Settler's Diary of Death Valley*.

I take the seat opposite from him. "Couldn't you have found a location a little closer?"

It was a thirty-minute drive from Wind Aerospace to here.

"This library has the best hours," he replies without looking up.

"I can set you up in a conference room with round-the-clock hours."

"But would it have this?" he asks as he turns the pages of the book toward me.

"What is it?"

"An account of a silver miner being terrified by giant owls tearing up their campsite at night," he explains.

"I'm sure you could find that on the internet."

"And how would it get there, Bradley? Do you think accounts like that just magically appear online? Or perhaps it's because of the efforts of people like me to find these details and make them available to everyone else? Don't you wonder how things end up on Wikipedia?"

"Let me guess, you're also a wiki editor." That wouldn't surprise me.

"Actually, I have aliases for over a dozen Wikipedia editor accounts."

"I think you told me that at one point."

Tyler taps his forehead. "Did you forget to stash it away in your mental palace?"

"It seemed like a waste of space," I joke.

"You may think so. But I'm the last line of defense between you and a Wikipedia page on all of your dirty exploits," he says with a smile.

I did forget that Tyler is as good at burying information as he is at surfacing it. It shouldn't be surprising that a lot of what gets said about major political events is filtered through someone like him.

It also explains why certain things that should get more coverage don't. While research papers were circulating showing credible evidence that the COVID pandemic may have originated from an accidental lab leak, a certain group of Wikipedia editors were working tirelessly to block any references and citations that didn't label it as a lunatic conspiracy theory.

While I wouldn't go as far as to suggest that the Chinese government was influencing that policy, I know that the US government wouldn't hesitate to do so if it was in our interests—or the interests of the people that decide our interests.

People like Tyler are handy when they're working for you. The danger with him and his ilk is that they're more driven by curiosity than a political compass. That makes them unpredictable.

"Did you look at the photos?" I ask.

I sent him images of the spider hole we found.

"I did. What did the FBI say?"

"Nothing yet. They have a forensic team there right now. What do you think?"

"The metal rod was a gun rest. I'm sure you thought of that," says Tyler.

"And a gun rest would imply a gun. The problem is, nobody heard a gunshot. None of the microphones picked one up either."

"No. Just a ping. I heard the sound file. Either that was something firing or something being hit."

"We haven't found anything that resembles a bullet puncture," I reply.

"So no evidence of a bullet and no sound of a gunshot? What does that leave?" Tyler loves to test me.

"No gun?"

He shakes his head. Apparently, I failed.

"A gun that doesn't use gunpowder and doesn't use bullets," he explains.

"Like a contained piston gun? You think the saboteur used one of those?"

A contained piston was a type of firearm developed by the KGB. Instead of a shell that shot a bullet down a barrel, this gun used the explosion to push a piston that propelled the bullet.

The explosion never left the barrel and made the gun much quieter. You could only get one shot out of them, and they had a big kick that could sprain your wrist if you didn't hold it right. But from a few meters away, the gun sounded like a champagne cork popping. From a few hundred, it wouldn't even be noticeable.

"But those guns still used conventional rounds," I point out.

"They didn't have to. You could put anything in that chamber. Bullets worked best because they're the most aerodynamic shape. But other objects would work as well."

"They did a gunpowder residue test on the metal bar while I was there. It was negative," I tell him.

"It could have been compressed air or some gas with a better expansion ratio. We know Russian snipers have been using something stealthier than silenced firearms," says Tyler.

"Anything that would leave a hole like this?" I show him the photograph of the part with the slot going right through it. "An ATF and

FBI agent both told me that couldn't be a projectile because it was so two-dimensional and didn't have a radiated exit pattern."

Tyler sighs. "Well, if you have those experts, why come to me?"

"I'm just telling you what they said."

Talking to Tyler was a chore when he was a teenager too. Now he's a smarter, more sarcastic version of himself.

"Point one: you could have a flat, arrow-shaped projectile that might leave a channel like that if it was hot enough. The excess material wouldn't melt around the surface, it would liquefy and spray.

"Point two: have a look at this." Tyler slides a printout from under a folder.

I'm looking at aluminum blocks with similar grooves shot through them. The holes could be twins of the slot I viewed in the hangar.

"What is this?"

"Test photos from the Russian space agency. They were testing different materials and how they would hold up against impact from different kinds of space debris. This was a ceramic chip, like what's in orbit up there now from their satellite-impact tests."

"A ceramic bullet?"

"You're asking the wrong question. You should look at this and wonder what shot it. That chip had to be going much faster than any bullet. Faster than it could with compressed gas," he adds and takes out another printout. It shows a meter-long device that has a long, square barrel and a large block underneath. "This is what they used to fire that ceramic chip into the piece of spacecraft."

"Is that a . . . rail gun?"

"Yes. They did the tests in orbit. This used a battery and could accelerate the projectile at over Mach 5. Because the ceramic was non-conductive, they used a metal piston that would also exit but break apart quickly. You should tell the forensics specialists to be looking for tiny metal pellets," he suggests.

"And where does somebody get a rail gun like this?"

"The plans were leaked in a hack years ago. Anybody with access to a metal shop and an electronics supplier could build a version. The capacitor is the most complicated part. The batteries have to charge that up for several minutes. I imagine it would get quite hot," he speculates.

And would be invisible to thermal imaging if underground.

I place a U-shaped magnet with a bullet floating between its arms on the chessboard in the Time Traveller's study.

"So anybody could make one of these."

"Just about. But you're asking the wrong question. Again."

"Okay, Tyler, point out the error of my ways."

"Finding someone to make this gun is easy. Finding someone capable of shooting it—that's a different matter. You need an experienced sniper who is not only comfortable taking a shot from two hundred yards, but doing so at night with an unconventional weapon. Just getting the wind right would be a challenge," he explains.

"Going faster should make it easier, as should the venting gas from the Sparrow."

"If you say so," says Tyler.

"What is it?"

"There are maybe twenty men for hire that are capable of doing this. That's assuming . . ." His voice trails off.

"Assuming what?" I reply.

"Assuming that this was a hired gun and not someone who is active-duty military," he suggests. "There's an air force base within spitting distance. I'm sure they've got a few people who know something about taking out high-value targets with unconventional weapons."

"Okay. Back to the giant owls terrorizing gold miners for you," I reply as I fold up his printouts and slip them into my pocket.

"It was silver. Anyway, feel free to stop by. I'll be around. Next time we can talk about Ms. Connor's aircraft," Tyler says as he raises an eyebrow.

"And what about it?"

"That's a question for another day. Anyhow, pleasure to see you. You really need to come to the Hamptons next summer. Everyone is dying to see you."

"No, they aren't," I tell him.

"No, they are not," Tyler echoes. "But it's a nice thought."

"Thank you. Don't go far."

"I'll be lurking. Don't worry. There is one other thing . . ." Tyler lets his voice trail off for dramatic effect.

"Yes, Tyler?"

"You've made a very interesting assumption," he says.

"I've made a lot, I'm sure. What is this one?"

"You chose the word 'saboteur' to describe who did this."

"What else would you call him?"

"What's another word for a sniper for hire? That's easy—'assassin.' Was the goal to blow up the plane or to blow it and Ms. Connor up with it?"

Damn. He has a point. I've increased the security around Kylie because of the possibility of someone coming after her, but I hadn't really thought that she and not the Sparrow was the target.

Whoever did this must know that she'd built backups of the Sparrow. While an explosion would lead to an investigation that could slow development, a quick resolution could put it back on track.

Killing Kylie, on the other hand . . . it wouldn't matter if it was revealed that she was assassinated. If the culprit was never found, the motive would remain speculation.

I need to get back to her and ask more questions.

I also need to double her security detail.

MISSED CONNECTIONS

As I drive back to the facility, I ask myself if I'm slipping. There's no doubt that I'm out of practice. I've been sitting on the sidelines for a while now. The fact that I saw Kylie only as a potential target and not *the* target is a colossal blunder.

It's the kind of thing a younger me would have been called in to clean up.

I have to do my best, not fuck up like that again.

Good pep talk, Brad. Now focus. Take a look at that chessboard and figure out what else is missing.

I've placed a gremlin with a futuristic rail gun crouching in a hole on the chessboard. He's aiming at the Sparrow, but Kylie stands in the same line of sight.

Huh . . . in my mental model, Kylie is an action figure. I guess that makes sense.

What else?

Over in the corner, I have three metal dogs from the Monopoly game board dancing in a circle.

Damn it, man. You missed something again.

The last mutt to get dognapped was picked up earlier that day. How did our Sniper Gremlin manage to get them to a part of the facility where they'd set off the sensors, then travel to and from his foxhole without being seen?

Trick question.

He didn't.

He was there all along.

Someone else released the hounds.

But why?

To keep Sniper Gremlin from being found while he was in the act of sabotage?

Maybe. But also to clear the area for when he made his escape.

We're not dealing with one gremlin. We're dealing with at least two.

Damn it. Things just escalated.

Hiring one assassin is complicated enough. Finding a solid two-man team . . . that's another level.

Assuming they're hired guns, that means whoever hired them knows what they're doing. This indicates state-level action.

It doesn't mean the Russians or the Chinese are behind it. But it does suggest that someone who worked for them is.

Or someone who worked for us. Someone like me.

#

"Explain to me what you mean by 'state-level,'" says Morena.

As Wind Aerospace's chief counsel, she must know what I mean.

I'd gathered Morena, Kylie, and Sophia Elad, my friend who I just put in charge of security, into the conference room for an adults-only conversation about what happened and who might be responsible.

"It means that whoever is behind this has access to resources that normally only state actors or people working on their behalf do. Like when Iran or Russia provides terrorist groups with advanced weapons or training."

"Do you mean . . ." Morena begins.

"No. That doesn't mean a country like Russia, Iran, or China is involved. But it does mean we might be dealing with people who've worked for them."

"People?" asks Kylie.

"One sniper and one lookout—possibly with a getaway vehicle. Considering the difficulty of the shot, our sniper was a professional. And that implies there was someone to do the hiring."

"What do we do?" asks Morena.

"Give everything we can to the FBI, but be as proactive as possible. We need to find out who's behind this at *our* pace, not theirs. I need to know who could have hired these guys. Who could benefit from this and who could pay for it?"

"Anybody from a foreign government to a rival firm. Half the people at the launch party have their hands in so many things, it could be any one of them," says Morena.

"How many of them could afford to pull this off?" I ask.

"How much would it cost?" she replies.

"Two hundred grand for the snipers. Another hundred for the gun. Maybe a hundred for visas and travel documents. Plus another two hundred for margin."

"Five hundred thousand? That's it?" Kylie responds, shocked.

"Half a million, yes. That's the running cost of a political hit in many countries. Less if the country has a low GDP."

"Trasker, half the people at that party spent as much or more on a stupid JPEG image of a cartoon monkey when everybody was crazy over NFTs. Any of them could have afforded this. Heck, so could most of my employees who have been here for a few years."

"So that leaves motive," offers Sophia. "And apparently there's an infinite supply of that."

"You know, there is one other factor," I tell them.

"Yeah, of course. Willpower. It's one thing to have motivation and resources to pull this off. It's another to be willing to go through with it. And that either means you've done it before and gotten away with it, or you're so desperate that you see no other option," Sophia explains.

"So we just need to find someone desperate to blow up our work who's cold-blooded enough to actually do it," says Kylie.

"That's assuming the Sparrow was the target," I reply.

"Wait, what?" she asks. "It took one heck of a trick shot to destroy it. It would have been a lot easier to just aim for my head."

"Yes. And more obvious," says Sophia.

"There's a version of events where the Sparrow exploded, took your life, and everyone decided that it was mechanical failure and not an assassination. Unfortunately, we don't know the plan or the players," I remind them. "Which brings me to the other reason I asked to meet with you. We have to face reality. We're at war. Someone is out to destroy either Kylie or this company. They're well funded, and they know what they're doing. This isn't just a matter of adding extra security guards and putting up more cameras. We need to be proactive in defending this facility and Kylie."

"Whatever it takes. They put one of my guys in the hospital. I want to punch back twice as hard," Kylie tells us.

"That's good in theory, but there's something else to consider."

"And that is?"

"They very likely had help. Help from inside. At the very least an unwitting person who gave them information about the Sparrow and your security setup."

"One of my people?" asks Kylie.

"You have four hundred and twenty employees here, Ms. Connor. Statistically, nine of them are sociopaths," says Sophia.

"We have zero people with criminal records for violent offenses, so I'd imagine that number is lower," Kylie fires back.

"You don't have to be a sociopath to do the wrong thing or betray someone's trust. Like we said before, desperation can lead people to do just about anything. More than a few people here have been passed over for a promotion they felt they deserved or had a project killed that was their life's work," I explain.

"Anybody who has a problem can come to me. We're not like other companies," says Kylie.

"Not everyone here may like you. No matter how fair you are, somebody is going to resent you. Either because of something you did or some deficit in their character. Or the simple fact that they don't think they're being compensated enough."

"Cough, cough, Ben Kohl," says Morena.

"Kohl?" I ask.

"More bark than bite," says Kylie, shaking her head. "I know I'm being naive, but I just wanted to create the kind of company I'd like to work at."

"You did," says Morena. "Employee satisfaction is through the roof here. But you can't please everybody."

"But anger them enough that they would destroy what we're doing?"

"Like I said, they may not have known. They still might not know. It could have been a simple request, like inserting a thumb drive."

"Our security team disabled all of those," says Kylie.

"You know what I mean. I had to intervene in a situation where US government emails were showing up in Russian intelligence circles. We looked and looked for a hack and couldn't find one. When we went back and looked at the oldest emails, they were from a certain city in Europe.

"When I went to the embassy there and shadowed their employees, I found a man who liked to take his laptop to a local bar and work from there. Which is a violation of protocol in and of itself. Worse, he'd get blackout drunk and pass out while still logged in.

"Somebody noticed what was on his screen and the next thing you know, there was a Russian asset there every night to buy the guy free shots so they could access his computer."

"I get it," says Kylie. "So what now?"

"Sophia's going to take a closer look at your employee records. I know you screen them because of the sensitivity of your work, but I also know there are plenty of back doors and ways that can be faked."

"Faked? Like I could have a spy working here?" asks Kylie.

"The Chinese have spies at most of the top tech companies and university research programs. They're not formally trained spies or ex-military, but they're typically compromised in some way. It could be as simple as an American researcher that takes payments to give speeches at Chinese technical colleges, or a Chinese national that knows the well-being of his family requires working for Chinese intelligence. And there are people in China doing the same for us. It's the game." I shrug.

"I'd like to do a physical sweep too," says Sophia. "I want to put in cell phone sniffers to see if anyone is carrying more than one transmitting device. I also want to search cars as they come and go."

"People will be upset," says Kylie.

"They'll be a lot more upset if something else happens that could have been prevented," I tell her. "Can we order a few hundred lint brushes? The kind that you peel off?"

"Sure. Why?" asks Kylie.

"I want us to look for dog hair in every car that comes or leaves. I know you have a lot of dog owners. Few would have three different kinds of hair in their car. It's a long shot, but I want to rule it out."

Kylie's face remains expressionless, which I take to be the way she processes things when she's not happy.

"We can put extra people at the security gates to make sure it goes quickly. We'll just write down their employee ID on each sheet and look more closely later," adds Sophia.

"I'd also like a short list of anyone who could benefit the most. I know you mentioned X-Lifter as a potential competitor. Who else would raise a red flag?"

"Ben Kohl," says Morena again.

"Who is he?"

"Former head of propulsion. We had a disagreement. He left," says Kylie.

"And then threatened to reveal our intellectual property to anyone who would pay him," adds Morena.

"He was just bluffing. The guy was angry and got a little drunk and wrote an email he shouldn't have," Kylie says.

"He could have faced federal time. You went easy on him. He even went public with our cease-and-desist," says Morena.

"And a lot of good that did for him. He just looked like an asshole."

"An asshole with a grudge," Morena points out.

"What about Timothy Watkins, your missing engineer?" I ask.

"Nothing so far," says Morena. "Police still have nothing. He's a little loony tunes and may not want to be found."

"Well, we need to find him."

"If there's a rock to turn over, they haven't found it," she says with a shrug.

"In that case, I'll take that on." I remember a burned hundred-dollar bill next to Watkins's screwdriver in the black box I placed in front of the Time Traveller's fireplace. "What about . . . Douglas Gallar, the venture capitalist who died?"

"He was an early investor. He died in a car accident. I don't think there was anything suspicious about it. Just unfortunate," says Kylie.

"Unfortunate and suspicious are the same thing in my book. After I look into Watkins, I'll dig into that."

I've got a missing engineer, another with a grudge, and someone connected to Wind Aerospace who died at a very inconvenient time.

Maybe one or two of them are unrelated to what happened, but my gut says they can't all be.

HOUSE CALL

Timothy Watkins's apartment is in a new development that began springing up outside Lancaster as the Mojave Spaceport became operational.

I use a thin key marked GARAGE that's actually a skeleton key and the shim in my nail clippers to pick the lock to his front door. I could have asked the police for a wellness check or talked the landlord into letting me in, but this is much easier.

Watkins didn't have too many friends, so who's to say I'm not one of them if someone shows up at random and asks why I'm here.

For extra cover, I brought a shopping bag with beer and cereal in case somebody actually does wander by and ask what I'm doing.

Burglars don't generally bring groceries.

My four most useful disguise accessories are (1) a walkie-talkie headset that makes me look like the technical staff at a hotel or event, (2) a large metal clipboard, (3) an Amazon delivery uniform, and (4) groceries. Those plus reading glasses hanging around my neck can get me just about anywhere.

When I was younger, I used to practice walking into places that I had no business being in. I found that I could get to the CEO of almost any company by carrying a registered letter that required a signature.

For places with more locked-down security, I could walk in as an AC repairman with a tool belt and get the building manager to let me in anywhere, then leave me alone once I was up on a ladder.

The grocery bag is overkill for this situation, but you never know.

I set it down on the counter that divides the kitchen from the living room and look around.

The place is a single-bedroom apartment with a washer/dryer in the closet straight ahead of me. A bedroom to the right and a bathroom to the left. A yoga mat is rolled up in the corner.

I checked the floor plan from the apartment listing for the unit so I have a clear picture of the layout and exits.

Watkins has minimal furniture. There's a couch, a chair, and a console with a television and PlayStation.

Inside his bedroom there's a bed and a desk with his company laptop sitting on it below a widescreen display. On the nightstand by his bed is a stack of books ranging from the philosophical to the technical.

There's no sign of a struggle, and the door didn't look like it had been forced open.

Of course, if two men showed up dressed like police officers in the middle of the night and asked him to step outside, there would be no struggle. A disturbing number of kidnappings in other countries are committed by people disguised as law enforcement. In some countries, they *are* law enforcement.

I don't think that's the case here. There's no set of keys by the door, and his car is gone. That suggests he drove—or was driven somewhere.

I call Sophia.

"What's up?" she asks.

"Do me a favor and run Watkins's license plate to see if he parked his car at an airport," I reply.

"On it," she says.

Post-9/11, every license plate that comes near an airport gets logged. Not just to track where suspect terrorists might be going but also to flag for potential car bombs.

Ten kilos of plastic explosive in a car in front of the international terminal at JFK airport could shut down air travel for days simply by creating chaos and increased security.

Access to license-plate tracking data isn't a public service, but Sophia has semiofficial channels to acquire such information.

I open up Watkins's closet and find a small collection of dress shirts on hangers and a pile of T-shirts and jeans on the floor next to several pairs of shoes.

I take out my phone and scroll through the photos I pulled from his social media. It's a simple way to see what outfits are missing and what he might be wearing.

Between the clothes in the closet and what I found in the washer and dryer, there is at least one T-shirt missing, as well as a pair of sneakers, a pair of boots, and a hiking jacket.

I search through his drawers and find a folder with a birth certificate and other documents, but no passport. I also can't find the backpack that he appeared with in a photo on a mountain in Mexico.

It certainly looks like he took a trip out of the country.

But was it for fun? A change of life? Or was he running from something?

My phone rings. It's Sophia.

"What do you have?" I ask.

"His car was tagged at the parking lot at Meadows Field Airport in Bakersfield a week ago," she replies.

I scroll through his social media once more. He's been to Mexico three times in the last year. Romantic or other reasons?

"Do you think you can get a cell number search done in Mexico?"

"Mexico? That's easy. It'll cost fifty bucks. Give me a couple hours. You want Watkins's data?"

"Yeah. I really just care about the last seven days. Trips before, too, if you can."

"Do you think he went willingly?"

"It looks that way. It's what happened at the other end of the trip that has me curious."

"If you need someone to go down to Mexico, just let me know."

"Ha. I need you near Kylie. My Spanish is terrible but serviceable."

"Too bad you didn't inherit your mother's gift for language," she observes.

My mother speaks more than a half dozen languages, plus various dialects. Her capacity for language and disguise was legendary among the intelligence community.

ENTREPRENEUR

Peter Strausman, CEO of X-Lifter, greets me in the lobby of the Los Angeles headquarters of his company. A full-size replica of the Wright brothers' *Flyer* made from aluminum and Mylar hangs from the roof of the atrium.

Alongside Strausman is an older man in a business suit who I assume is Jordan Metz, his legal counsel. The two make for quite a contrast. Strausman with his tan complexion and blond hair looks like he should be out on the Pacific with a surfboard, while Metz belongs in a dark boardroom planning a hostile takeover.

"You like the plane?" asks Strausman. "It's by an artist named Angie Glassler. She takes old technology and re-creates it with new materials. She's working on an all-Kevlar Stingray that I'm dying to buy for my living room."

"I'm sure that will be a talking point."

"I'm sorry, Mr. Trasker, but we don't know much about you. Do you mind if we have this conversation in the lobby?" asks Metz.

"Jordan is worried that you might be here to spy on us," explains Strausman.

I am, of course. But not for industrial secrets.

"I'd prefer a place a little more private," I tell them.

"This will have to do." Metz crosses his arms.

I check my watch to estimate how much traffic I'll be stuck in, then reply in an almost bored voice. "In that case, I'll let the FBI explain the situation to you—I assume you'll be more accommodating to them."

Metz was trying a power play with me. It was a rookie move. If he were smarter, he would have been glad-handing me while marching us to a swanky conference room. Maybe even offering me a drink and seeing if it loosened me up.

"We'll get a conference room," says Strausman.

"I don't know if there's anything available," growls Metz, frustrated at being overruled.

"How about the one we did the interview with the *Los Angeles Times* in? I think we can trust Mr. Trasker in there, don't you?"

It's clear to me that while Metz may guide him on some things, Strausman gets his way when he wants. The threat of me walking away without finding out what I was here to tell them was enough for him to overrule his attorney's silly intimidation game.

"This way," says Strausman, leading us through a security gate and down a hallway. "Please remember to turn off the flash on your spy camera."

"It's infrared," I joke back at him.

I'd bug the hell out of this building and have all their computers hacked if I thought they were hiding a secret that was a physical threat to Kylie, but their corporate secrets are theirs, and I would never divulge anything I didn't discover through legal channels. (Getting an engineer drunk and listening to his stories is perfectly legal, by the way.)

We seat ourselves in a glass-walled conference room and Strausman flips a switch, turning the walls opaque gray.

From the million-dollar art piece in the lobby to the science-fiction conference rooms, X-Lifter puts Wind Aerospace to shame in the competition for most ostentatious headquarters. Wind Aerospace looks more like a community college campus than a state-of-the-art technology industrial complex. But appearances are skin deep. Wind Aerospace has three times the valuation of X-Lifter and a better track record. Kylie isn't the type to lurk around Art Basel trying to find the perfect showpiece for her lobby.

"You know quite well about the incident that happened," I explain.

"Terrible. But for the grace of God go us," says Strausman. "I'm glad Kylie is okay. She's one of a kind."

"Yes, she is. As you also know, there's an FAA investigation. And you heard me mention the FBI in the lobby."

"What's their angle?" asks Metz.

"You're going to find out soon that we think this was an act of sabotage and have evidence to prove it," I explain.

I study the reaction of both men and place Strausman in a metal airplane on the Time Traveller's writing desk. Alongside him, Metz holds an old fountain pen menacingly over the ink blotter. I don't know if there's a rhyme or reason to how my brain makes up these images. I just know that they stick.

"What evidence?" asks Metz.

"We can't go into that."

If they *are* connected, I don't want them knowing what we know. There could be other clues out there for us, provided that they're not sanitized first.

"What I *can* say is that we don't know if this was specifically targeted at Wind Aerospace or more generally at the advanced aviation industry. We'd like to share information with you, and hopefully you will share with us anything that might pertain to security."

"Such as?" asks Metz.

"Disgruntled employees that have made threats. Contact from foreign governments. Anything unusual."

"Why not just go to the FBI?" says Metz.

"We are, and we encourage you to as well. We just ask that you pass on anything you can to us as well. Especially if it's actionable."

"Do you have any actionable things to tell *us*?" says Metz.

"Yes: however many security cameras you think is enough, it's not. I'd want eyes on every part of your facility—especially your testing grounds. If someone goes near an engine stand, you want to know. I looked at the Google Maps images of your Nevada facility, and it seems pretty wide open. You have one guard shack and a few miles of barbed wire that would be easy to get through." I point to the offices behind me. "Forget what's on your computers. If I wanted to know how your engines work, I'd just use a pair of wire cutters to go in and examine them."

Metz falls silent. He wasn't expecting useful advice. I just gave him a large download.

"Yeah . . . we're a little negligent there," admits Strausman.

"We're still picking up the pieces from our explosion. It might have been preventable. I hope you have better luck."

"Is this going to be a big setback for you?" probes Metz.

I shrug. "Not my area of expertise."

My phone vibrates with a text from Sophia:

I have the last location in Mexico for Watkins' phone.

I rise to leave. "Let's stay in touch."

Strausman follows suit and shakes my hand. "Please let Kylie know that I'm happy to help if there's anything I can do."

"I will."

Strausman seems sincere. Metz, on the other hand, I'm not so sure about. He was watching me closely the whole time.

I realize now that the whole "let's meet in the lobby" ploy wasn't a petulant power move but a calculated tactic to see how I handled it.

I'm not sure if I overplayed my hand or not. It might have been better to look like the type who can be bullied around. Sometimes the absence of ego is the best camouflage.

CELDA

The Municipal Police Center in West Cuernavaca, Mexico, sits across from a playground filled with brightly painted monkey bars, swings, and workout stations. It's a warm afternoon, and nobody is using them at the moment, but I suspect that when the neighboring school lets out, the playground will be full.

The police station itself is located between a tae kwon do school and an auto repair shop. The station takes up most of the block—a tall blue wall from end to end with only a doorway and a closed gate for cars to enter and exit.

On Google Maps, the station is actually three buildings. One for administration, another that appears to be some kind of storage or repair shed, and a third with bars on the window that must be a pre-transfer holding area for prisoners.

The last place Watkins's phone was used was inside the perimeter of the police station. He didn't make a call—it was simply the last location where the phone sent its location to cell towers.

For my craft, cell phones were a godsend. I'd feel differently if I were an old-school surveillance hand, harkening back to the days when you could dress like a telephone lineman and climb a pole down the street from your target and tap their phone. But I was a HUMINT—human intelligence—operative. I like to know where people go when they move around.

When I had Sophia call the police station, she was told that there was no American there and definitely nobody by the name of Watkins.

I listened in while standing outside the station, in case her call set off an alarm and someone decided to move our missing engineer. In truth, I'd be surprised if he were still there. Prisoners are usually transferred to larger facilities while awaiting trial.

I press the button by the entrance, and a moment later a mechanical catch unlocks the door.

Inside the doorway is an open lot with half a dozen police cars and three motorcycles. The jail building is to my right and has a tall barbed-wire fence enclosing an asphalt yard where two young men dressed in casual clothes are playing cards and listening to a radio.

I step through the glass door in the building directly in front of me and find myself in a small lobby, where an older woman seated in the guest area chats with a woman in a police uniform sitting behind the counter scrolling on her phone.

The officer puts her phone down and greets me. "How can I help you?" she asks in Spanish.

She's friendly. It's the reading glasses around my neck and colorful sweater vest. People see me as either a warm father figure or harmless professor type.

"Hello"—I look at her name tag—"Officer Marta. My name is Donovan. I'm from the US consulate. I was asked to drop off a prescription medication for an inmate you have here, Timothy Watkins."

"The American?" she asks.

"Yes." I place a prescription bag on the counter. It contains sugar pills. The prescribing doctor's name on the label is Watkins's supervisor at Wind Aerospace. The instructions say that "Relief will come soon."

I don't know if he's here or somewhere else or even for what reasons they might be holding him. It's quite possible he shut down his phone in front of the police station and is sitting at a remote beach, drinking bad rum.

Marta takes the bag from the counter. "Let me see."

She walks through a door, and I hear the sound of a male voice but can't make out the words. He seems curt. A moment later she emerges and places the bag down.

"There's nobody here by that name," she says without making eye contact.

"Was he transferred?"

"I don't have any other information," she replies.

I can see the shadow of two feet by the door she just walked through. Somebody else is listening in.

"I'm terribly sorry," I say as I pick up the medication. "I probably have the wrong address. If you'll excuse me. I need to hurry and make sure he gets these."

I exit back onto the street. Marta saying "the American" and a person listening at the door were pretty good confirmation that Watkins came through here or might still be at this location.

If I suspected this were cartel related, I would have had four armed men waiting for me so we could stop any car leaving here and check if Watkins is in the trunk.

My intuition is that this was strictly a commercial venture and that the captain of this precinct was bribed to apprehend Watkins. For what reason, I don't know.

To get to the bottom of this, I need a good local lawyer who understands the lay of the land here.

There are plenty of local law firms that gladly represent Americans in trouble with the law. They'll take your money, show up at your bail hearing, and make some defense, then throw up their hands when the judge either doesn't grant bail or requests one that's so ridiculously high you can't afford it and no bail bondsman would take on because they know you're a flight risk the moment you step out of a Mexican jail.

Everything you need to know about the heart of my craft can be found in studying the prisoner's dilemma—the philosophical question of when you should trust someone.

It's not easy when you don't understand the other party's incentives.

I could call a prestigious LA law firm and get a recommendation for an attorney down here, but it's not going to be their first-tier choice because I'm not a client who spends millions of dollars on their services. They'd be more incentivized to let me pay an attorney they want a favor from than send me to the best—especially if I have a complex case.

Instead, I call a contact at the consulate, ask who they use, and get the name of a Mexican attorney who wants to maintain a high-value relationship with US officials.

While I wait for a call back, I need to find out more about Watkins and why he was apprehended.

I might be able to learn more by finding the local cop saloon. There're always one or two within walking distance of a station house—but not so close that their supervisors will see them grabbing a drink in the middle of the day.

INFORMACIÓN

El Nido del Halcón ("The Falcon's Nest") is three blocks away. Balthazar Espinós, a deputy who works in the jail facility at the Municipal Police Center, is about four cheap beers into his afternoon happy hour.

I found him sitting at a table in the back corner of the bar, playing a word game on his phone. The Falcon's Nest opens to the street when the shutters are rolled up, and electric fans placed on the sidewalk displace the slightly warmer air inside.

It's hot at the back of the bar, but Balthazar didn't seem too bothered. He seems perfectly happy with his beer and his game.

I set two bottles of premium beer on his table before taking a seat.

Balthazar seems more amused than bothered. "This isn't the kind of bar you apparently think it is," he says to me in Spanish, implying this may be a come-on. "But I'll take your drink."

"I don't think there's enough beer in this whole bar to make that work between us."

This brings about a fit of laughter that doesn't seem proportionate to the level of humor in my joke. I guess he's an easy audience.

After twenty minutes of small talk, I learn that Balthazar has lived in this town since he moved here with his mother. He now supports her and has his own place. His favorite television shows are telenovelas he watches with his mother but that he assures me are quite well written.

When I ask about the uniform he's still wearing (although untucked and unbuttoned at the top), he says he works in the local jail. His uncle got him the job when he ran the police station. Unfortunately, when his uncle retired, so did his chance of advancement because of "that prick Allendo."

Balthazar is an easygoing, happy-go-lucky kind of guy. He says he's never had much problem with the prisoners, and the worst part about the job are days when it gets really hot and the air-conditioning breaks.

With his fingers clutching his nose, he says the smell of the men stacked in there reminds him of the gorilla enclosure at the zoo.

The average police officer makes less than $700 a month—which is even below what's considered the national living wage. Balthazar's salary amounts to even less than that.

The fact that he's sitting here drinking his salary and still has money to support his mother implies that he has supplemental sources of income.

For a corrections officer on either side of the border, that usually means looking the other way when someone wants to get something into the prison. This could be anything from a cell phone to a prostitute.

Since most of the people locked up in his jail are street criminals, payment often comes in the form of narcotics. Which means that Balthazar has on more than one occasion accepted a bribe in the form of contraband.

I don't think this makes him a bad man. But the honest correctional officer would be home with Mom right now, not getting drunk in his uniform.

"Tell me about the American in the jail," I say after setting down another round of beers.

Balthazar nods. He knew I had a purpose when I came over to his table. He was curious to see what I was about and how many rounds I would foot him.

I up the ante with an open box of cigarettes that I place on the table. Clearly visible inside are several rolled-up hundred-dollar bills.

Balthazar pushes the carton back to me. "You've been good company. No need. Any chance to screw over that prick Allendo."

Allendo is the new captain at the station. I suspect he was the person on the other side of the door when I went there and asked about Watkins.

"I show up one day and there's an American in a cell by himself. I ask Javier, 'Who is this?' There's no paperwork. No file. Just a man who speaks almost no Spanish sitting in the cell. Javier tells me not to worry. He says Allendo is holding him for the Federal Ministerial Police and needs to be kept hidden because the cartels are looking for him.

"Well, I laughed. There is no way the FMP would trust Allendo for something like that. He'd tell every whore and mobster he could, that prick. Maybe if the FMP wanted the man killed . . .

"So I ask Allendo, 'What's with the gringo?' Allendo tells me that it's not my problem. I tell him that I have to feed this man and take out his shit, maybe I should know why.

"And this is where Allendo gets stupid. I know someone's paying him to do this. Does he pay me anything? No. Why would Allendo give you a peso when he can lie for free?

"He says, 'This man is a drug trafficker, and they arrested him on the bus to La Alameda with cocaine in his baggage.' Why anyone would want to bring cocaine to La Alameda is lost on me.

"Well, Javier said Allendo stopped the man and brought him into the station himself—because Allendo was too cheap to pay any of us. Not even a token." Balthazar taps the cigarette box.

I show Balthazar a photo of Watkins. "Is this the man?"

"Yes. That's the one. Are you a private detective?"

"A friend of a friend. I was asked to look into this. Any chance you can get me in there to talk to him?"

"No. Javier has a mouth on him, and it's better to swear behind Allendo's back than to cross him where he can see you."

"I understand. How is Timothy doing?"

"I see some people cry the moment they step inside. Others? It does not bother them. This man, he sits there in his yoga pose and doesn't seem bothered. I suspect he may be a little crazy."

"How is he being treated?"

"Allendo made it clear that he wasn't to be harmed. And Javier and the other men aren't violent. Greedy, yes. But not mean like in other places."

I push the cigarette box toward him. "Who is Allendo's biggest enemy?"

"Besides me?" Balthazar lets out a cackle. "Maybe his wife when he comes home late."

"Anybody else?"

"Harold Perdigó. He's with the state police reform office. I've heard Allendo use his name as a swear word. Perdigó wants to change the way things are done. Allendo likes the old way." Balthazar shrugs.

If you're going after someone, make sure you know what they're afraid of.

"Thank you," I say as I get up.

Balthazar slips the cigarette box in his pocket. "My pleasure. Hopefully you can get your friend free and I can have Allendo's job," he says with a laugh.

I reach out to shake his hand. Balthazar stands up, surprisingly steady for as much as he has drunk, shakes mine, and then contorts his face for a moment.

"Fuck it. Prisoners are allowed visitors. Allendo never said this man couldn't have one." He checks his watch. "And the fucker's probably gone by now. Let's go."

Balthazar walks out of the bar and motions for me to follow.

On the way to the police station, I text Sophia an update and instructions in case I find myself on the wrong side of the bars.

RETREAT

"Hey, you speak American!" says Watkins as I introduce myself to him at the little table in the small prison yard where the men were playing cards earlier. I think he meant "English," but I don't correct him.

"Kylie sent me," I reply.

Other than the fact that Watkins could use a shower and has been wearing the same clothes for days, he seems surprisingly well for someone who has been in a Mexican jail cell for seven days with no outside contact.

I've had more experience inside foreign prisons than I care to remember—and the scars to show for it. I'm pretty sure nobody was putting out cigarettes on Watkins's back or whipping him with a garden hose.

"Oh man. I hope she's not pissed that I missed the unveiling," he says.

"She's more concerned about you," I explain. "So how did you end up here?"

"Crazy story. Apparently, I'm being charged for drug-running. I heard about stuff like that happening but never thought it would happen to me."

I don't know if it's the lack of human contact or his nature, but Watkins seems a bit spacey.

"Tell me how you got here."

"I was on the bus to La Alameda when it got pulled over," he says.

"Why were you going to La Alameda?"

"There's a great silent meditation retreat up there. I was going to chill for a couple days. Only as the bus is pulling out of town, a police car pulls us over. Next thing I know I'm being escorted off the bus and into the police car, then brought here."

"Did they tell you why?"

"The woman at the desk spoke pretty good English. The captain had her tell me that I was being charged for trafficking because they found several kilograms of cocaine in my bag under the bus. Which was BS, because I only had my backpack and that was in my lap.

"But they said my name was on the bag and that was enough to arrest me. Although I don't know if I was actually arrested. Everybody spoke Spanish most of the time, but nobody took my picture or my fingerprints. They said they were holding me until their version of the FBI came to talk to me."

"And did anyone come?" I ask.

"Yeah. Not from their FBI. Another man, named Wagner, came who said he would be my lawyer."

I drop a man in a white suit next to a jail cell and a jailed yogi near the model of the Time Traveller's time machine.

"Mexican or American?"

"Both. Fluently. He told me that I was in a lot of trouble and could spend the rest of my life in jail. But he said he could help me.

"I told him I had money. But he said it would be for free. I just needed to do a favor. This is where it gets weird. He said that a man from the Mexican Air Force wanted to ask me some questions and that if I was helpful, he could pull some strings and get me out of here."

Ah. Now we're getting to the bottom of things.

"Would these be technical questions?" I ask.

"I assume so. Unless he wanted to talk about UFOs. I can talk about those forever. But I got the feeling it would be technical questions about what I worked on."

"And what did you tell him?"

"I said I was under a nondisclosure agreement and couldn't talk about anything work related. He said it was okay because this man was from the government and we were in Mexico."

"What did you say?"

"I said I'd have to talk to my boss first. He got really angry and told me that if I didn't help, things would get bad for me. He said that if he wasn't there to look out for me, then I could end up in a cell with other inmates and they'd . . . you know. Do stuff. The thing is, I don't really respond to threats. I was bullied a lot, so I just kind of tune it out," Watkins says with a shrug.

"Have you seen this man since then?"

"No."

"All right. First, we'll get Allendo, the captain here. I want you to tell him that you'll speak to anyone they want and tell them whatever they want if they can get you free and give you one million dollars."

"Kylie would *kill* me if I said anything," Watkins says, horrified.

"You're not going to tell them anything. I just need Wagner to come here. You'll tell him you want an answer by the end of the day."

This man, Wagner, arranged to detain Watkins illegally. Which means he's competent enough to know who to bribe and use them to get what he wants—which I assume is the knowledge in Watkins's head.

When I asked Kylie if Watkins might be a target for intellectual-property theft, she said that he was one of only a handful of people who knew the application process they used for the coating that made working with hydrogen so much easier. She said this process alone could be worth much more than the aviation part of the company and that they'd come upon it based on sheer dumb luck. Other companies know she has solved the problem, but they don't know how.

Industrial secrets that can be worth billions of dollars often seem like the most innocuous things at first. A slightly better drill bit can help tap into vast oil reserves. A simple chemical compound can reduce the size of a microchip that makes a next-generation iPhone possible.

I don't know if the party behind Watkins's abduction is also directly responsible for the destruction of the Sparrow, but the timing and brazenness can't be coincidental.

The tricky part for me is that this Wagner fellow can cut and run if he thinks something suspicious is afoot.

I'm counting on Allendo not wanting to scare Wagner off by telling him someone was snooping around. Allendo's probably getting paid by the day for Watkins's imprisonment.

"So I just tell him I want the money?" asks Watkins.

"Exactly. Don't give him any other details."

"Then what?"

"I'll deal with him. While that's happening, someone should be coming here to get you out. And to do that, I need you to hold still while I take a photo."

I take out my phone and get several images to use as evidence that he's being held here.

"Proof of life, right?" Watkins says with a grin.

"Something like that."

I don't tell him that Wagner's other option is to hire gang members to torture him until he tells them everything—and then kill him. Hopefully that won't eventuate. If it does, I'll be speed-dialing kidnap rescue experts and forming a small mercenary force.

My best guess is that using the cartels would be plan B. Plan A was to scare Watkins, get him to talk, and then send him back home with the threat of prosecution if he told anyone what happened.

They might have been hoping that plus the shame of being charged with a drug crime would be enough for Watkins to keep his selling of company IP secret.

What they weren't counting on was their kidnapping victim already being mentally prepared to spend days on end not talking to anyone and going to the bathroom in a bucket.

While I hope to have Watkins home by tonight, my other concern is getting to this Wagner and finding out what he knows.

In the old days, kidnapping one of my people would be reason enough to take the gloves off, but this is a different game. I can't start pulling out fingernails with pliers . . . yet.

POINT MAN

The man known as Wagner exits through the door in the blue police wall and steps onto the sidewalk. He's not dressed in a white suit as he is in my memory palace but instead wears dark pants and a light-blue blazer that are immaculately tailored and well fitted to his athletic build.

He appears to be in his thirties, is tan, and has the posture of someone who carries a certain amount of authority.

Wagner's far from the schlubby fixer I was expecting. The same SUV that dropped him off arrives to pick him up when he steps outside.

The meeting lasted less than ten minutes.

My guess is that Wagner scoffed at Watkins's request and departed, ready to escalate the plan to the next level.

Fortunately for Watkins, Christine Leyden, an attorney who came highly recommended from the consulate, is on her way to the jail along with a court order from a judge and two Mexican federal police agents to free Watkins.

I pull my rental car onto the road and follow Wagner's SUV. Although my consulate contacts were able to find Leyden, nobody knew a thing about Wagner.

This suggests that he's a gun-for-hire not from the region.

The SUV has local plates that belong to a Mexico City executive security firm, which means both the vehicle and the driver are rented.

These are the people you hire to make sure you don't get kidnapped.

With the crackdown on the drug trade and demand shifting to more domestically produced narcotics in the United States, kidnapping is on the rise in Mexico and other countries with a heavy cartel presence. Despite the predictions of economists, slowing down the international drug trade didn't change the net amount of vice in the world. It only shifted it.

Wagner's truck turns down a street and I follow from a safe distance. His driver takes another turn and I wait before crossing the intersection.

Following without being obvious is tricky. I make it a point to rent small, ugly cars that blend in with the other vehicles. The SUV, on the other hand, is easy to follow from several blocks away.

I lose sight of it as it turns a corner but don't worry because traffic isn't moving that quickly. I make the next turn and come to a stop at a traffic light. The SUV is visible down the block.

I'm so focused on where the SUV is heading that I don't notice the man approaching the passenger side of my car until he opens the door and climbs inside.

"Hello, Mr. Trasker. I thought I might save you some trouble and tell you myself where I'm headed," says the man called Wagner.

There's no gun in his hand. No implied threat.

His only weapon is his extreme confidence.

"Where to?" I ask, trying to stall for time and figure out how to make up for my carelessness.

"The executive airport at Atizapán. It's about an hour drive. Maybe we could have a little conversation."

I can't tell if he's improvising or if I'm the next fly to fall into his web.

COUNTERPART

I pull over to the side of the road and park to let the bus that's been honking pass. Wagner is making this into a cute little game, but I don't have to cooperate.

"Well, you know my name. What's yours?"

There's no bulge under his arms or by his ankles. If he's strapped, it's in a holster in the small of his back—which I can't see because he's turned toward me. That would make it a small, low-caliber pistol.

"We'll just use Wagner for now. When I heard that I might meet the infamous Bradley Trasker, I couldn't tell you how excited I was."

"And why would you be excited?"

"I've heard quite a bit about you." He's resting one arm on the top of the seat and bracing his body with his other to keep himself facing me. It's a bit of an odd posture. I can't tell if it's some kind of power pose or if he's trying to make me focus all my attention on him.

I keep an eye on my rearview and side mirrors in case he's having someone sneak up on me.

I could slam the knife under my thigh into the flesh under his jaw in less than a second. I keep a blade there for carjackers. It would work equally well on him.

"Nobody is coming for me, and I'm sure you can think of a hundred more ways to kill me than I can to kill you," says Wagner. "This is just a friendly conversation. Consider it a professional courtesy from a fan."

I don't relax. I keep my eyes moving between him and the mirrors.

"In that case, why not tell me who's paying you?"

"Unfortunately, Brad, we're not that good of friends. Not yet."

"Then I don't think this is going to be a very long conversation. I took your photo when you entered the police station and sent it to my colleagues."

"Sophia Elad? She was a great hire. Good move on your part. I suspect as you get older you have to worry about the little details—like leaving this car door unlocked. But I can save you some trouble and email you my LinkedIn. I'm very easy to find."

"I'm sure that will be helpful to the FBI."

Wagner closes his eyes and lets out a laugh.

While his mouth is open, I see the spot where my blade would penetrate through the roof of his mouth if I pushed hard enough through the soft part of his lower jaw.

"The look in your eye, Brad. You're visualizing how you'd kill me right now. This is priceless. There aren't many guys like you left. A few Russians, but they're psychopaths. You're a special breed."

I could also go for his throat. A stab or a slash, depending on his posture in the moment. He'd have a hard time cracking wise with a pair of severed arteries.

"I'm going to slowly reach into my pocket and take out my phone. Don't murder me, okay?"

I don't stop him. If he'd wanted to kill me, he could have done it the moment he opened my car door. He's playing some other game I don't understand.

"You see this?" says Wagner, holding out a sleek Android phone.

I don't respond to the rhetorical question.

"I want to make a point." He turns the phone away from me and enters a code to unlock it.

I can see the code in the passenger-side mirror as he enters it: 287577.

I begin to store it away but pause when I realize he may be messing with me.

28-75-77 is "knife kill quick" in the mnemonic major system—the first method I learned to memorize numbers. It can't be a coincidence that his passcode spells out the kind of words a hired fixer might use. Is this another mind game?

Wagner angles the screen at me. It's tuned to a Telegram app channel. The name at the top of the screen is in Cyrillic.

"I know you're an adaptable guy, but I don't know if you understand how much things have changed in the last few years while you've been out of the game." He points to a string of numbers in a text. "Do you know what that is?"

"A bitcoin wallet. Let me guess: you can send some cryptocurrency to that address and have a hit put out on someone."

"You're so old school. I love it," says Wagner. The smile fades. "I press this button and you're erased."

"That sounds the same to me."

The cocky grin returns. "That kind of thinking is why I'm sitting here knowing everything about you and you're sitting there, clueless, thinking all the ways you could fillet me with that knife under your leg . . . because that's the best you can do."

He sits back and waves at the cars passing by. "What do you see? If we roped off the entire block and counted all the pesos in their pockets and all the money in their bank accounts, do you think that will even come close to what's sitting in your bank account? Not counting that trust fund you've never touched?"

I don't respond.

"How much did it cost to bribe the guard at the jail? A hundred bucks? That's not even your hourly rate," he says, answering his own question.

"This is why people hate Americans."

"No, Brad. This is why people hate the rich. Because 'rich' is another word for 'power.' You can't run for office in America without having a friend who's a billionaire. Down here it helps to know someone in the cartel, because they have all the money. Drugs, social-media likes, political votes—it's all about money. Where it comes from is irrelevant."

"This is your big insight? Money equals power? I hope your parents didn't have to pay for your education."

"You're missing the bigger picture. That's always been the case. What's changed now is the rate of acceleration. Think for a moment . . . you have no idea who I am. Ten years ago you'd probably be able to guess who I worked for because there was only a handful of players and you knew them all.

"And now? I could be working for a foreign government or some kid who built a crypto coin-miner in his grandmother's basement. He could be the one that presses the button that pays me to do what I do. Or it could be someone sitting in some office in Langley with a black budget and carte blanche to do whatever he thinks is necessary in the American interest."

"Is bribing a cop to fake a drug charge so you can steal intellectual property in the American interest?" I ask.

Wagner shrugs. "Who's to say? I don't need to know who's on the other end. All I need to know is if the transaction went through."

"Don't you care?"

"Did you care when you helped get a visa for a Pakistani intelligence officer who ended up providing false information that led to carpet bombing three different villages that hadn't had a Taliban presence for months?"

I don't have a response. I've lost sleep over that. It wasn't my call but Azmat's, the Pakistani intelligence officer who gave me a bad vibe. I didn't trust him . . . but I didn't trust anyone.

"Would you rather have some tech bro inconvenienced for a few days on your conscience? Or the deaths of dozens of innocent people? I know my answer," says Wagner.

"Is there a point to this?"

"Yes. I'm trying to tell you that the game has changed. There aren't any superpowers anymore. There are just people with power. Putin and Xi aren't politicians. They're businessmen who know where real wealth can be found. Even a socialist like Hugo Chavez, born dirt-poor, left behind a billion-dollar fortune.

"More than ever, money talks. Powerful people don't need to build spy networks or raise armies. They just press a button and the dirty deed's done for them."

"I wish I could say this monologue has been enlightening or at the very least interesting, but that would be a lie," I reply with a sigh.

Wagner sighs back at me. "Brad . . . What's the reason you followed me? What piece of information did you hope to extract?"

I wanted to know who he was working for. I realize now that he was giving me the answer in his own, long-winded way.

"Were you going to zip-tie me to a chair and beat it out of me? It's not my kink, but damn, I'd actually like to try that at least once."

"I can arrange it."

Wagner laughs. "Slow down. I'm doing you a favor. You're just not picking it up."

Oh, I picked it up. Wagner's telling me that he has no idea who he's working for. Nor does he care. He doesn't see a difference between me and himself because in the end the results are the same.

"You're probably saying to yourself, 'Hey, I only work for the good guys.' But you saw how that worked out with Azmat Haq and probably a dozen other times like that. And now you're working for Kylie Connor—as innocent as can be. You finally found somebody worthwhile to put yourself in service to. Maybe it helps you get over the pain of losing your son. Jason, right?"

Wagner stops yapping when he sees the knife in my hand.

"This is your problem, Brad. Violence is your go-to solution," says Wagner. "I meant no disrespect. All I want you to do is to take a real close look at what Kylie's trying to do. Is she solving world transportation or making it cheaper to kill anybody anywhere in the world? Do we really need that?"

I relax my hand and bring the blade back down.

"I only have one more thing to say before I make my exit," Wagner says. "Ask your friend Sennet to look up 'Nochnaya Sova.' Then have a conversation with Ms. Connor. It should be interesting." He opens the door. "I'd stay and talk, but I'm getting paid a stupid amount of money to go to some other part of the world and solve a problem. Look me up. Send me a DM if you ever want some work."

"I'm sorry this job didn't work out for you," I tell him.

Wagner leans in through the open window.

"Brad. You still don't see it. It did."

THE GAME

Wagner occupied way more of my mental space than I would have liked on the flight back to California. I don't know if his parting shot that he'd accomplished his mission was intended to play with my head or if he was serious. Either way, it got to me.

The smug grin on his LinkedIn profile only makes it sting even worse. He'd already sent a connection request to my account, which lists me as a boring-sounding foreign trade consultant.

Michael Charles Wagner lists his entire résumé and educational history. Everything is legitimate. Even his corporate consulting firm. All of it checks out.

He doesn't need a disguise because nobody can see what he's doing. I'm sure if they pressured Allendo to reveal who'd bribed him, it wouldn't come back to Wagner. It was probably done anonymously. Allendo didn't care as long as the money cleared. He wouldn't know if the person who told him to let Wagner speak to Watkins was actually Wagner himself or some other individual.

In my profession, we worried about the effects that untraceable electronic currency and complete anonymity would have on terrorism and global politics. We figured it would make it a little harder to catch the bad guys. None of us was expecting someone like Wagner, who could do his dirty work almost completely out in the open because nothing could be traced back to him.

Even law firms that move drug money between cartels and terrorist groups make an effort to pretend to be legitimate. They have some sense of shame.

Wagner's too smart to fall for a wiretap or any of the other ways you'd catch someone well versed in the digital realm but ignorant of the real world.

But the existence of people like Wagner isn't the real problem I'm dealing with. It's the revelation that even *he* doesn't know who is pulling the strings.

I believe him on this because the notion made him gleeful. He loves this new order because there *is* no order. Dinosaurs like me are being pummeled by the asteroid while scrappy mammals like Wagner are thriving in their little underground burrows.

I came to Mexico hoping to find out if Watkins's disappearance led back to whoever was behind the destruction of the Sparrow. Instead, I got an update on how the world really works today.

It's a world in which even using an old-school method like "truth serum" (actually a drug that lowers one's inhibitions) and interrogating Wagner wouldn't reveal anything of value.

Terrorist cells are hard to disrupt because they keep members ignorant of the identities of one another. Hence, capturing one doesn't reveal the rest of the network.

Satellite surveillance, invisible trackers, and intensive electronic eavesdropping combined with supercomputers dedicated to information processing helped break those terror cells up and limit their impact. Al-Qaeda wasn't able to pull off another 9/11 because of that.

Now technology has outpaced our ability to disrupt organized bad actors. Who needs a terrorist cell when you can just send some crypto to a desperate person to get them to perform your evil deed?

You don't have to be a spymaster working for the CIA or the CCP to reach around the globe. You simply need an address to send bitcoin.

I'm agnostic on technology. I can bemoan how much it's changed my craft, but that doesn't change the facts. The world is very different from the one I started out in.

I either have to adapt or die.

Right now, I'm struggling with how to adapt. My first warning was the fact that I didn't consider the possibility that Kylie could be targeted as seriously as I should have. Second is this realization that I'm playing a game I don't understand.

It reminds me of the parental disconnect I felt whenever I sat down with my young son and tried to play one of his video games with him. The controls baffled me, the graphics made my head hurt, and everything moved so *fast*.

I remember thinking to myself that Jason's brain was wired so differently from my own. I didn't feel *old* so much as *alien*.

The way Wagner looked at me wasn't all that different. I was a piece of amusing nostalgia. The idea that I might slide my knife into his jugular was exhilarating for him.

I was an *experience*.

I can imagine him at some tapas bar in Ibiza regaling his friends with the story of the old spy that held a knife to his throat—like I'm some hip escape room he made it through.

Everything's an experience. Nothing is real.

Maybe there's some advantage in there for me in this, but I don't see it. How do you threaten someone who doesn't have the common sense to accept that their life's in danger?

And threaten them for what? The untraceable account they were communicating with?

Wagner doesn't know anything about who hired him because he didn't want to know—precisely because it would be a liability for him.

That doesn't mean whoever hired him is untraceable. Believing you're completely anonymous leads to mistakes. The trouble is detecting those mistakes—and not making them at a faster rate yourself. Something I've failed at thus far.

The game isn't what it used to be.

And damned if I can't figure out what it is.

But I didn't come away entirely empty-handed. For some reason, Wagner decided to leave me a breadcrumb: "Nochnaya Sova."

I sent that to Sennet, as Wagner suggested. Five minutes later he texted me back.

Do not mention that to the client until we have spoken. Urgent.

Sennet telling me not to tell Kylie about this is . . . concerning. She's the person I'm working for. If I can't trust my employer with new information, then why am I working for her?

I drive straight from the airport to the rural library Sennet has been using as his makeshift office. I call Sophia and have her relay to Kylie that Watkins is in safe hands and being put on a flight back to the United States.

Other than that, I decide to hold off contact with Kylie until I get the skinny on Nochnaya Sova.

All I know is that it's Russian for "Night Owl." Beyond that, it's a mystery to me.

NIGHT OWL

"How much do you know about Kylie Connor?" Sennet asks me from across the table in the back of the public library in California City.

"What I've read and what I've observed. What *should* I know about her?"

"I just wondered if you had a feeling or an instinct about her."

I can tell when Sennet's being evasive and when he's playing one of his "I know something you don't" games.

"Get to the point. What is this Nochnaya Sova thing?"

"Nochnaya Sova or 'Night Owl' was a proposed aircraft developed by the Soviets in the 1980s. They wanted to project power across the world and not be limited by access to aviation fuel. They took early work on hydrogen rockets and applied it to a jet engine and the infrastructure to support it.

"One of their key developments was the containment and fueling system—which was going to be applied to their Buran space shuttle," says Sennet.

"I'm not sure I get what the connection is," I reply. "It seems like a logical course of action to follow."

"Yes. If you're trying to make routine use of liquid hydrogen in aerospace, it's one of the factors that has to be dealt with. Look how long the Artemis rocket sat on the launchpad because of issues relating to hydrogen containment. But this is what I want you to see." Sennet removes a printout from a folder and hands it to me. He loves his printouts so much that he travels with a portable printer and shredder.

I'm looking at a black-and-white diagram of an angular engine with notations in Russian.

The notes explain inlet valves and include a breakout box describing how much each section should be coated with something called "NV3001."

"Okay? Now this," says Sennet as he places another diagram in front of me. "This was taken from an FAA design specification that Wind Aerospace filed."

The designs are strikingly similar. There's even a box that says "Proprietary coating to be applied to interior surfaces."

"It's not just that." Sennet pulls out more documents. "There are designs for valves, storage tanks, and other equipment that are close to the Soviet specs."

"How did you find this?" I ask of the diagrams.

"There was a hack on an old British intelligence server that had digitized documents dating back to the Soviet era. Nothing was revealed that affected current security, so the leak was in the news for a few days and then it went away. Oddly, this apparently came from a KGB case file and not from the design bureau."

"So Kylie and her engineers took a little inspiration from this. That's hardly new. The aerodynamic and control systems for the Buran were based on our space shuttle, and we've copied countless innovations from them and others. Hell, our first space rockets were Nazi V2s we repainted."

I'm being a little more defensive of Kylie than I need to. Sennet is laying out the facts. I'm acting like my kid got accused of plagiarism.

"That's fine, but there are two things you should know. First, prior to this hack, US intelligence had no idea of any of the technical specifications of Night Owl. The designer died after the program was shut down. And the British didn't know what was in the documents they had on their server.

"Second, this leak happened three months ago. Wind Aerospace filed these specs with the FAA last year. That's the real mystery," he says.

"Wait . . . You're saying nobody knew about this until just recently? Are you sure there wasn't some other leak?"

"I've come up with nothing. The British files were encrypted with a method that was only recently cracked. If Ms. Connor knew about the Night Owl, it would have been through some other means."

"Such as?"

"There might be people on the Russian side who had the info. Connor might have paid them. Which would be a violation of Russian law and potentially ours as well—we have trade laws that prevent the purchase of stolen intellectual property," explains Sennet.

I compare the two designs and my head starts to hurt. I'm no aerospace engineer, but the choices appear to be more than coincidental. Even the style of the diagrams looks the same.

"What about the original designers?" I ask.

"Dead. Except for the head of the design bureau, who is senile and living in a retirement home. One possibility is that she didn't buy them but found them first."

"Which would mean hacking the British intelligence server," I reply. "That's not good."

Working for people who have done shady things is nothing new to me. But when I worked for the government, the theory was that in the long run it was in the best interest of America and global security.

Helping a private company is a different matter. Besides the ethical considerations, I could be breaking the law. I need to find out what's going on here sooner than later. If I don't, I'm little different from Wagner, whose ethics align only with the direction the money comes in from.

"Are you going to confront her?" asks Sennet, who seems almost excited by the idea of me putting Kylie on the spot.

"I'll ask . . . after I do a little more research. I'd like to talk to an outside aerospace engineer."

"How about a disgruntled former Wind Aerospace engineer who tweeted this, then promptly deleted it a minute later?" Sennet slides me yet another printout from his folder.

@DarthDarkwing

can't wait for the sh*t to hit the turbo fan when people look closely at a certain chick-led aerospace companys designs and notice the hammer and sicle.

"Let me guess: DarthDarkwing is Ben Kohl."

Kohl was already on my list of people to talk to. He left Wind Aerospace under contentious circumstances and started causing issues—to the point that Morena had to speak to him personally and warn him that the next visitor from Wind Aerospace would be bringing a restraining order and court summons.

He shut up for the most part, tweeting instead about dark forces coming for him and making angular references to Kylie as the next Elizabeth Holmes, the disgraced CEO of Theranos.

I didn't read his provocations as signs that he might be trying to do physical harm to Kylie or Wind Aerospace, but you never can be sure.

"One and the same," confirms Sennet. "Did you learn the specifics of why he left?"

"Some mention of a conflict of interest," I recall.

"To say the least. While he was working at Wind Aerospace, he was starting his own company that his partners touted as 'the next evolution in aerospace.' It was based around a cryptocurrency fund-raise. They made about ten million dollars."

How did I not know this?

"Ten million? Who are his partners?"

"Nobody can say. There were several other crypto wallets attached to the project—and they had backed other successful projects. The selling point was a slick web page and a computer-animated video."

"Ten million for an asshole running a side hustle and several unknown investors who could be cartel bankers?"

Although crypto enthusiasts insist that most transactions are legitimate, that's hard to know for sure. More than one run-up of an NFT or a coin has been connected to money laundering in the narcotics trade.

In fact, that could have been a huge factor in driving up the crypto bubble. Instead of sending bricks of cash across the border, the cartel bankers back an NFT release and the drug buyers purchase those as proxies.

It's a world I don't know too much about, because most of it happened after I retired. After my encounter with Wagner, I'm realizing that this lack of knowledge is now costing me.

If I'd known Kohl had raised that much money and had shady connections, I would have put him first on my list of people to talk to. He's every bit as suspicious—even more so—as X-Lifter or any of Wind Aerospace's other competitors.

"Morena said that Kohl got paranoid and moved after she visited him. Do you by chance have his current location?"

"By chance I do. I am sure you'll be cautious, but know this: as Kohl's gotten more paranoid, he's started posting in gun forums and associating with a rather . . . lunatic fringe."

RECLUSE

If you visit the museum at the FBI headquarters in Washington, DC, one exhibit that stands out more than others is a tiny one-room cabin filled with books, survival supplies, maps, and bomb-making tools.

The cabin is the former home of Ted Kaczynski, known as the Unabomber. The name "Unabomber" was used to describe his targets: University and Airline Bombing targets—Un A Bomb*er*.

The reconstructed cabin is a demonstration of how dogged persistence and the help of citizens (Kaczynski's own brother, in this case) can be critical in fighting crime, even when it seems like there's no hope and all the leads are dead ends.

Kaczynski's cabin is also a window into the kind of mind that would mail bombs to professors and company executives whom he'd never met and had done him no harm—other than working on the other side of Ted's war against modernity.

Ben Kohl's home isn't a tiny cabin in a forest, but it's odd in its own way. It's located on a hilltop north of the San Francisco Peninsula in a rural area surrounded by dry grasslands. The setting sun makes the desolation and isolation all the more apparent.

On my way there, I pass a few horse stables and farms that appear to be in a state of neglect. This is more than an hour from the city and the kind of place you go if you want to be close but not too close to civilization.

He'd purchased the property shortly after he raised funding for his aerospace effort. The listing price suggests that he spent a significant amount on the house and surrounding buildings.

I assumed he bought it because of its remote location and large storage barn that could be used as a workshop. Some of the photos he posted to a Discord server for his backers show various pieces of equipment he was building. The location in the background resembles what I see around me.

I reach the top of the hill and drive through a broken gate that's wide open. Since there aren't any No Trespassing signs, I assume I won't be shot on sight. But you can't be too careful. One of my closest calls happened when I went to get some information from an informant who had been holed up in an abandoned building on the outskirts of a South American city. He had been working for a cartel, handling weapons trading, and had information about a connection between the cartel and a terrorist group.

His reasons for reaching out to us weren't altruistic. He'd stolen a significant amount of money from his employer and was looking for an exit strategy. When I went to speak to him to find out if he had anything useful to tell us, nobody informed me that he had a cocaine addiction that could put an LA nightclub to shame. As a result of the addiction, he was both paranoid and delusional.

Proof of this was delivered to me when I knocked on the door and a bullet punctured the door and plowed into the wall behind me. There were wooden splinters on my jacket, and bits of concrete hit me in the back of the head from the impact.

"Hey! Cut that out!" I yelled.

Hearing my American accent, he opened the door and apologized.

I needed to know what he knew and tried not to think about the fact that if I'd been standing three inches to the right, I'd have been a dead man. Ever since that day I travel with a bulletproof jacket that I keep for house calls like this.

The main house is a mansion with a nonfunctioning fountain and a sloped walkway that leads around the side of the house to the back patio with a pool that overlooks the grassy valley. Small plaster statues of lions stand on either side of the steps leading up to the doorway. To the right is a three-car garage with its doors down.

It's clear that the home was in a state of neglect long before Kohl purchased it. From the cracked asphalt to the exposed wood left bare by the constant wind in this treeless valley, the place's fix-up cost probably exceeds the purchase price.

I decide to put a small model of Kohl's decrepit house on a black workbench in the Time Traveller's workshop. His study's full, leaving me to use the other areas of his home for this investigation. While I'm at it, I create two more workbenches, one white and one gray. I put the Sparrow on the gray one in a detonation crater. Beside it, I place the Russian design plans for the Night Owl.

It's hard to describe, but when I fix objects in my mind, I see my hands putting them in place. I feel the objects' textures and even imagine I can smell them. The burning cinders of the Sparrow's crater smell like sparks from a welding rig. Kohl's house reeks of rotten eggs.

This habit of applying multiple senses was taught—or rather ingrained in me—by my mother. When I was a little boy, she'd have me place something in my mind, then ask me, "What does it smell like? Can you taste it? Does it have a sharp edge that frightens you?"

As I get closer to the house, the smell of rotten eggs increases in my mind.

The actual scent is a mixture of dry grass and—

I smell the fumes of something that was recently on fire. The wind should have blown it away by now, but it may have saturated the ground.

I press the button on the electronic doorbell.

Nothing.

I knock on the door and call out, "Hey, Ben? Are you home?"

No answer.

There's a video camera at the upper left of the doorway. I glance around and spot four more visible from this spot.

I don't think Kohl is the kind of guy to buy cameras and not hook them up to a system that would tell him when somebody is knocking on his door.

I also don't think he's the kind of person to come rushing to the door if there's a strange man standing there—even one as friendly looking as me with my sweater vest and reading glasses.

"Hey, Ben? I'd like to talk," I call out.

No answer.

Even if he's on the toilet, he should be able to respond through the electronic doorbell. Either he's ignoring me for some reason or he's not home.

I have an easy way to tell when someone is hiding from me. It's also how I avoid ambushes.

The BlackFox Pro is a $3,000 device I keep in my travel kit that tells me if there are any active cell phones in the vicinity.

If a cell phone isn't being used, it can take a few minutes to pick up the signal it uses to tell the nearest tower that it's in its cell zone. If someone is actively texting or talking, the sniffer will pick them up right away.

Mine is a short-range, handheld version of what Sophia is using to monitor communications at Wind Aerospace.

I take it from its case in the trunk of the rental car and switch it on. After a minute of calibration, the radial display shows the direction of three distinct signals.

The two antennae are too close together for a precise fix, but they can let you know if you're hot or cold.

When I aim the BlackFox at Kohl's house, I'm very warm.

One or more of the signals could be from a cell modem in a computer, a tablet, or an Apple Watch. One of them might also be from his cell phone.

Since opening his front door could be an invitation for getting shot, I decide instead to walk down the sloped path to the back of the house.

The sniffer keeps pointing toward the house, even when I reach the back terrace with the murky pool half filled with dark-green water.

I realize my assumption that Ben Kohl has his cell phone on him is likely incorrect—based on the presence of a body floating facedown in the pool.

PERSON OF INTEREST

"You said you found him facedown in the pool?" asks Detective Chandler from the Novato Police Department.

Chandler is a tall man with a buzz cut on a balding head. From the moment he arrived, he's been watching me out of the corner of his eye.

"Yes. I was doing a check-in and went around the back to see if Mr. Kohl was there," I reply.

A Novato Police patrol car arrived an hour after I called 911. I'd explained everything to the officer on the scene, careful to remember all my details so I'd be consistent the second, third, and fourth times they asked me to recount what happened.

I had to keep the details straight because there were certain ones I wouldn't be telling them—like how I used a cell phone sniffer or that I'm a former intelligence operative with a background that should make me a suspect.

The moment I saw Kohl's body, I had to make a decision. Do I retrieve the body of the clearly dead person and, in so doing, transfer forensic evidence like fibers to his body that could be used later to make the claim I killed him? Or do I let first responders recover Kohl, keep clear and clean, and maybe look a little callous?

The hopeful part of my brain took over, and I stepped into the algae-covered water to retrieve his body and perform mouth-to-mouth resuscitation.

"I tried to revive him but I was too late," I say with the appropriate amount of reserve.

"How did you know Mr. Kohl?" asks Chandler.

"I only knew him professionally. He worked for the same company I did," I reply.

"Is he still employed there?"

"No. He left several months ago," I explain.

"So why were you here?" Chandler gets to the point.

I have little doubt that drugs will be found in Kohl's system—enough to explain an accidental drowning—but probably not enough to explain why he would take a swim in a filthy pool.

In a potential murder investigation, the first person on the scene is also your first suspect.

"I've been checking with other people involved in aerospace to see if they've received any threats," I reply.

You normally don't want to bring up the topic of foul play when you could be a potential suspect, but in a way, the truth was better told up front rather than found out later. I don't point out that Ben Kohl could have been a suspect in the Sparrow sabotage, because it'd make me seem too paranoid.

"What do you think happened here?" he asks, inviting me to incriminate myself.

"I have no idea. You know as much as I do."

While I was making a statement to another detective, Chandler went through the house with two police officers. At this point he knows more than I do.

"Did you go into the house?"

As much as I wanted to do my own investigating, I didn't. I had no idea what the cameras would be recording. If I were caught strolling through the house while Kohl's body lay dead on the back terrace, it would have raised a lot more questions.

"No."

"What was your relationship like with Kohl?" asks Chandler, rephrasing a question from before to see if I'll answer it differently.

"I didn't know him. He was just one of the people we wanted to speak to."

In some cases, referring to Kohl by his first name or acting more emotional could elicit more sympathy for me, but I decide it's best to respond like one professional to another.

Right now, Chandler is testing me. Do I get defensive? Do I slip up?

"We're going to take a look at the video footage. Is there anything I should know before doing that? Did you maybe go inside to use the bathroom?"

I think he's trying to give me the illusion of an out. If Ben was killed and I was the killer, I'd probably have been inside the house with him. Nervous of that fact, I might try to concoct some innocent reason that my footprints or fingerprints could be in there or why I might be on video.

"I rang the doorbell, then went around the side to see if he was in back. That's as far as I went," I respond matter-of-factly—as if I hadn't even considered that Chandler's trying to trip me up.

"We'll see," he says, still suspicious.

"I can call our head of legal and have everything sent over about Mr. Kohl," I offer helpfully.

"That would be useful." He takes out a business card and hands it to me.

Nearby, Ben Kohl's body is being placed into a pouch to be taken to the coroner's office.

"Do you know who his next of kin is?" asks Chandler.

"I have his emergency contact form from his file. That would be his mother. She lives in Kentucky. I'll email you that too. I'll also forward you the contact information for the FBI agents we've been working with."

I intentionally keep using the words "we" and "work" to frame the dialogue around the idea that this is a professional conversation.

Chandler's investigation only started an hour ago; depending on what he found inside the house and what the coroner tells him, it could go in any direction. My goal is to know what he knows as soon as he knows it.

I take out a recently printed business card and give it to him. "Please contact me for anything else you need. I can also put you in contact with others who knew Mr. Kohl if that's helpful."

I can tell Chandler is still trying to read me, because I haven't slipped up in any way that he can detect.

"What do *you* think? Could he have been killed?" he asks me directly.

"I have no idea. But I do know that I have a thousand pieces of an experimental airplane scattered across a runway and a CEO that was almost killed in an explosion that I don't think was an accident. So I'm paid to be suspicious."

A police officer pulls Chandler to the side and whispers something to him.

My lip-reading skills were never the best, but I can usually get the context of a conversation. Since the officer's mouth is only twenty feet away and I can pick up the higher-pitched sounds, I have a fairly clear idea of what he just said:

He was in Mexico yesterday when this happened.

By "he," he means *me*.

Interesting. While Chandler was questioning me, he had his officer checking me out. I'm not sure who his sources were, but they were resourceful enough to pick up that detail.

My estimation was that Kohl had been in the water for about a day. It seems that's what their on-site forensic examiner determined too. If so . . . lo and behold, I have an alibi.

The officer shows Chandler something on his phone. He looks at it, then glances at me for a moment, then asks a question I can't make out because his head is turned.

Chandler returns to me. "You were in Mexico yesterday?"

"Yes. I got back last night. I was there on company business."

"You didn't mention that."

Of course not. Blurting out that I was a thousand miles away at the time of the potential murder would only have made me look extra suspicious. It would only prove that I wasn't physically present here, not that I had nothing to do with Kohl's death.

"My apologies," I offer.

Chandler would have found out I was nowhere near here yesterday if he'd hauled me in for questioning. But in the long game it's better to let him discover that fact for himself rather than call attention to it in a suspicious manner.

He assesses me for a moment, trying to decide if he can trust me. "You worked for the Bureau of Intelligence and Research?"

Chandler has connections and made some useful inquiries in the last hour.

"For five years," I reply. "I then went into the private sector."

For those that know, that's a subtle way of saying I took a job with another agency but had a civilian cover.

"What did you do?"

"Paperwork, mostly."

"Bullshit," he replies. "I was NCIS before this job. I think I understand who I'm talking to."

Chandler makes more sense to me now.

"Maybe you can help me out," he continues.

"Anything," I offer.

"I'm going to show you something. But I want your honest opinion. Not the carefully calculated way you've been talking to me. We both know if you killed the victim, you wouldn't be standing around talking to me right now."

Fair.

"Follow me." Chandler walks through the sliding glass doors of the house.

I stop at the entrance and point to my still-wet clothes.

"Let me see if we can get you a bunny suit," he replies, referring to the white protective suits worn to keep the crime scene free of contamination.

DESPERATION

Kohl's home is sparsely furnished. Everything looks like it came on an Amazon delivery truck or from a quick trip to IKEA. Inside the living room a flat-screen TV rests on the floor next to the box it was delivered in.

There are two mismatched chairs at the kitchen counter and a card table and folding chairs in the dining room. Opened delivery boxes with gaming consoles, VR headsets, and collectible action figures litter the rooms like quickly abandoned Christmas toys.

It reminds me of the apartment of a Russian drug dealer in Marseille whose income got a massive increase when his boss went to jail. He spent his money recklessly and agreed to do a gun buy for a Sudanese terrorist group we needed intel on. This was a dumb move and put him on our radar.

While Kohl's cryptocurrency windfall might not have been as enormous as the Russian drug dealer's income, at least the Russian didn't blow his loot on plastic figurines of video game characters.

Chandler leads me up a flight of stairs and past a landing that leads to the front door. Leaning next to the entrance are a large hockey stick and a baseball bat with a nail pounded into it.

"Was there a gun in the home?" I ask.

"We haven't found one yet," Chandler replies.

We go up another flight of stairs and into a hallway that ends in a master bedroom. Although calling it a "master" bedroom is overstating it a bit.

The bed is a mattress on the floor. In front of it are three large-screen televisions. One is hooked up to an Xbox, another connected to a small multimedia player, and the third one shows several camera feeds—all showing views of the outside.

"Any interior cameras?" I ask.

"No. And notice the black screens? At least three of the cameras aren't functioning. I don't have access to the recordings yet, but right now it looks like he only had visibility at the front of the house."

I get the sense that this is an important detail.

"I want to show you this, off the record," he says as he points to the bathroom. "Don't touch anything."

I walk to the edge of the carpet and look inside the large black-tiled bathroom. There's an open door to a toilet and bidet, a shower, a huge bathtub, and a long vanity with a mirror.

Chandler didn't call me in to see the 1980s aesthetic. He wanted me to see the pill bottles and the writing on the mirror.

There are three prescription pill bottles and scattered pills. The labels have been scraped away, leaving it to a lab to identify the drugs.

The writing on the mirror is less hard to decipher.

TELL KC SORRY

"Could 'KC' be Kylie Connor?" asks Chandler.

"It certainly feels like someone wants us to think that."

Chandler nods. "I think we're on the same page."

That page being that this all looks incredibly convenient and staged. We have a body for someone that died of a drowning from a drug overdose, and we have the pills.

Barring any suspicious bruising that suggests Kohl was restrained, or video evidence, it's going to be hard for Chandler to prove he was murdered. "Convenient" isn't persuasive when it comes to proving foul play.

There's also the inconvenient fact that, to outsiders, the only person who had anything to gain by Kohl's demise is Kylie. I don't know if Chandler has arrived at that realization yet.

Or he has and I'm still his suspect in the orchestration of all this and he mostly wants to see my reaction.

A key to my craft is envisioning all the different scenarios and choosing a winning path that succeeds in most of them. Sometimes you make a move that'll be weak in most scenarios but will increase your overall chance of success.

"Was there an issue between Mr. Kohl and Ms. Connor?" asks Chandler.

"More of an issue with Kohl. He was let go for a conflict of interest and made some threats in the heat of the moment."

"Does this look like something he would do?"

"I have no idea. I didn't know the man," I respond.

"Given what you do know?"

"I don't think he felt he did anything wrong that he needed to seek forgiveness for," I reply.

I keep it to myself, but Kohl seems like the kind of paranoid personality that would take his own life and then try to implicate somebody else for it.

"Here's my problem. I'm willing to bet the toxicology report is going to say he had drugs in his system, and the likely explanation is that he tried to overdose and stumbled into his pool. While to you and me it looks like a very easy way to conceal a murder, my chief isn't going to go for that unless there's some other factor."

There's little forensic difference between someone who intentionally overdoses and someone who is forced to keep swallowing pills with a gun to their head and then dropped face-first into a pool.

While friends and family might say that Kohl never had a drug problem and his liver might be perfectly healthy, without a suspect, witness, or evidence, it's the kind of case that sits around for a while, then gets shelved in favor of more pressing crimes.

"*Is* there some other factor?" asks Chandler.

"None that I can think of. And to be honest, I have no idea why anyone would want him dead. He was a pain in the ass, but not enough to warrant a professional hit."

But do I really know that? Did his crypto-funding scheme rip off someone who decided to hire a person like Wagner to give Kohl his due?

I don't know.

I do know that his death is extremely suspicious in light of recent events. Not to mention inconvenient for me. A suicide would have made my life less complicated. Kohl taking his own life would mean I don't have to try to figure out how that plays into all this.

"So what now?" I ask.

"I'm going to make sure our good medical examiner is the one to do the exam and not the other one who tries to check 'em off as quickly as possible. Other than that, speak to your contacts at the FBI and hope we get the video and find something useful."

Inside the Time Traveller's workshop, I place a large mirror frame. Where the reflection would be is an image of Kohl's bathroom with the message scrawled above the vanity. The bathtub is a swimming pool with his body facedown in dark water.

"I'll walk you to your car," says Chandler.

We go down the stairs and through the back sliding doors. Kohl's body has been taken away. A crime-scene analyst is taking photos of the pool.

As we walk up the path around the house, I see a light coming through the open door of the large shed at the edge of the property. A police officer is walking toward us.

"You guys want to take a look at this?" she asks.

Chandler follows her to the shed. I tag along behind, trying not to be too obtrusive but appreciating how the bunny suit helps me blend. (I add a bunny suit to my mental disguise closet, noting that it conveys authority, expertise, and caution.)

We get to the edge of the door, and I can see a large worktable surrounded by shelves full of tools and pieces of machinery. On one side of the table is the prototype jet engine that Kohl had shown off and used to fund his addiction to action figures and impulse Amazon shopping.

But it's what's on the other side of the table that has my interest.

It's a square tube about five feet long with a large battery in a protective case attached to the bottom, a professional sight on the top, and mounting brackets.

"Have you seen this before?" Chandler asks me.

Technically, no.

But it's a rail gun exactly like the one used to destroy the Sparrow.

"Not exactly, but you should talk to the FBI sooner than later."

GAP

Kylie is on a scaffold examining the interior machinery of a Sparrow while two engineers stand below with tablets, taking notes.

This jet's an exact copy of the prototype I watched blow up with the exception that part of the outer skin of the fuselage has been removed. I can see two others in various states of construction with engineers and robot arms working them over elsewhere in the hangar.

Kylie climbs down from the scaffold and walks to me. She's wearing the black jumpsuit I see her in whenever she's at work. The jumpsuit, like her bob haircut, is purely practical but carries a touch of style.

"Morena filled me in, but I have questions," says Kylie as she leads me to a bench out of earshot from her workers.

I called Morena and Sophia the moment I left Kohl's compound and gave them every detail, from what Chandler and I found to my suspicions.

They concurred that while Kohl being the saboteur would make things simple, not to mention resolved, we shouldn't let our guard down.

"Dead?" she asks.

"Yes. I pulled his body from the pool."

She frowns. "Damn. He was a jerk, but that's just sad. What about the rail gun?"

"There was what appeared to be a rail gun in his shed—exactly like the kind we were looking for."

She thinks something over, then shakes her head. "I don't see it."

"What do you mean?"

"Kohl wasn't much of a builder. On his résumé he seemed to be, but that was basically other people. His research papers were good and he was clever, but finishing things wasn't his strength. He'd get bored and move to something else when it got hard. That was one of the problems he had here. He was happy to tell everyone why their idea was dumb, but he wouldn't lift a finger unless it was his project."

"In all fairness, I call ideas dumb all the time, but I'll still test them if someone feels strongly." She points to the Sparrow. "If we only did things my way, we never would have gotten this far. I listen to people."

And that's why she's standing in the middle of her own billion-dollar facility and Kohl died in a dirty swimming pool at a house with a bunch of half-opened impulse purchases.

To be honest, I'm a little surprised that Kylie isn't jumping all over the prospect that Kohl was behind the attack. Her degree of emotional detachment is rare.

"So what happened?" she asks.

"I'm still trying to figure that out."

Kylie crosses her arms. "Humor me. Give me some theories."

This is an order, not a request, I realize. Well, she is signing my paychecks.

I glance over at the second prototype and envision its twin next to the Night Owl on the gray table in the Time Traveller's workshop. I have questions for Kylie, and if I don't like her answers, I might not be accepting any more paychecks.

"The first hypothesis is that it's exactly what it looks like. Kohl built the rail gun and destroyed the Sparrow. While it doesn't fit all of our assumptions, they are only assumptions. People still can't agree if one person or twelve killed John F. Kennedy," I tell her, leaving out the fact that I know the actual number.

"Second hypothesis is that Kohl is the architect, but he had help. The man I met in Mexico, maybe a professional sniper, and someone to build the gun.

"Third hypothesis," I continue. "Kohl is part of it, but not the architect. Perhaps his partners on his cryptocurrency fundraiser. That still leaves motive wide open."

"Okay, which—" Kylie starts to ask.

"Hold on," I interrupt her. "There's a fourth and fifth hypothesis." She closes her mouth and nods for me to continue.

"Fourth hypothesis: Kohl's death and the rail gun are purely coincidental. Maybe he heard about rail guns and was curious and had one built.

"And fifth: Kohl is a scapegoat. We were supposed to think the Sparrow's destruction was a design flaw—but we found the sniper's nest and the rail gun evidence. We were looking for a saboteur, so the real ones set up Kohl to take the fall."

"Is there a sixth hypothesis?" she asks.

"I could go on all night. These are the ones that at least make some kind of sense. Although I don't like any of them. In the fifth scenario, which feels the most likely, killing Kohl and planting evidence creates too many opportunities for exposure. While there's a good chance the FBI will tell us it's an open-and-shut case, there's also the chance a neighbor saw something or they got captured on a hidden camera. You don't commit a larger crime to cover up a smaller one. Until now, this wasn't a murder investigation. Now there's a body," I explain. "See?"

"Man, and I thought my job was convoluted," she replies.

"Your job is a lot more complicated, but you have the benefit of putting something on a test stand and finding out the truth. In my world there's often not a lot of closure."

"So what are our next steps?"

"They're still the same. We need to chase down all the anomalies and keep our guard up. How has it been working with Sophia?"

"She's a pain in the ass. But I get it." Kylie points to two security guards visible at the entrance to the work bay. "I'm pretty sure I'm being followed," she jokes.

"If it's any consolation to you, being the person that has to watch someone else's back is even more tedious than having your back watched."

"That's right. You used to be one of those marines who stood outside of embassies for hours at a time."

"For a brief period in my life."

"I have to know: What the hell did you think about while you were doing that?"

I've never had anyone ask me this. Leave it to one of the most mentally and physically active people I've ever met to pose this question.

If it were anyone else, I'd give a joke answer about my mind being naturally blank. But because it's Kylie asking, I want to be sincere.

"When I was young, my mother taught me how to build memory palaces—but from books I'd read rather than constructed purely with imagination. When I was a marine standing at attention, I'd go through my library and take down a book and look through the memories I'd stored there."

When I mention my library, I envision one particular book: *The Lost World* by Sir Arthur Conan Doyle.

It was Jason's favorite story. I helped him remember the names of different dinosaurs by placing them in the book. The incorrect ones used by Doyle complicated this a bit, but it was still effective.

I stored a lot of memories of Jason in that book. Instinctively, I've kept it out of my mind since he passed away. Opening it makes his absence feel so . . . real.

"Your mother taught you this?"

"Yes. Among many other things of questionable utility," I reply.

"Is she still around?"

"Very much so. If things get too out of hand around here, I may have to call her in," I say only in half jest. Suddenly I find myself blurting out something I've never told anyone before—even those who knew.

"My mother was a spy."

"For real?"

"For real. Master of disguise, Cold War undercover operative, all that."

"So that's where you get it from."

"I didn't get a fraction of it." For some reason my mother's legendary bluntness takes control of me. "For example, she'd be asking *you* right now why the Sparrow looks so much like the secret Soviet spy plane called the Night Owl."

"Really? A lot of times people end up with the same solution, though. Like in evolution. Dolphins and sharks couldn't be further apart in the animal kingdom, but they're almost identical from a structural point of view," she replies without any hesitation.

Kylie's tell is that she's feeding me an explanation so I'll stop thinking about the puzzle. Her mistake is understandable: she's an engineer, schooled in the world of certainty. You stop when the equation balances out.

I'm from a world of infinite nesting dolls. It never ends. The better answer for me would have been, "I don't know."

The conversation stalls awkwardly. I went from sincere to painfully direct in the span of a minute. We both know this took a turn.

Maybe I struck a nerve by insinuating that she didn't come up with this herself. I know that, as a woman running an aerospace company, Kylie's dealt with plenty of that kind of second-guessing. Or perhaps there's something more going on . . .

"I'm not an engineer. It's all magic to me," I reply, trying to put the conversation on sounder footing.

"What are our next steps?" she asks, trying to move on as well.

"Between you almost getting killed in the explosion, Watkins getting targeted for an intellectual-property ransoming, and Kohl's murder,

I'm concerned about the unusual amount of bad luck happening to people who work here. The other big stone to turn over is what happened to Douglas Gallar."

"Poor Doug," she replies. "He was one of my biggest early supporters."

"Yes," I say. "And now I'm very curious about exactly how he died."

FAST LANE

Janice Gallar, the widow of Doug Gallar, is seated across from me in the living room of their Malibu hillside mansion overlooking the Pacific Ocean. She's in her early fifties and has gray hair and piercing blue eyes that convey both gravitas and warmth.

"Kylie sends her regards," I say as I take a seat on a sofa that probably cost more than my SUV.

"She said some very kind words about Doug at the celebration of life," she replies.

I'm still not on board with calling a memorial service a "celebration of life." I've seen a lot of death in my life; glossing over it doesn't give it the solemn respect it deserves. It sounds as though someone didn't want to take the elevator down through all five stages of grief and got off on the bargaining floor: *If I call it a celebration, I'm still acknowledging that they're dead without having to think about it too much . . .*

I don't look forward to the gut punch when a coffin lowers into the ground, but I can tell the difference when I've had that moment and when I haven't. My philosophies surrounding loss don't matter, but I'm curious how it goes in Doug and Kylie's world.

Did everyone accept and forget? Do people ask questions?

This is important. You can hide great evil in the shadow of avoidance.

If we'd paid more attention to the number of journalists disappearing in countries run by "allies," we might have stopped authoritarian monsters on the rise before it was too late.

If Doug's death was part of this—and there is a "this"—maybe his friends and family saw more than they realized?

"When Doug died, what happened to his investments?" I ask.

"They became part of the family trust. I'm the administrator for that," she tells me.

Janice is an investment banker and an obvious choice to take over.

"What about partnerships?"

"Doug had a clause that I could take over any board seats that he held. I know, looks suspicious." She laughs.

She knows why I'm here and doesn't dance around the issue. I appreciate that.

"Right now, I'm sorting through them and deciding which investments we hold on to. What we sell and in some cases what we increase our stake in. One of them is Kylie's company," she explains.

"It's none of my business to ask how you're feeling about that," I reply.

"But you can. I have a good feeling about her. She's smart. The accident doesn't faze me."

We'll see how she feels about that when Morena does her due diligence and explains everything that's going on. Janice may still have faith in Kylie, maybe not so much the future of Wind Aerospace.

"Is there any reason someone might want to have killed Doug?" I ask bluntly.

"Whoa. You're more direct than I am. I'll admit that when I was first dealing with Doug's death, part of me started to wonder. He liked to drive fast, but he wasn't the kind to do drugs or get drunk and race around like an asshole. The only surprise about the death of those kind of guys is how long it takes before it finally happens."

"So Doug was a good driver?"

"Yes. But he did like to go fast, and these hills are dangerous. All it takes is a text or some distraction and a blowout happening at the same time. Next thing you know, your $300,000 sports car is rolling down a cliff." Janice takes a moment, then continues. "Motive? Like road rage and someone running him off the cliff?"

"Financial or some other reason. Would anyone gain by his death?"

"Nobody nearly as much as me," she responds.

"Other than you?"

"I don't want to speak ill of Doug's . . . uh, friends, but his body was still warm when I started getting calls from concerned people offering to help relieve the financial burden by buying some of his holdings. *Burden?* I made my first million before I was thirty. Look at what Doug left behind here. Anyway, I ran out of polite ways to tell people to go fuck themselves. Pardon my language," she replies.

"Nothing to pardon. I don't want to inconvenience you, but a list of the people who contacted you would be helpful."

"Yeah. I can put together a spreadsheet," she says. "To be honest, it's not like there's a huge advantage. If there's a company that Doug has a position in and somebody else wants, they can just go invest in the next round. Doug was usually at the seed or A level, so there was lots of opportunity for coming in later on."

"This is all pretty complex to me. I spent most of my life on a government salary," I admit.

I don't mention that to many of the old guys who taught me who are still around, "VC" still means a soldier in the Viet Cong army.

"How is Kylie dealing with the accident?" asks Janice.

"Nothing can stop her, I'm beginning to learn."

"I've only met her a few times, but I heard a lot through Doug. You'd think he was talking about his kid sister the way he enthused," says Janice. "It almost made me jealous."

Doug's widow seems an astute judge of character. I'm curious about her take on Kylie.

"She's kind of complex," I reply.

"Yeah. Doug said she had a really rough childhood. She and her mother were even homeless at one point when her father died. I think that made her more guarded."

I have to approach my next question delicately. I don't want to seem disloyal, but the Russian connection is still bothering me.

"Did Doug ever comment on that?" I ask.

"He said that she could be a bit secretive. When she first went to him for funding for Wind Aerospace, she wouldn't tell him what it was about. He'd already made a lot of money with her other company, though, so he was on board. Even when she had to cancel the investment round and start over," says Janice.

"What was that about?" I ask.

She waves her hand. "Not really anything. I think there was a problem with a cofounder, and Kylie had to pay him off and then start all over again with a new company."

Nobody mentioned this to me. It seems kind of important.

"A cofounder? Who was it?"

"I don't know. It only lasted a week or so. From what Doug said, it was no big deal and everything was fine. The other person had a family commitment and wasn't ready or something." She shrugs.

I have to go back into the Time Traveller's study and add an all-black figure standing behind Kylie like a shadow on the chessboard. The three dogs in the corner stop chasing each other and bark at the figure, then go back to running in circles.

"I have to ask: Do you think Doug's death *wasn't* an accident?" she asks me.

"I don't know. We may never know. He's gone and there's nothing really to investigate," I reply.

"What about his car?" she asks.

"Is that still around?"

"What's left of it is in the garage. I had it towed back here. Don't ask me why. I got a call from the impound yard asking what to do with it. They mentioned something about the McLaren having usable parts, but that sounded too ghoulish to me. I was a little mental," she explains.

I understand her state of mind more than I want to admit.

❧

She takes me to the four-car garage and raises all the doors. A Tesla Model S is parked on the far side, plugged into a charger, while the white McLaren 570S convertible is sitting in the third spot. The windshield is smashed, one of the doors is missing, and the whole frame is twisted.

I walk around the car to examine the damage. The passenger-side front wheel is bent outward. The back tires seem fine. The paint looks like a grizzly bear went at it, and the front driver's-side tire is completely gone. The rim's still there, but the tire is gone.

"The police say he probably hit a nail and it ripped apart the tire. They were off-brand because of the shortage and possibly defective," explains Janice.

I kneel and use my iPhone light to inspect the interior of the wheel well.

"Doug hit the corner at the worst possible point, the tire went out, and he skidded over the edge of the hill and . . . you get the point."

I glance up and see that Janice's icy reserve is gone. Seeing the car has brought back a flood of memories.

"Fucking car," she says as she kicks it.

I push my light deeper into the wheel well and take a photo.

Janice doesn't notice. I don't want to mess with her head right now. I need an expert to take a look and check my work. I can see how the police missed this. The car is so dented up it would be easy to not notice. Just to be sure, I align the beam of my phone's flashlight with a spot right behind the front bumper.

Damn.

A tiny sliver of light goes straight through the body of the car, from the front of the wheel well, through the space where the tire would have been, and through another tiny slit at the back of the well that looks exactly like the one that destroyed the Sparrow.

MOTIVE

Two days later, FBI Special Agents Shirley Broadhurst and Tiffany Morrel are sitting across from me in the conference room at Wind Aerospace. A few years ago, I'd have answered their questions openly and without hesitation. Then things got more political within agencies, and even what would have been a casual conversation became something that could be used as pretext for claiming a procedural violation if the people you were talking to secretly had it in for you.

Technically, not everything I was asked to do in other countries had clear legal standing. While certain laws would in theory protect me if I was following orders, if something got screwed up and the people who issued the orders wanted to pass the blame, I'd be left holding the bag.

What orders?

If, say, you were being debriefed by an agency about an unrelated topic and they casually asked you if you'd ever spoken to someone whose name you don't recall and you said no and then signed off on their report . . . Congratulations. If they have proof you did speak to him, you just lied to the federal authorities and signed your name to it.

They can then pursue you for a perjury charge—which is a felony.

It's also hard to win a perjury case, but if the feds are aggressive and start suggesting that they might go after friends and family, it's possible to wear somebody down.

I know the names of so many undercover assets and operations that the moment I sense a conversation is deviating, I end it.

I was once interrogated by a Justice Department official, who was a political appointee, about billing records, and he casually asked if I'd ever heard about a wiretap done on a diplomat that I knew was connected to his patron.

"I'm only authorized to talk about billing records," I replied.

"I'm just curious," he responded. "Why are you so defensive?"

"Like I said, I'm only authorized to talk about billing records," I repeated.

"We're both government employees, it's fine," he said, raising every alarm bell.

When I told my supervisors about the fishing expedition, they called up his bosses at the Justice Department and told them if he ever set foot in this agency again, he'd be arrested for suspicion of espionage.

It wasn't always like this. But then everything became political. And it was from every side and every direction.

I asked around about Agents Broadhurst and Morrel before meeting them. The responses I got said they're solid agents who build good cases. Broadhurst worked in corporate espionage, and Morrel has a background in counterterrorism. They seemed like a solid pairing.

"Here he is," says Broadhurst, looking across the table at me.

"We got the line on you." Morrel shakes her head. "How'd they get a guy like you to work here?"

Apparently, they've done some digging of their own. It's hard to know what they might have found out, but if they asked around enough, they'll have learned at least a few details I'd prefer not be known.

"I needed the money," I tell them.

Morrel takes a folder out of her bag and sets it on the table. "We read everything you sent. For a field guy, you know how to work a word processor."

I learned early on that it's wise to write down every single detail and interaction in order to cover your ass. With my memory tricks, it's easily done. I even got chewed out on more than one occasion by case officers over the "novel-like" length of my field reports.

A supervisor once asked, "Why can't you just write that you met the informant and got the copy of the letter? Instead of telling me the brand of glasses he wore and how many cups of coffee were sitting on the table in front of the man in the corner who was wearing black boots with a blue nylon windbreaker?"

"Because," I replied, "if I omitted the windbreaker detail in my first report, and then the second time I met with him there was also a man in a blue nylon windbreaker wearing black boots in the corner, it would be pretty important."

"Was there?" he growled.

"I only met with him once."

"Damn it, Trasker. In the future I want a short version as well. No more than half a page. Okay? That one I'll read. The other version I can ignore and you can publish when someone asks you for the most goddamn boring spy novel ever written."

"You never know what's important, so I try to be thorough," I tell the agents.

Well, you can also be *too* thorough. I decided to leave out anything that wasn't directly related to the explosion or the deaths of Kohl and Gallar. However, I did mention Wagner.

"When did you first start working here?" asks Broadhurst.

"A little over a week ago," I reply.

"Did you know Ms. Connor prior to that?"

"I'd met her a few weeks prior. I had a flat tire. She drove me to Walmart so I could get a tire repair kit."

Broadhurst makes a note of this. "You'd never spoken to her before or after?"

"Not until she invited me to the unveiling," I explain.

It's hard to tell if this is routine fact-finding or if Broadhurst is going somewhere specific.

"Did she or anybody she worked with mention a job offer?" asks Broadhurst.

"Not until after the explosion," I say.

"Did you discuss your background in intelligence when you first spoke to her?"

"No. It's not a topic I go into," I respond, becoming a little concerned about the focus of this conversation.

"Explain what your title, 'Chief Security Adviser,' means . . . ?" asks Broadhurst.

"In an organization like this, you have someone in charge of IT security and someone in charge of infrastructure and personnel. I help Ms. Connor coordinate with those departments and make sure everyone is up to date."

"When you went to Mexico to intervene on Mr. Watkins's behalf, was that within the role?"

"There are situations where I step in and provide assistance," I say, trying to keep the answer short.

Morrel enters the conversation. "Would 'fixer' be an appropriate way to describe your job?"

"Not if you associate it with all of the negative connotations. My job is to look out for the security of the organization. Part of that is making sure that we conduct ourselves in a lawful manner."

"Would you describe providing a bribe to a Mexican law-enforcement official as conducting yourself in a lawful manner?" asks Morrel.

Here it comes. I didn't write in my report that I paid Balthazar for access to Watkins. They're making an assumption to put me into a corner.

"If this is a conversation about my conduct, then we'll have to put a pause on it until I have an attorney present."

"Slow down, Mr. Trasker. Nobody is after you. We're just trying to understand the limits of your job," says Broadhurst.

I say nothing.

"We want to know what you do in this role and how far you'll go," adds Broadhurst.

I give them my "this is stupid" look and remain silent.

"Silence isn't a good defense. And bringing in an attorney only makes you look guilty," says Morrel.

I stand. "I'll have my attorney schedule a time for us to talk."

Broadhurst holds up her hands. "Hold on, Mr. Trasker. Just give me a minute. All you have to do is sit and listen. Okay?"

I sense some sincerity so I sit back down. Although I wasn't bluffing about the attorney.

"We're not after you. Yeah, maybe we just wanted to off-balance you, but trust me, you're not the focus. However, we don't know if we can fully trust you either," she says.

I keep my mouth shut.

"All right, I'll just throw this out there. We got the report from the Novato Police Department about Kohl's death. While the death's suspicious in its own right, the rail gun found in the shed is even more interesting."

Obviously, I stay silent.

"Some of the parts on it had serial numbers. They were traced to a supplier. That supplier kept records of purchases."

My mouth is still shut.

"Okay. I know you're curious. They were sold to Wind Aerospace," Broadhurst informs me.

"Kohl worked here," I remind them, breaking my silence.

"Yes. But these were purchased months after Kohl left. Someone *here* provided the parts to build *that* device."

I keep my reaction under wraps. But this revelation fits the "big if true" category. I still don't know if it means that someone from here was directly involved, though. There are a thousand possible explanations.

"While someone like Ms. Connor is clearly capable of building a device like this, she'd need an accomplice to fire it," says Morrel, jumping in with a damning accusation.

"Are you fucking kidding me?" Let them incriminate me for that.

"Hold up. Maybe on the surface it sounds crazy, but let's explore it for a moment. Rumors are circulating that the Sparrow project was way behind and had reached some technical problem they didn't know how to solve. Why not give yourself a little more time by making it look like you're the victim of sabotage?"

"Let's start with the fact that people assumed it was a design flaw," I reply.

"Until you and Ms. Connor found the sniper nest in the field near the tarmac," says Morrel. "That's when it became sabotage. Some would say it was convenient that you two found the evidence."

"I watched her almost lose her life," I tell them.

"Almost. She's brilliant and extremely capable of figuring out what a safe distance would be from the explosion."

"Did you ask the same FBI bomb expert who nearly killed himself and four other law-enforcement agents during a training exercise last year? Nobody can predict how far material will fly in an explosion like that. The fact that we're having this conversation should be professionally embarrassing for you."

"We have other reasons to be suspicious that we can't divulge," says Morrel.

"I'm sure you do. I've never been short of people willing to pass on dubious speculation as fact. And more often than I care to remember, I found myself chasing down some phantom lead someone higher up was too lazy to vet for themselves.

"I don't know what you heard, but you should also realize that anyone capable of pulling off an act of sabotage like this is more than capable of getting someone to pass on bogus information to you as if it came from a reliable source."

"Maybe so. But allow me to ask you one question. You can answer it or not," says Broadhurst.

"Fine," I respond.

"Has anyone suggested to you that the Sparrow may have been based on Russian technology?"

I keep my expression neutral. "I'll give you my attorney's contact information."

"Be that way. But everything we just discussed is confidential. Do not pass this on to Ms. Connor or her legal representatives," says Morrel.

That's not how it works and they know it. But maybe that wasn't the point.

Maybe their real goal—or the goal that was passed on to them—is to plant a seed of doubt in my mind.

FOSSIL

Morena catches me in the hall as I leave my meeting with Broadhurst and Morrel.

"Everything go okay?" she asks me as we round the corner and stroll out of earshot.

"Hell no."

I have a moment of hesitation. Morrel and Broadhurst asked me to keep their questions about Kylie confidential—but in reality, it was only that, a request. They knew telling me put me into a conflict of interest.

I might have afforded them some professional courtesy and curated the information I pass on to Morena and Kylie, but Morrel tried to back me into a corner with the perjury trap regarding my bribe to Balthazar.

I know a dozen different ways to skirt that if it ever came to a courtroom. Technically, I never offered him a bribe. I simply lost my cigarette pack with the cash in it. Trying to make a case out of that would require putting Balthazar on the witness stand, and ultimately what would they prove? That I had to pay a bribe to free a US citizen who was being illegally detained? That's not a bribe, it's ransom.

It was a dumb ploy on the part of Morrel and Broadhurst that I found insulting. I have no problem telling Morena what we spoke about because even if their allegations are true, I'm not going to derail their investigation.

If they had told me on the record at the start of the conversation that it was confidential and I needed to sign a statement to that effect, they knew I would have walked. They chose to gamble, doubled down, and lost.

"Wow, that's a lot," says Morena after I give her my debrief in a conference room in the securest part of the facility.

"Do you believe that Kylie used stolen Russian technology?" she asks me.

"I wouldn't know."

"Okay. Different question. Would you ever be willing to bend the rules in a way that would benefit the company?" Morena inquires.

"In what way?"

"Let's say there was some Russian prototype design and Kylie wanted you to go buy it," she postulates.

"First, I can't set foot in Russia. I'd be detained by their security services and declared a spy the moment I landed on the tarmac. Second, if you're asking me to buy stolen goods, the answer is a flat no. If you want me to find out if they're stealing your secrets, then I'd get the cooperation of a US intelligence agency so we at least have plausible deniability."

"What if the feds came to you with evidence of wrongdoing on Kylie's part? What would you do?" asks Morena.

"Call my lawyer."

"And if they had something incriminating on you and offered a plea deal?"

"We just saw a soft form of that happen, didn't we? But in answer to your question, I'm not going to throw somebody else under the bus for my screwup."

"I'm sure everybody thinks that until they fold," says Morena.

She's pushing me, but she's doing it on behalf of Kylie. I respect that. I respect it enough to be a little more honest with her.

"If you look into my CV, you'll see a five-month gap during which I wasn't employed by anyone, yet my address remained in the same building as an intelligence agency I previously worked for. I won't tell you what country I was in during that time or what I went through. But I still have the scars. I don't talk."

Even when the fuckup wasn't mine and an asshole State Department staffer tried to get back at me for an imagined slight by "accidentally" slipping my name to the wrong person.

"I believe that about you," she says.

"I also don't like being lied to. And if the allegations were true, we'd have a problem. I'll put my life on the line to protect someone, but I won't throw my reputation away. And by reputation, I mean my willingness to take a fall if it protects someone worth protecting."

Morena nods.

"If there's more to the Russian question, then I need to know so I can decide if I should keep working here or not."

"What if I told you it's complicated?"

"Uncomplicate it for me," I tell her.

"What if I told you that if you knew the whole picture, you wouldn't have a problem?"

"It would be a lot easier to tell me and let me decide," I say with a sigh.

"Let me put it this way. You went to Mexico and brought Watkins home. Everyone assumes that you had to bribe a Mexican official to pull that off. I know it's illegal for a US citizen to do that. But I also understand how Mexico works and that if you didn't, Watkins would still be down there. So what is my legal responsibility here? By the letter of the law, I should contact the authorities and have you reprimanded. But like you, I'm more concerned about my and your *ethical* responsibilities. You made a decision that was in the best interest for everyone and also had no direct benefit to you. So I ignore it. I may have to explain it down the line, but I know that the act was done in good faith.

I'm okay with getting disbarred for doing the right thing in a situation where the rules are broken. If it had been a US law-enforcement officer and there were legal ways to accomplish our goal, then it would be a different matter."

"You want me to accept that there's a good explanation that I'd be happy with and move on?" I ask.

"Basically."

"I appreciate your directness. So I'll be direct. If I found out you lied to me about this, being disbarred would be the least of your worries."

She gives me a smile. "Then I think we're going to be fine. Out of curiosity," she continues, "does this 'old-fashioned straight-shooter with a dangerous edge' act work for you?"

"I'm not sure what you mean."

"Yes, you do. I have to imagine some women even find it attractive."

"I think to most women I look like a fossil that belongs in a museum."

"Hey, I loved the T. rex skeleton at the Natural History Museum. Even in fossil form, he was still pretty awe-inspiring," she says, staring straight into me.

I'm decades past the time when strange women would buy me drinks in bars, so now it's hard for me to tell if someone is flirting with me.

"Maybe when we're on the other side of this we can grab coffee and talk about dinosaurs . . . and bones," she says at last.

Yep. She's definitely flirting with me.

Is it manipulation? Probably. Oh well. It's interesting.

"Hey! There you guys are," says Bianca as she bursts into the room. "Did I just walk into something?"

"It's fine. What's going on?" asks Morena.

"Social media is blowing up. Someone is using Ben Kohl's account to accuse Kylie of faking the explosion and working with the Russians," she says breathlessly.

"That didn't take long," says Morena. "Where is everybody?"

"Wilbur Conference Room," replies Bianca.

"Okay, we'll be there in a minute," Morena tells her.

After Bianca leaves, Morena turns to me. "Are we on the same page?"

Frankly, we're dealing with two different books here.

"Trusting me isn't the problem," I reply.

"Fair enough. And the same goes for me. Now, let's go see what kind of disaster we're dealing with."

UNROLL

I'm in the conference room named after the milder-mannered Wright brother, Wilbur Wright, looking at a stream of tweets berating Kylie and Wind Aerospace and wondering what ol' Wilbur would have made of all of it:

> @DarthDarkwing
>
> If ur reading this. I'm dead. lol. This tweet stream is automatic in case of my untimely demise
>
> 1/11
>
> @DarthDarkwing
>
> I've been trying to revolutionize aviation as you know. This is a fools errand. But hey. I'm good at playing the fool. If I'm dead its because THEY didn't want it to happen.
>
> 2/11
>
> @DarthDarkwing

Since I'm dead. RIP. Boohoo. Poor Darth, I can name names. They can't sue me in hell. Ur. Can they?

By names I mean name: Kylie Connor.

3/11

@DarthDarkwing

Yup. Everyone's golden girl is actually the Elizabeth Holmes of aviation. I worked with her. I know the facts. Buckle up. Lock your doors. You don't want to get Epsteined.

4/11

@DarthDarkwing

I was asked by Kylie Connor to look over some designs once. I asked where they were from. I was told none of my business. Whatever.

5/11

@DarthDarkwing

While going through the typically messy work she does (if you really saw lol) I noticed something under a photocopy of the plans . . . letters . . . Russian letters.

6/11

@DarthDarkwing

So I googled them:

Novoye kosmicheskoye konstruktorskoye byuro = New Space Advanced Design Bureau

Huh. Weird right?

7/11

@DarthDarkwing

So I ask Kylie why do we have plans from a Russian aerospace company?

Crickets.

"Oh, your services are no longer needed."

LOL

8/11

@DarthDarkwing

I then started looking into the funding for Wind Aerospace. Spoiler: There are some very shady people with connections to the Russian government.

Russian plans + Russian investors = Holy Crap.

9/11

@DarthDarkwing

Don't believe me? Check out these images of the Sparrow and the New Space Advanced Design Bureau's Night Owl.

You could look at her plane…but she blew it up.

I tried to tell people Kylie was a con woman. But it's worse. She's a traitor.

10/11

@DarthDarkwing

I let responsible authorities know. Now you're seeing this and Kylie Connor is probably being treated like America's darling and I'm literally dead. I mean literally. God bless America.

It was fun while it lasted.

11/11

Kylie is handling it fairly well. Sophia is stoic, Morena is pissed that she can't sue Kohl, and Bianca is having a bit of a meltdown. None of her media training told her what to do when someone accuses you of being a traitor in a series of tweets that have already gotten more than one thousand likes.

I'm the only one here who's been through a crisis like this. My takeaways:

Rule 1: Don't panic.

Rule 2: Don't overreact.

"We need to get on top of this *now*," says Bianca. "We should have you on CNN tonight, calling bullshit."

Perhaps I should have spoken that last rule out loud.

"What if he'd said Kylie was in league with the Martians? Would you want her on the news then?" I ask.

"No. Don't be ridiculous," Bianca replies.

"So why are we treating this any differently? If Kohl was a nut saying crazy things, then treat him like that. You only swat back at things you think are real threats."

I keep the possibility that what Kohl said was true to myself. In that case, there's nothing to do and I'm out of here.

"What do I tell the media?" asks Bianca.

"You tell them that our thoughts are with Ben Kohl's family and that he will be missed by people who worked here," says Morena. "If they want a quote about the tweets, ask them if they have a specific question. Make them ask out loud, 'Are you colluding with the Russians?'"

"And what do we say if they ask us that?" asks Bianca as she bites at her nails.

"You say no, you nitwit!" shouts Morena. "Make them flat-out ask. Don't let them push us into a vague statement about the tweets that could bite us in the ass. Firm questions get firm responses, and I'm sorry for calling you a nitwit," she adds.

An unwritten rule in a crisis is that everyone needs to calm the heck down. Don't become your enemy's ally by attacking your friends.

"Did the Wright brothers have to deal with this?" I ask, trying to puncture the tension.

"Well," Kylie responds, "the criticism they would relate to. Long after their flight at Kitty Hawk, the press refused to believe that two self-taught high school dropouts could have solved the biggest mechanical challenge of the age. And when everyone and the media finally accepted it as a fact, then came the claims that lots of people had already achieved flight and it was, like, no big deal.

"It's the real innovator's dilemma. They tell you that you can't do it. They don't believe it when you do. And then they tell you that you weren't really the first, you stole it, whatever, and anything you did wasn't important."

"Yes, but all of this starting by a tweet from a nobody? A dead nobody, at that?" I ask.

"I think they would have appreciated that most of all. Orville and Wilbur had all the experts telling them they didn't know what they were doing. When they finally ignored the experts and did their own wind-tunnel calculations, they realized everyone else was doing it wrong. That's why they flew and the others didn't. I'm an outsider to aerospace, yet here I am. Ben was . . . well, Ben, and at least he gets to be heard in the end," she says, shrugging.

I'm surprised by how well Kylie is taking the accusations. I hope it's just her being pragmatic and not the somber reflection of her own guilt.

"What is he talking about regarding the Russian design firm?" I ask.

"The New Space Advanced Design Bureau went defunct in 1986," says Kylie.

"Is he telling the truth? Do you have any documents from there?"

"Are you asking if I stole Russian technology?"

"I'm asking if someone could claim there's proof that we did," I say calmly.

"Follow me," she says and abruptly leaves the table.

❧

I follow her down a hall past a room full of engineers staring at massive monitors and drafting tables.

She leads me into a side corridor and to a door with a biometric scanner and electric keycard. Kylie waves her hand over the scanner.

"Don't tell anyone, but I'm always losing my keycard," she explains. The door beeps and she pulls it open.

"Step inside," she tells me as she walks into a huge room with a long row of filing cabinets and shelves to the rafters full of boxes.

Kylie strides to a cabinet, opens a drawer, pulls out a folder, and hands it to me. I look inside and see Russian blueprints for a massive airplane bigger than anything that ever flew, at least as far as I know.

Kylie pulls another folder from a cabinet and drops it into my hands. This one contains the plans for a UFO-shaped craft that uses turbo fans.

She leans back on the filing cabinets and stares at me. "I lost track of how many different documents I have here. I stopped counting at twenty thousand. I've been obsessed with aviation my whole life. I started with blueprints on eBay when I was twelve. I'd go to online forums and talk to men five times my age and ask questions. Old engineers who worked on Apollo, the SR-71. People sent me notes, blueprints, old design specifications.

"Was all of it officially declassified? I don't know. The men who sent them just wanted to share something they helped make. After talking to Morena, I took their names off of everything in the event that something maybe shouldn't have been divulged. But I never asked for anything illegally. I was just a curious girl who loved to see how people solved problems. There's a lot of brilliance here.

"I spoke to a Japanese engineer who built planes during World War II who figured out how to work around shortages by doing things like making tachometers out of soup cans. I've got the only copy of a book on exotic fuel mixtures written by a chemist with a workshop in his garage who spent thirty years trying different combinations.

"Did I ever ask Ben to look at something that I pulled from here that may have come from a Russian design bureau? Maybe. I don't recall. I'm not saying he's a liar . . . *was* a liar, but it wouldn't mean what he said it does.

"The heads-up display in the Sparrow was actually created by a toy designer who found a simple way to make volumetric displays. I borrowed from everyone I could that I was legally allowed to."

"And the Russian investors?" I ask.

"I think he means Victor Chelomey. His grandfather was from Russia. Victor is a second-generation American. He does global investing, including in Russia until the Ukraine war. Do you know what he did? He liquidated every holding there at a huge loss and donated it to Ukrainian charities. Does that sound like a Putin crony?"

Kylie's defense is passionate and I believe her sincerity, but I still get the feeling she's not telling me everything.

Maybe I'm too cynical. I don't know.

"Can I still count on you?" she asks.

Do I tell her I still think she's not being forthcoming? What if she is? How could she prove that to me?

"Yes," I reply.

The answer comes easily when I think back to the first time I heard her voice, when she offered to help me in a time of need. I was in a much more broken place than I am now.

I can at least offer her that much.

RETALIATION

"Happy now, Bradley?" Morena taunts me as Kylie enters the conference room.

"It's my job to be suspicious," I tell her. I don't expand on that by detailing all the times I've been screwed over for not being suspicious enough.

I've resigned myself to the simple fact that there's a small possibility I could find myself behind bars for the next ten years. It's not like I had any plans to begin with. What really bothers me is the thought of being betrayed by someone I so want to trust.

"So, what are we doing next?" asks Bianca.

"I'm still getting the Sparrow ready for its next flight. I think we're a week away. Once we get FAA approval, I say we run with it," says Kylie.

"That's assuming they give us the go-ahead," adds Morena.

"We've identified the problem. It wasn't a design problem, and we were able to put in extra plating to prevent that from happening again," Kylie tells me.

"Yes, but the wheels of bureaucracy don't move that fast," says Morena.

"Trust me, I know. But we can push."

"Not to be the killjoy here, but there are two important points to consider. First, there's an active criminal investigation," I point out.

"The FBI's investigation is separate from the FAA's. I can push on the commissioner not to let one impede the other," says Morena.

"Fine. But the second, more critical point is that whoever destroyed the Sparrow and killed Gallar and Kohl is still out there."

"I thought Kohl destroyed the Sparrow," says Bianca.

"No. It wasn't him," says Kylie.

"Why am I always the last to know?" Bianca moans.

"Well, it's going to get worse. The FBI says some of the parts for the rail gun found in his shed came from *here*—*after* Kohl left Wind Aerospace," I explain. This is the first time I've had the chance to break the news to anyone besides Morena.

"That would mean . . ." Kylie's voice drifts off.

"That the saboteur may have an accomplice that still works here. Either someone who built the rail gun or provided parts."

"Damn it," says Sophia.

I know she's been going through all the employee records and logs. The search for dog hair came up empty—but we have a much better idea of how many of our employees are pet owners.

"Why would somebody do that? These people are their friends and coworkers," says Kylie.

I point to the tweets still on the screen. "It's going to get worse. The fact that some of the parts came from here will surely leak."

"Can't we ask the FBI to keep that a secret until they investigate it?" asks Bianca.

Sophia and I let out a laugh.

"What's so funny?" she asks.

"Nothing. The short answer is there's no guarantee, and besides that, whoever planted the rail gun did it to point back at us here. They're gonna leak it. We can't avoid that," I explain.

Bianca's face goes pale. "What are you saying?"

I nod to the tweets on the screen. "This is nothing. Get ready for headlines and cable news programs jumping all over this. Every enemy you have—which, by the way, ranges from Strausman and Boeing to the Chinese People's Liberation Army—is going to amplify this."

"But it's absurd," says Bianca.

"But it's also a great story. The media will spend years on bullshit if it gets them an audience. They're dying for another Elizabeth Holmes—this time while they're paying attention," says Morena.

Besides lying to people with medical conditions about fake tests, the saddest part of the Holmes and Theranos case was that she'd been in the media spotlight for years and the media never scrutinized her properly.

Now Kylie and other female entrepreneurs have to pay the price. One of the largest newsrooms in the United States has a stated policy that all tech coverage has to be negative. They're going to be thrilled when they find out about the rail gun.

"I don't care," says Kylie. "We have plenty of funding. We know the truth. They can say whatever they want. I'll be in the work bay getting the Sparrow ready."

"Not if they're pulling you into Senate hearings and we're flooded with more FBI agents going through every inch of this place," says Morena.

"Should we move the archive?" asks Kylie, glancing at me.

"No," I reply. "If anything, put glass doors on it so everybody can see inside. Does anybody else have access?"

"Anyone with a keycard," she responds.

"Perfect. Then you're not hiding anything. Moving it would be worse. Have you ever given tours of your archive to any government officials?"

"Several. Last one was Senator Hallacy. He's a big aviation nut," says Kylie.

"We took a photo of him in there," adds Bianca.

"Great. Keep that on hand. If word gets out about 'secret files,' then we post that picture, explaining it's a research library. You should also make an agreement with a technical college to help digitize the archive and make it publicly available," I suggest.

"There might be some problematic files in there," says Morena.

"It doesn't have to happen overnight or ever. But starting it now will provide you cover if it comes up."

"Wouldn't moving it be better?" asks Bianca.

"And what will you tell the FBI when they ask you why we moved it? What will your quote be to the *New York Times*? You don't move things from a high-security facility to a self-storage unit to make them more secure, or yourself seem more innocent. It's shady. Don't run from it.

"There'll also be a convenient explanation if we get asked about the plans Kohl said Kylie passed him. 'Do you have any secret Russian jet plane plans?' 'Probably. We're still sorting through everything in our collection. Want to come take a look?'" I demonstrate.

Morena is nodding. "Okay. This makes sense. We can also see what university collections are out there. Maybe offer a grant to a scholar to come look at what we have—a friendly one. Very clever, Trasker."

"It wasn't my idea. It was Kylie's," I tell her.

"Me?" Kylie says, surprised.

"When I challenged you on the Russian plans, you brought me to the archive. It was the most convincing thing you could have done. Any reporter who hears you wax on about how you built the archive is going to have a hard time spinning it as something sinister. Not that they won't, but their narrative won't be as strong as yours."

Assuming there's nothing dreadful to be discovered . . .

"So, busy as usual?" asks Bianca.

"Within limits," says Sophia. "We still have one or more killers out there. You can worry about the media; I'm concerned about them."

"About that. I want us to hire an outside detective agency to shadow our team whenever we go with Kylie somewhere. Make it discreet. Hire someone you trust, but it can't be connected to you," I explain.

"What's that for?" asks Morena.

"It's a good bet that Kylie is being watched. Maybe by the killers, possibly by someone they hired. They want to know her routine and security detail. We need to know who's watching us. We can't use our own people because the enemy apparently has someone inside Wind Aerospace."

"What about Elevation? Are you still doing the keynote there?" Bianca asks Kylie.

"What's that?" I ask.

"Elevation? It's a conference connected to the Miami Air Show. Kylie is scheduled to give the keynote talk. We're also putting a prototype of the Sparrow on display."

"Pardon me?" I turn to Sophia. "Did you know about this?"

"I was going to tell—"

"I said not to bring it up until I spoke to you," Kylie cuts in. "Don't blame her. Elevation's very important to me. I know it's a security risk, now. But if I can't go share what we're working on there, what's the point? It's a huge recruitment tool as well," she explains.

"It would also put us in front of this mess," adds Morena. "I'm not thrilled, but not showing up would make it look like we're hiding."

"We *are* hiding!" I exclaim. "We've got trained killers out there who might want your boss dead. Being predictable is the *last* thing we want to do. An event that large? It's a nightmare."

"I can handle it," says Sophia. "We've been talking to the organizers, and I think we can get her in and out safely. The vice president is giving a talk there the next day. I know his Secret Service advance team supervisor. We can coordinate."

"I don't like it," I reply.

"Of course you don't. We'll put her on an unscheduled flight, get her to a private airport, and have a security detail the whole way," says Sophia.

I growl something like, "Okay."

The room falls into sudden silence.

"Can you ride a dirt bike?" asks Kylie, apropos of nothing.

I look at her. "It's been a while. Why?"

"I want to take a ride tomorrow. I also want to do a little investigation of my own," she says. "I have a theory about something."

ROAD WARRIORS

Kylie races ahead of me on her dirt bike, passing her vintage P-51 Mustang parked on the tarmac and crossing the point where the runway meets the desert. A spray of dirt kicks into the air. I follow, but upwind to avoid the tan cloud of dust.

Far to our left, an army of wind turbines slowly turn in the breeze. To our right lie miles of desert and the tiny glimmer of an office park at the outer edge of the Mojave Spaceport.

"Keep up," says Kylie over the intercom in our helmets.

"One of us has to stay in one piece to carry the other one back. I'm also not too excited about surprising a rattlesnake," I reply.

"They'll hear you coming long before you see them," she responds.

"Even electrics like these?"

"They still vibrate and make a racket."

"That's for sure," I reply as my front wheel hits a rock and sends a shock wave from the handlebars into my forearms.

"When was the last time you were on a motorcycle?"

Afghanistan, twelve years ago.

"It's been a while," I tell her.

"I'm sensing a lack of trust between us . . ."

No kidding.

"I'm not very interesting."

Kylie takes a leap over a small hill and catches air. Her lithe body looks almost acrobatic as she handles the jump.

"I doubt that. Let's try this again. When was the last time you were on a motorcycle? I know you've ridden before."

Fine. It's not a state secret. Well, the specifics are . . .

"Twelve years ago in Afghanistan."

"That doesn't sound like a pleasure ride."

I watch a jackrabbit in the distance leap in a zigzag pattern away from our commotion. I feel a sense of kinship with the creature. There's also a lesson to be learned about how to get away from a threat when you're smaller and plumper—don't flee in a straight line. The faster, sleeker animal will always catch you. Going in a zigzag pattern makes them use more energy and exhausts them sooner.

I'm used to running in straight lines. I need to practice my zigzagging.

"It wasn't. A journalist was kidnapped by the Taliban. They were waiting for their leader to show up so they could behead the poor bastard. We got an intercept that told us it was going to happen. While one team went to grab the leader, it was my job to go in and grab the reporter.

"We didn't have any air support or backup. So I came straight through the desert on a bike we borrowed. This was when electrics weren't practic—*ooph*." A large rock interrupts me as the seat slams into my testicles.

Kylie looks back at me. I give her a thumbs-up.

"Like I said, it's been a while." *Goddamn.* "Anyway, this bike was actually turbocharged. It wasn't exactly quiet, but you couldn't tell what direction it was coming because the high-pitched noise threw you off."

"What happened?" asks Kylie.

"I parked the bike behind the compound. They were sitting under a tree listening to a soccer game. I waved at them, dropped a backpack filled with cash, and they turned over the journalist. I put him on the back of the bike and drove off."

"No bullets?" asks Kylie.

"Not that time. They weren't exactly committed. They were sheepherders bullied into joining. It was their leader we were concerned with. Two Afghan pilots in A-29s took out his convoy on the road to the compound." I add with some hesitation, "Then they blew up the compound."

I had been asked if I was willing to put an explosive in the backpack full of cash. I declined.

"I bet the reporter was grateful," says Kylie.

"He was."

The entire reason we saved his ass was to exploit that gratitude. For better or worse, I was able to use him as an asset to plant stories afterward, as needed.

Kylie races her bike up a hill. I lean forward and follow, still trying to keep the dust out of my face and my ass firmly on the seat.

She comes to a stop and takes off her helmet. She wipes locks of black hair from her eyes and looks out at the plateau behind us. I pull beside her, put down the kickstand, and hop off.

The Mojave Basin stretches out into the distance. I recognize most of the scattered patches of civilization and can see Nellis Air Force Base way off near the horizon.

"It doesn't look like much, but there's a lot of history here," says Kylie.

I know of at least two secret facilities behind visible mountain ranges that Kylie's probably never even heard of. On maps they have names like "Desert Reclamation Project" and look like mineral mines. One of them is a surveillance station with a laser that could take out a satellite in orbit, the other a bioweapons lab that develops the stuff of nightmares.

Kylie parks her bike and sets her backpack on the seat. She pulls a small drone out of it and unfolds the arms and rotors.

"I was thinking last night," she says. "Ben Kohl and David Gallar are dead because of me. I still haven't, you know, processed it all. I don't know that I will. I can't think of something I should have done differently, but it still hurts. If I never existed, they'd still be alive."

"That's not the way to look at it. The net amount of evil in the world isn't going to diminish if there are fewer good people," I assure her.

"Yeah. I can do the math and say that if we succeed and make travel safer, we'll save X lives. But still, that doesn't lessen the pain."

"No. But wishing you didn't exist isn't the answer," I respond.

"I know. I know. I guess the other thing is that I don't really want to wait for something to happen. I thought I could spend some more time around you and learn a little about how you think. Like how you're about to say something self-deprecating to deflect the indirect compliment. Or why you always pause before entering a doorway. My guess is that you're making sure you know who's on the other side."

I had no idea she'd been watching me this closely.

"Sophia's been giving me firearms instruction. But there's a lot more than that to learn. I want to be several steps ahead, like you."

I'm about to say that I don't feel like I'm several steps ahead, then realize Kylie already nailed me on the self-deprecation.

"Some of it can't be taught. It comes from surviving," I tell her.

"Then teach me the parts that can."

Kylie starts up the drone and it flies into the air. She uses the control to send it out over the desert toward a junkyard in the distance, where half a dozen airplanes in various states of disrepair sit behind a metal fence among hills of old parts and rusted machinery.

"First lesson: ask questions. What's with the drone?" I ask.

"I was thinking last night, 'What would Trasker do?'"

"Fly a drone?"

"Maybe. I wanted to show you first and walk you through my thinking and see how I'm doing."

"With a drone?" I ask.

"I'm getting to the drone. The shot that took out the Sparrow, that was tricky. There were all kinds of conditions that had to be right. They had to practice it. Where's the best place to practice? In a place as close as possible to where you're going to have to pull it off.

"A friend of mine is a film director. He once took me to this town that's about fifty miles from here that looks like a small city in Afghanistan. The military uses it to train, and film productions rent it for movies," she explains.

I've been there. I can name a few others like it that no film crew has ever seen. Including one that's completely underground and is used to practice missions inside countries with satellite surveillance.

Kylie flies the drone around the far side of the scrapyard. I can't see it because it's too far away, but the display on her controller shows objects I recognize, giving me a general idea of its location.

"If I had to take that shot at the Sparrow, I'd practice it in conditions as close to that night as possible. That means shooting at a similar target from a similar position in the same weather. Since there was no way to predict the weather that night, that means practicing it in different weather conditions," she says, describing 90 percent of sniper training without realizing it.

She flies the drone to the ground outside the fence.

I think I know where this is going . . .

"The best place to practice? The same spot where they took the shot from. The second-best place? Somewhere nearby almost exactly like it. So I looked at some high-res maps of the area and found this spot."

"The scrapyard?"

"It's just a hunch."

"Well, remember: we were standing over the sniper's nest and didn't even notice it."

"We didn't know what we were looking for." She brings the drone a foot off the ground, and the rotors send up a cloud of dirt that I can see from here. The screen is completely obscured by it.

Kylie fires the drone upward and the cloud vanishes from the monitor. Then she brings it back down into a hover.

Damn.

There, under the dissipating dust cloud, lies a rectangular lid the same size as the one we found covering the sniper nest.

Kylie flies the drone close to a derelict Learjet that hasn't flown in decades.

The camera swivels and pans along the fuselage, and we see hundreds of tiny little slot holes like the ones in the Sparrow wreckage and Gallar's wheel well.

Each has a circle around it and a number written by it. Several of them are close to a tiny green sticker.

This is exactly how I've seen snipers keep track of their shots. The sticker is what they aim for. The number tells them which shot and under what conditions.

"I figured this is the kind of thing you would do," says Kylie.

I know she means it as a compliment, but I'm kicking myself for not thinking of it first.

"Think they left behind any clues?" she asks like an eager child.

I smile. "One way to find out."

TARGET PRACTICE

There are 422 holes in the Lear's fuselage. The sniper had a lot of practice. Since the old jet's inside the chain-link fence, that meant that someone had to climb over and open the gate in order to mark and label the practice shots.

When Kylie and I approached the scrapyard, I looked for an entrance while we waited for the police to show up. FBI agents Morrel and Broadhurst were notified, but they had already returned to their Los Angeles office and won't be able to make it until tomorrow.

Which is fine with me. It doesn't matter when they show up. That Kylie and I found the second sniper's nest will be suspicious to them, regardless.

"Well, this certainly is interesting," says Jack Douglas, the undersheriff who responded when we found the original sniper's nest. He's standing on the edge of a hole identical to the last one, except it has no metal rail to use as a mount.

One of his deputies is crouched in the pit, panning its walls with a video camera with a macro lens.

Kylie and I keep our distance so we don't contaminate the scene. Although I don't think the sniper expected anyone to find the second nest or connect the tiny holes in the fuselage to what happened to the Sparrow, they wouldn't be sloppy enough to leave behind any additional evidence. At least not intentionally.

"How did you find this?" asks Douglas.

"Drone," says Kylie. "I have a recording if you want it."

"Yes. That would be helpful. I'm sure our friends at the FBI will want to see that too. Let me get Sean Nicholson on the phone. He's the one who owns this scrapyard. Although I don't know if he's been out here in a while."

He walks away to make the call. I wander back to the fence and watch as a deputy takes photographs of the ground near the fuselage. Kylie joins me.

The deputy, a young redheaded man in his early twenties, notices her and gives a shy grin.

"How's it going?" asks Kylie, not wasting the opportunity to get more information.

Working in a field dominated by men who don't socialize much with women must have been a challenge for Kylie to navigate. One thing I've noticed is that the men around Kylie respect her, joke around, and feel comfortable using her first name, but there is still a distance. It could be a bit of awe on their part. Or a guard Kylie keeps up.

My mother was different. She could control any situation. I've witnessed the tone of voice that she used when she wanted something done. It's like being scolded by your favorite teacher.

Mother said she learned it from her mom, who grew up with five younger brothers.

"It looks like a stepladder was used here," says the deputy, pointing to four indentations in the dirt. "We might figure out the weight of the suspect by looking at the depth. We might even be able to tell what brand it is from the diameter," he adds, trying to impress Kylie with his forensic acumen.

"A five-foot aluminum Werner ladder," she says.

The deputy scratches his head. "Maybe. We'd have to look it up."

"No," Kylie says with a girlish giggle I've never heard before. "Right there, behind the oil drum. There's a five-foot aluminum Werner ladder, folded up."

Was the giggle calculated, or is the Kylie I normally see a mask she wears to keep people at a safe distance?

The deputy walks over to the ladder and kneels down. "Huh. We'll take this back and look for prints. You never know, we might find a partial."

He might be right. I don't know if they have the resources here or if Morrel and Broadhurst will go through the effort of sending this to one of their labs, so I don't get my hopes up.

Douglas puts his phone in his pocket and walks back to us. "I spoke to Sean Nicholson. He says he hasn't been out here in over a week and didn't know anything about the plane being shot up. He actually forgot it was out in this section. And to be honest, unless you made me look closer, I'd have just thought it was buckshot or something the scrappers did when they brought the plane here. Anyway, Nicholson did say that he was out here two weeks ago at night because he had to grab a part and there were two men on dirt bikes driving away from where we are now.

"He didn't think much about it. There was nothing worth stealing that you could carry out on a bike. Nothing worth stealing you could haul away at all, to be honest," says Douglas.

"Men on motorcycles were spotted near the complex two weeks ago," I reply.

"That does sound suspicious," he says.

"Did you say two dirt bikes?" asks the deputy.

"Yeah, Lonnie. You see something?" asks Douglas.

"It might have been a little more than two weeks ago, but I pulled into the gas station by the spaceport at Mono and 18, and I saw two guys with a pickup truck and a trailer hauling dirt bikes. I didn't think too much about them, other than they were kind of watching me," explains Lonnie.

"You got a description for us?" asks Douglas.

"I only got a good look at one of them. Stocky guy. Well built. Black hair pulled into a ponytail and a beard. He reminded me a little of Roman Reigns."

"Roman Reigns?" I ask.

"Professional wrestler," Kylie answers for him.

"Oh. I haven't been keeping up. What about the other one?" I ask.

"He stayed in the truck. I didn't get a good glimpse, but I think he had a beard too. And no, I didn't get the license plate. But we can check the security camera footage there."

Kylie turns to me with a raised eyebrow. "Well?"

"Well what? I think I should be learning from you."

BAD NEWS

Sennet is sitting across from me in the library three hours later. The library is closed, but for some reason they trust him with the key. I have to hand it to him: with a certain crowd, he has his own brand of charm. I've noticed that crowd mainly consists of blue-haired women twice his age, but in his circles, they're an important constituency.

"You want the bad news or the worse news?" he asks.

"Just give it to me," I reply, shaking my head.

I sent him the frame grabs from the gas station security footage. I had a feeling his connections would get answers faster than anything the sheriff or even the FBI has access to.

"I've got a seventy percent match for the one man caught on camera. Based on the description of the other one from the deputy, I'd put it at closer to ninety-five percent," says Sennet.

"Let me guess: A known team?"

"A suspected team. The Drako brothers. They go by Nikhil and Dusan or Adrik or Luka—depending on the rap sheet you're looking at. Their real last name is Kolker. They're not brothers but cousins. Given how crowded some of those rural gene pools are, though, they might as well be brothers. Anyway, they had an uncle who worked for the *mafiya* in Russia. He was also politically connected. The brothers started working as a team and doing hits as teenagers. They both then went into the army for three years, saw some action, and learned some skills. They went from mob work to political assassinations and now overseas kills. Early in the Ukraine war, they were sent in to infiltrate and kill officers and politicians. They were quite good at it," says Sennet.

"How's their English?" I ask.

"Apparently pretty good. Although they grew up in a poor area, one of their mothers and a sister both taught English. It seems they picked it up. Nikhil also speaks French fairly well."

You generally don't worry about Russian hit men outside of Russia because they tend to stand out. While Moscow has a few operatives that are both highly trained killers and skilled linguists, they're rare and only used for the most important assignments.

Skilled killers that understand enough English to navigate their way through America are a frightening prospect. I need Broadhurst and Morrel to get their heads out of their asses and start taking this seriously.

"At least the local police know what one of them looks like. They've already issued a bulletin. But I doubt anyone outside of Kern County will pay attention," I tell him.

"I don't know how useful that bulletin will be if they switch up their ride and shave their beards. I'm also sure they've got driver's licenses and all the documentation they could possibly need," Sennet says pessimistically.

Not to mention that if we do catch them, pinning them to a crime that the FBI isn't treating seriously could be next to impossible.

The local police could pull them over, but if their documents are in order, there'd be no cause to arrest them. Our evidence against them is all circumstantial.

"Do we have any forensics on file for them?" I ask.

"Someone I know in the DIA says they have a print from a rifle they think one of them used," he replies. "They don't exist as far as Interpol is concerned. And since they have clean records in the United States, they could be traveling under their own names, or at least Russian IDs that would check out."

"Would the Russians give them that much coverage?"

"Probably not. But that doesn't mean they don't have it," says Sennet.

"Can you get me a copy of the print?" I don't know how helpful it will be for the FBI investigation, but at least for my sake it could confirm who we're dealing with.

"Yes. But one more thing. Remember how I said there was worse news?"

"Yeah?" I thought this was bad enough already.

"These aren't just highly skilled killers, Bradley. These men are killers. And what I mean is that it comes natural to them. About a year after they got out of the military, two men wearing full body armor shot their way into a bank in Chechnya, robbed gold bars from a safe-deposit box, and killed three police officers on their way out. Twenty people got shot and eight killed in total. There were over thirty police officers on the scene, and these men went through them like they were nothing.

"Rumor has it that their gold bars belonged to an anti-Russian politician. The Drako brothers got the go-ahead because it was politically beneficial. It didn't matter that half their victims were bystanders."

"I'll be careful," I promise.

Sennet shakes his head. "You need to get the hell out of here. I'm leaving once I lock up. It's been fun helping you out, but I've had my fill."

I've never seen my friend this agitated. He's never hidden the fact that he doesn't have a desire to be anything other than the person you go to for information, but he's always loved the thrill of being close to the action.

Now, not so much.

I could tell horror stories for days about vicious killers and sociopathic hit men. I've had to deal with a few of them directly. And in a few situations, work side by side with them. But that was in my younger days. I'm not as quick on the draw now. I can't pretend otherwise.

I've brought Sophia in, but that might not be enough. I need to make sure Kylie has as much coverage as possible in Miami. As if that could protect her from this pair of Russian killers.

I trust the team Sophia has put around Kylie, but I need to be close by as well.

Not because I could do a better job than Sophia, but because I'd never be able to live with myself if something happened and I wasn't there.

"We need more people," I say to Sennet.

"You need to find out who's paying them," he replies. "Because that might be the only way you stop them."

I sigh. "I still don't even have the first clue. Everything is convoluted. If the Sparrow doesn't happen, a lot of people benefit. Corporations, foreign militaries, you name it."

"Okay. Slightly different question, then. You and I come from a world motivated by greed and political ambitions that tie back to greed. This one is only driven by greed. Who stands to make the most money if she's dead and the Sparrow doesn't happen?"

"Good question," I reply.

"Okay, here's another one. I know you won't like it, but I have to ask. Between the Russian hit men and the secret Russian plans that match the Sparrow, I'm picking up a bit of a Slavic vibe . . ."

"What's your question?"

"Maybe there's more truth to what Ben Kohl tweeted. Maybe Kylie doesn't have Russian investors, but maybe someone in Russia helped her out and was expecting something in return and she didn't give it to them?"

"That's reaching," I tell him.

"And yet here we are discussing the motives of politically connected Russian hit men. If this isn't a political hit, then it's a financial one. The angle might be more complicated than what I suggest, but you have to consider it."

"I trust her," I say flatly.

"You trust that Kylie wouldn't do anything wrong *intentionally*. But mistakes happen, and sometimes they escalate."

GROUND CONTROL

I'm in a conference room talking to Sophia via video. She's in Miami with our advance team preparing for Kylie's visit.

Our current security details cover the Wind Aerospace facility, the route from here to Kylie's home five miles from here, and her property itself.

Her house is a simple three-bedroom home she bought because of its practicality. Under Morena's advisement, she purchased four other homes around the chosen property and had a wall built around them all, complete with security cameras. These precautions were put in place long before I started working for her.

Sophia and I made changes, including creating three security zones. The first is round-the-clock private security watching every car that comes and goes from the small neighborhood.

The second layer is an off-duty deputy we pay to park in front of the home and keep watch.

The third layer is the security team posted in the house next door.

We also placed cameras in locations that we don't own but want to keep a watch on. This includes her neighbors' houses.

Sophia went through the added trouble of going door-to-door to meet the people who live near Kylie. She gave them a contact number in case they saw anything suspicious while taking careful note of Kylie's neighbors.

Some of our security exists as a physical deterrent; some of it is psychological.

A small hit team could shoot their way in, take out the deputy, and possible overwhelm our security team, getting to Kylie.

The problem is, it would be a suicide mission. We're also monitoring the home from here and can have the Kern County Sheriff's Department there in minutes, blocking roads and sending up helicopters.

This only gives me slight comfort. Every assassin has a price at which they will take on outsize risk. This may apply doubly to the Drako brothers.

"How does the hotel look?" I ask.

"We've booked five rooms in three different hotels. I'll decide two hours before she departs the venue which one we'll take her to," Sophia informs me.

One way to keep the bad guys from finding you is keeping your next location a secret, even from yourself.

"What about event security?"

"That's been doubled up because of the vice president's visit, and they've been doing background checks on all staff. Secret Service is also using their facial and electronic identification systems. I told them about our situation as well."

The Secret Service tries to record every person that comes close to the people they protect. They then analyze faces and look for people that show up multiple times. If you follow a presidential candidate from city to city and they notice your Facebook posts are extremely critical of them, you're going to get flagged. Electronic surveillance also offers a way to do this. Cell phone sniffers can track which phones keep showing up at events.

You may think you're attending anonymously, but some government agency has logged your face and the unique ID for your mobile device.

So why not leave the device at home or use a burner? It's what I'd do, but 99 percent of the people who'd threaten the life of a public figure don't think this way.

"How is it on your end?" asks Sophia.

"We've got three private jets booked at three different airports. We booked them under an outside company's name. We had the crews file different flight paths. We'll change it up at the last minute."

"Okay. We'll have to meet them at Opa Locka Airport. It's the only one I feel we can keep a tight security screen around," explains Sophia.

This concerns me, but I trust Sophia's decision. Sometimes being random can put you in a vulnerable position, and the better policy is to double down on security.

"What about the venue?" I ask.

"We'll have a team watching the crowd. There are metal detectors at the entrances, and the staff has to use biometric identification. I have three teams in place to handle disruptions," she assures me.

One vulnerability to prepare for is a diversion—when a bad actor creates a distraction that attracts all the security personnel to one part of the facility, leaving the person they're protecting thinly covered.

To handle this, you have two other teams standing by. While Group A responds to the initial threat, Group B gets your VIP out of the building, and Group C covers their flank.

You also have to make sure you have a clear path and the exit point is protected. I can show you case after case of amateur protection details that lost the person they were protecting because a diversion flushed them into an ambush outside the location.

There are entire tactical schools in the United States where federal agents and military personnel practice different scenarios against people who do nothing all day long except think of ways to penetrate security.

"What's your gut say?" asks Sophia.

"I think we're being paranoid enough. But I don't know. Since we discovered the rail gun, anything that happens to her will look suspicious. Either they've given up, or that doesn't matter now and they'll try to take her out any way they can. That makes me nervous. The rail gun was pretty exotic, to begin with. Using plastic explosive to collapse a hotel on Kylie wouldn't be that big of a stretch. Anything is possible."

One of the problems laypeople have in planning this kind of strategy is getting into the heads of the bad guys. If I asked someone to figure out how to take out the financial district in Tehran, recruiting volunteers to hijack airplanes for a suicide mission wouldn't immediately come to mind. Neither would killing two hundred innocent people with a truck bomb simply to take out a political rival. But it happens.

I can think up some pretty ruthless scenarios, but even then, I'm only role-playing.

AIRSPACE

Later that night, I'm standing in Kylie's living room while she finishes packing in her bedroom. Her mother and a security team member, Brenda Antolí, are both sitting on the edge of her bed, keeping her company.

While Kylie's mother is occasionally present, she's a quiet person who tends to be happy in the background. Her stepfather, Evan Fimley, is the opposite. He's known for unscheduled drop-ins that disrupt Kylie's workflow. But she handles it well.

Despite Brenda's rather flippant first encounter with me, ever since I took down her ex-boss Ruskin, she's proven to be dedicated to her job and has clearly earned Kylie's trust. She hangs out with Kylie in her off-hours and sometimes even crashes on her couch.

In the best scenario, your bodyguards like their protectee enough to be concerned with their well-being even when off the clock, but not so familiar that it interferes with the job.

I think the two of them have the right balance. Kylie is a workaholic who still needs an hour a day to make small talk about the boyfriend she doesn't have time for and what pair of shoes she should wear for an interview. Brenda seems more energized being around Kylie and has been asking Sophia about taking on a larger role.

This is what I'd hoped for and why I didn't fire the entire security team. Sometimes there are great people in bad systems. Unfortunately, the world is filled with bad systems.

"All set," says Kylie as she emerges from the bedroom.

She's carrying her own bag because Brenda and I need to keep our hands free.

I have a contact in the Secret Service who spent eight years dealing with the irate wife of a politician who was upset that her bodyguards wouldn't act as her personal valets. If you really want to know what a person in power is like, listen to what their bodyguards say. Or rather what they don't say. If they don't effuse about the kindness and generosity of the protectee, that tells you a lot.

It's often surprising to find out who has a good reputation and who doesn't. I know of some politicians described as tyrants in the media who are beloved by the people sworn to protect them. I know some who are regarded as saints but treat their protectors like furniture.

Brenda calls into her throat mic. "How are we outside?"

"Way station is clear," says Savoy over the radio.

He's also become one of the faithful since the Ruskin meeting. Right now, he's scanning the area with thermal binoculars for anything suspicious.

Brenda and I flank Kylie as we walk to an SUV parked between two identical vehicles. Kylie climbs into the back seat with Brenda. I slip into the passenger seat next to Benoit, our driver, who's been through tactical training and worked mobile security.

I keep my phone in my lap on dark mode so I can watch for any alerts, but most of my attention is on the road and buildings around us. Driving her around Mojave has become routine, but routine breeds laziness.

"You guys are going to love the nightclubs in Miami," Kylie jokes.

"We'll be sure to tell you what they're like," says Brenda.

I know Kylie's not the clubbing type, but my heart skips a beat at the thought of her making us escort her into a densely packed nightclub. She's the boss and could insist, but she knows it would make our lives more difficult.

I also know that the murders of Gallar and Kohl have made Kylie more appreciative of the extreme measures we've been taking.

We reach the end of the neighborhood, and the SUV ahead of us comes to a stop, waiting for me to tell him which way to go.

The airport Kylie's scheduled to depart from is something that even I don't know.

"Siri, give me a random number between one and three," I say into my iPhone.

"Your random number is one," the voice assistant replies.

"Skybridge Airport," I call into my earpiece, informing the other drivers.

"You know that algorithm is actually fairly deterministic," Kylie observes.

"I'll take my chances these people aren't math prodigies," I reply.

"I've been thinking about motive," she continues as we head down the highway.

"Any conclusions?"

"No, but a thought. We can only look at theoretical, down-the-road upsides for someone trying to stop our work. That makes the probability cone effectively infinitely wide at one end."

I raise my eyebrows, not exactly giving away my ignorance while encouraging her to explain.

"A motive could be as simple as the Sparrow poses a threat to the revenue of an existing air-transit company. Or it could be that, a hundred years from now, the Sparrow will bring about the destruction of humanity, and we're actually dealing with benevolent time travelers trying to save the world," she explains.

"I assure you these people are not benevolent time travelers," I reply, automatically thinking of the book that's always in the back of my mind.

"I agree, but there's nonzero chance of that. It's effectively zero for the purposes of this mental exercise. You basically made my point," she says.

"I'm glad to hear that. Could you explain how I did that?"

"The chance of it being someone who perceives the Sparrow as some far-future threat is possible, but assuming they're a rational actor, spending this many resources to stop us doesn't make sense. There are an infinite number of distant theoretical threats. Choosing me to stop one of them seems random.

"If, on the other hand, there was a much shorter-term reason with a large-enough incentive, then that might justify taking action."

"I think I follow you," I tell her.

"Basically, putting in this much effort implies a tremendous reward for our saboteurs. A reward that's either very short-term or highly probable. It's an investment. The question is, What *kind* of investor and what do they know that we don't? Historically, seemingly random large bets with huge payoffs happen when the person making them sees something others don't," she says.

We take a corner and head down another highway toward the airstrip. The road is deserted, and the only visible lights are our headlights and the blinking of the control tower in the distance.

"If I get what you're saying, there might be something obvious that we're not realizing."

"Not quite. I'm saying that someone sees an obvious benefit that we don't. Like they know there's a diamond mine nearby and we haven't seen it."

"You're pretty business-savvy. How come it's not obvious?"

"It might be like insider trading. Someone has information they shouldn't have and they're acting on it."

We pull through the entrance of the airport, and a Kern County deputy waves at us. I requested one at each airport.

Our entourage drives past the mostly empty parking lots and toward the hangars.

Skybridge is a small airport mainly used for private planes. The runway is long enough for small jets, and they have a fuel truck that can handle a limited amount of business.

As we drive past the space between two hangars and onto the tarmac, our jet is waiting with its door open and a small set of retractable stairs leading up to the cabin.

"Kong, this is Greaser. Everything nominal?" I ask over the earpiece.

"Affirmative," replies the voice of Edwin Carver, the bodyguard I assigned to this plane.

"What's the catchphrase?" I ask.

"Don't knock twice," he replies, letting me know that neither he nor the pilots are at gunpoint.

The lead SUV in our convoy brings us to a stop twenty meters away from the jet.

"Wait here," I say.

I get out to visually inspect the interior of the plane. As I exit the vehicle, I scan the tarmac. It's wide open. The only sound I hear is our jet's turbines.

I reach the top of the jet stairs, and Carver steps aside to let me in. I give the cabin a quick check and look inside the bathroom.

"All good?" I ask.

"Affirmative," he replies.

I walk to the cockpit. The two pilots match the photographs on my phone.

"Gentlemen, I need you to call in a new flight plan." I take the document from my jacket pocket and hand it to Renwood, the copilot.

"Damn. I should have packed sunscreen," he says with a smile.

"Why am I not surprised there'd be a change of plans?" says Captain Jensen. "You people are worse than the CIA."

Guess where I learned this kind of clandestine air travel from?

"Why don't you bring aboard your cargo while we call this in?" says Jensen.

I leave the jet, return to the SUV, and open Kylie's door.

She steps out and glances over her shoulder, saying, "You know, it's odd . . ."

And that's when the first bullet flies.

CONTROL TOWER

It makes a sound like an ice pick punching through a refrigerator, followed by the tinkling of glass. I shove Kylie back into the vehicle and yell, "Drive!"

But Benoit can't. The first bullet was meant for him. His head is tilted to the side, and an exit wound the size of a half dollar has cratered his right temple.

I catch light flickering through a hole in the roof and realize they took the shot from a high angle, *through* the body of the SUV.

"Out!" I yell to Kylie as I slide down onto the tarmac, pulling her with me.

I shove her under the SUV and try to put as much metal as possible between me and the sniper.

"Dispatch! We need backup! We're pinned down by a sniper in the control tower!"

Brenda slides across the seat, her body low. "What do we do?"

I grab her wrist and yank her out and onto the ground an instant before another bullet penetrates the roof and tears a hole in the seat.

Bang. Bang. Bang. Bang. Four more bullets follow.

From the sequencing, it sounds like there's just one person shooting at us. But assuming this is the Drako brothers, there's at least another person spotting and waiting to shoot us when we expose ourselves.

"Alpha?" I call, using the call sign for the first SUV.

"Paolo's hit!" shouts Savoy over the comms.

"Get under your vehicles!" I yell at the top of my lungs. "Stay away from the control tower side!"

Bang. Bang. Thump.

My head's flat on the asphalt, and I see the body of one of our people fall in front of the lineup of SUVs.

Damn it.

"Gamma?" I call over the comms to the driver of the third SUV.

"Leeds is down!" says Minter.

There were nine of us, plus Kylie. All three drivers have been taken out, leaving us with no exit.

I could try to pull Benoit from the driver's seat and take control, but that would be asking for death. The sniper has us pinned down from the control tower. When I reconnoitered this airport, that was a distant but not particularly plausible scenario. The tower was locked down and in constant radio contact.

They'd have to move in right after the deputy at the gate waved us through, and then act fast.

There was also the fact that the tower was much farther away from the hangar than seemed practical for a sniper.

I was expecting something conventional. This wasn't.

While we were driving through the parking lot, they were taking the control tower.

How did they know we'd be here? Was it a lucky guess? They must have covered all three airports, because even I didn't know where we were headed.

That's a question for another day. Right now, we have to stop them.

I call up the Time Traveller's workshop and study the tactile map I'd placed on his worktable. I used a 3D map to remember the layout of each airport, placing objects like milk cartons and mailing tubes for the buildings. This airport has one main tower with an administration building on the side opposite of the hangars. In my mind it's a box of Ritz Crackers lying on its side.

Paolo, Leeds, and Benoit are all down. That leaves Minter, Savoy, Brenda, Kylie, and me here under the SUVs and Carver in the plane with the pilots.

The sniper hasn't shot at the plane yet, that I'm aware of. I assume they want to keep the hope of escape alive and get us to make a run for the jet, then take us out in the open.

In theory, our best strategy is to wait until backup arrives and Kern County SWAT takes on the snipers in the control tower.

The problem is, they know that too. They've planned for this contingency. They know we'll choose the rational option and try to wait them out.

That means it's no longer the rational option.

If I were them . . .

"Keep her covered," I tell Brenda.

She assumes my position, shielding Kylie.

"Savoy, fire at the tower!" I say through the comms.

A barrage of gunshots echoes across the tarmac a second later as he follows my order.

I use the momentary pause to run from our SUV to the rear one, closest to the hangars.

Bang.

I feel something whiz past my head and hit the concrete a meter away.

I dive and roll to a painful stop next to Minter behind the final SUV.

He has his gun drawn and is sitting in a crouch, waiting for something to do. I notice a spray of blood on the left side of his face. That's probably from Nathan Leeds, the driver.

"Lie flat. Keep an eye on the area in front of the control tower and back there." I point. "They may try to flank us," I say to the team through my throat mic. "Savoy, more suppressing fire."

While he unloads another magazine's worth of ammunition at the tower, I make a run from the SUV to the closed hangar doors.

Bang. Bang.

Two shots ring out and send chips of pavement into the air.

I hit the metal doors hard, not daring to slow before escaping the sniper's line of sight.

As I ran, I caught a glimpse of the tower and saw the shattered windows.

The sniper had us in his sights the moment we pulled up. The spotter probably smashed the window with a crowbar the instant before the shooting started.

That took us by surprise and gave them a few seconds' head start. That was almost enough time to get us all, but not quite. Under the body of the cars, we have some protection from the tower sniper.

To get to us now, one of them has to do it from the ground. Coming at us from the opposite direction makes the most sense. It's what I would do.

Ping.

A bullet hole appears in the hangar door a foot from my head.

God*damn.* The sniper's shooting through the roof of the hangar and the door!

The accuracy is insane.

I don't wait for his aim to improve and run in the opposite direction of the tower, toward the far side of the hangar.

When I get to the edge, I wait. The second brother could be on his way toward us at ground level. I listen closely for footsteps. I don't hear any.

I bolt around the corner, gun aimed straight ahead. The fence separating the parking lot from the tarmac is wide open.

I catch a shadow behind a parked van. It could be the other shooter or it could be the deputy at the entrance.

I fire two shots at the back of the van, breaking windows, and run to the far edge of the lot to get a look behind the vehicle.

It's the deputy. I lower my gun, openly, but he panics and fires.

I'm far enough away that he misses, but now he realizes that it's me and is lowering his weapon.

"Sorry!" he yells.

I put a finger to my lips, then motion for him to come to me.

He makes a break for it. A gun fires from the parking lot in front of the hangar. While the deputy keeps running, I make my way around the van and toward the edge of the building.

I hear the *bang-bang-bang* triple burst of a machine gun from only a few feet around the hangar.

The ground shooter comes around the corner, plants his feet, and carefully aims his gun at the retreating deputy.

He catches me from the corner of his eye.

But it's too late.

I squeeze the trigger and put a hole in the side of his head. His body collapses on the tarmac, legs twitching as he expires.

I put another bullet in his skull, grab his machine gun, and sprint for the control tower, keeping close to the buildings in case the sniper still up there takes a look out the side.

One Drako down. One to go.

STAIRMASTER

Adrenaline surges through my body like nitrous oxide in a race-car engine. If I survive this, there's going to be hell to pay throughout my body.

The smart move would be to wait for SWAT to arrive and take out the remaining sniper, but there's a catch:

He's in such a strategic position that there's no way he doesn't kill more of my team, and possibly Kylie, if he's not taken out first. He's already turning the SUVs into swiss cheese. And once he's finished with them, he'll start on the jet.

The deadliest mass shooting in the United States happened when Stephen Paddock started firing at people attending a music festival from the thirty-second floor of the Mandalay Bay resort in Las Vegas. From the time he opened fire to when he took his life an hour later, hundreds of people were wounded and sixty were killed.

Charles Whitman killed fourteen people from an observation deck at the University of Texas at Austin before he was killed.

A gunman in a strategic position is extremely difficult to take out.

When Micah Xavier Johnson ambushed police officers, killing five of them, he retreated to a position so well protected the only way the police were able to stop him was by strapping an explosive device to a bomb-disposal robot and blowing him up.

There's also another critical factor: our sniper is firing conventional bullets now, but that doesn't mean he doesn't have other weapons.

A drone with an explosive charge targeting our aircraft wouldn't be beyond him.

I run along the row of hangars, trying to keep out of view of the control tower.

I don't know if the tower sniper realizes that I took out his brother yet, but it's safer if I make sure I'm not seen.

My knees are killing me by the time I reach the administration building. I ignore them and step through the shattered glass door the hit men came through during their initial assault.

Something moves in the dark lobby. I aim the assault rifle in the direction of a man sitting on the floor with his hands zip-tied to a railing.

I put my finger to my lips. He nods. I strip the duct tape from his face.

"Who are you?" I ask.

"The . . . the pilot," he stammers.

"How many?"

"One . . . one up there and one . . . one outside."

I use my pocket knife to cut his hands free. "Go over to that car-rental desk and stay hidden until someone tells you it's safe to come out." Hopefully he's smart enough not to run outside, but better safe than sorry.

"Which way up to the tower?" I ask.

He points to the far end of the lobby.

"I'm heading up to the tower. Stay low," I call into the comm.

When I get closer, I see the door has a fist-size hole where the doorknob used to be. They must have used a plastic explosive to circumvent the security keypad to the right.

I slowly open the door, careful to not make a sound.

After I step through, I put my pistol back in my holster and check the number of rounds in the HK416 I'd lifted from Drako brother #1. It's a thirty-round magazine that's still two-thirds full.

I only need one bullet . . . but so does the remaining sniper.

I take off my shoes so I'll make less noise as I climb the stairs. It's a minor precaution. The other sniper will suspect in minutes, if not already, that his partner is gone.

There's a chance he might decide to flee. In that case the stairs would seem the obvious route, but the Drako brothers are the kind of people to know that's a possible choke point.

They'd want another way out of the building. Given their training, that could mean rappelling out of the tower . . . or something else I haven't even considered.

I still don't know how they knew we were coming and got past security so quickly.

I take the first flight of stairs, keeping the HK aimed into the gap between landings that affords a clear view all the way to the top.

I take another two flights of stairs and push my back against the wall.

Bang!

A shot rings out, but it's muffled by the door at the top and likely aimed at my colleagues still pinned down.

I take the rest of the stairs in quick strides, ignoring the breathtaking pain in my aging knees, and plant myself against the wall next to the doorway.

There's no lock on the door. But I still have to open it . . .

I could fling it open and burst through firing, but chances are he's already well barricaded inside. That would be a suicide mission.

If I had a flash grenade or two, this would be a lot easier.

I glance to see what's around me. There's a fire extinguisher on the wall and a plastic trash can in the corner.

Okay . . . that's something.

I carefully move the fire extinguisher next to the door. Then I grab the trash can.

Exposing only my left hand, I take hold of the doorknob, pull the door open toward me, and slip the trash can into the gap to keep it from shutting.

Bang. Bang. Bang.

Shots strike the metal door and ricochet off the concrete at the back of the stairwell.

I'm crouched low behind the wall, hoping his ordnance won't penetrate cinder blocks.

Bang. Bang.

I feel lead slam the wall behind me, but no bullets get through.

He's probably using armor-piercing rounds. They have little problem penetrating metal, but they're not quite as effective on concrete.

I wait a beat, then put the fire extinguisher nozzle through the gap and squeeze.

Fire-retardant powder blasts from its nozzle and clouds the control room.

Another series of bullets hits the door. This time a wild pattern, top to bottom. He's not taking any chances.

I wait him out. As long as he's focused on me outside the door, he's not taking shots at my team.

In the distance, police car sirens wail as they race toward the airport.

"I surrender!" shouts an accented voice from inside the control tower room.

Bullshit he does. He'd rather take his chances getting the drop on me than wait for the police to show up in force.

"Throw down your weapon!" I call out.

I hear a clatter of something.

I take my iPhone from my pocket and turn on the camera.

When I slide the lens past the edge of the door frame, I see a figure in the cloud of dust standing in back with what looks like an HK aimed straight at the door.

He glances down and sees the screen. I pull my hand away before a spray of bullets fills the space where it was a moment ago.

The sirens grow louder.

I hear footsteps and the sound of breaking glass.

Bullets hit the doorway again, but too high to hit anyone. It's a bad shot from an expert marksman.

I burst through the doorway and into the control room.

The sniper is crouched by the broken window with a climbing harness around his torso, trying to tie a line around the opposite window frame.

He stands as I enter, raising his gun.

I fire first, putting a round through his shoulder and slapping him backward. His body tips out over the window edge. He tries to recover, dropping his rifle to grasp at the window frame, but he misses awkwardly and falls instead.

I hear a thud as I race to the window and see his body sprawled atop the administration building four flights below.

I scan the room, then check the pulses of the bodies of the two air-traffic control officers. Both are dead.

I grit my teeth at the renewed pain in my knees and race back down the stairs to Kylie and what remains of our team.

ESCAPE CLAUSE

Red and blue lights from the police cars and ambulances splash across the hangars of Skybridge Airport. Crime-scene tape twists and curls in the wind blowing across the tarmac.

Broadhurst has her hands tucked into her FBI jacket while Morrel watches a photographer take photos of Benoit's body, slumped over the steering wheel. Paolo didn't make it either, yet through some minor miracle, Leeds was only bloodied and knocked unconscious. He'll recover fine.

Savoy took a ricochet to the side of his face while I was making my charge on the tower and has been airlifted to the hospital. The round didn't penetrate his skull, thankfully, but his face was a mess.

The only other injury on our team was Brenda. A round made it through the SUV and singed her shoulder. The slug had lost a lot of momentum by then, but it will still leave a scar.

The only other bodies found besides the Drako brothers' were those belonging to the air-traffic controllers and the guards.

"You were lucky," says Broadhurst. "This could have been a lot worse."

"It could have been a lot better if you weren't barking up the wrong tree and ignoring what we we've been trying to tell you."

"Easy, now. We've followed up every lead you sent us."

"That's the problem. I'm one guy with only one person with any field experience and you're the fucking FBI. I shouldn't have been the one chasing down leads. The only reason we're alive is because my client took matters into her own hands and got curious. If we hadn't found the second sniper's nest and realized who was after us, she and I both would be on the pavement here with our brains spilled out."

I walk away in disgust.

"We still have questions," Broadhurst says to my retreating back.

I ignore her. As far as I'm concerned, this is a Kern County Sheriff's Department investigation and the special agent is merely a tourist.

I have questions as well. Although part of one mystery has been solved: how they were here ahead of us, even though I didn't know which airport we were going to go to until we got on the road.

The tied-up pilot I found in the tower lobby was a *helicopter* pilot. The Drako brothers had charted a helicopter in Tehachapi, thirty miles from here, then put a gun to the pilot's head and told him they had new plans.

While we were escorting Kylie from the house, they were watching from a chopper several miles away and tracking our convoy.

Once they realized it had to be Skybridge, they had the pilot race there, asked the control tower for permission to land at the empty heliport, and waited until the right moment to storm the admin building and take the tower.

I should have foreseen that the former Russian operators would look at airport security differently from a terrorist. They were trained how to take control of airport facilities and not just blow things up.

It's an oversight I'll regret for the rest of my life.

Undersheriff Douglas is talking to a group of forensic technicians. He sees me and sends them off.

"Dumb question, but how are you doing?" he asks.

"I'm about to make a couple of difficult phone calls," I reply.

"That's never good. Let me know if you want me to handle that," he offers.

"Thanks. But I gotta do it."

I glance over and see Kylie sitting in the back of a police car with several deputies around her. Brenda, who refused to leave her side, is having her wound dressed by a paramedic.

"This could have been a lot worse," says Douglas as he looks up at the control tower.

"You're the second person to tell me how lucky we were."

"I didn't say 'lucky.' I'm just saying that the body count could have been a lot higher. See that ambulance over there?" He points to the far end of the parking lot, which deputies have started to seal off with tape.

"That was here before," I recall.

"Yes. We found a cache of guns and body armor inside it. That was their backup escape route."

I think back to the sequence of events. While the tower sniper had us pinned down, his brother was working his way around to flank us.

If I hadn't run into him, he would have had a wide-open shot from the side of the hangar.

If we left the shelter of the SUVs, his brother would have taken us out in the open.

It would have been over in two minutes. The two of them could have made a run for the helicopter, if that were still viable, or used the ambulance.

In either scenario I don't see the responding police following an ambulance or helicopter leaving the scene. It was too sophisticated a ploy.

"In my thirty years I've never seen anything like this. Have you?" asks Douglas.

"The planning? Yes. Enough that I should have seen it coming."

Kylie sees me through the crowd of police keeping watch. She gets up and runs to me and wraps her arms around my neck and shoves her head into my shoulder.

"They're dead," she says.

At first, I think these are tears of relief that the Drako brothers have been killed.

Then I realize that she's talking about the people in her security detail, colleagues she's come to know over the past several days while they were around her constantly.

"I'm sorry," I whisper.

"It's because of me," she says softly.

"It's the job. They understood it," I assure her. But I really want to say it's because of *me*.

"I don't know if I can keep going," she says.

"Yes, you can. We'll get you someone to talk to. But in the end, you'll do what you do. You'll do what you were doing, and they were willing to die to protect you so you could," I explain.

My speech feels hollow. I'm pretty sure Benoit didn't really expect that being a bodyguard meant that someone was actually going to take his life on his next job. He did everything by the book. The only reason he's dead and I'm alive is because I took the passenger-side seat.

I've had too many close calls like that to give me anxiety. It's a perpetual miracle that I'm still alive, today more than most. Most days I'm grateful for it.

Some days, like when I'm watching the body of someone who worked for me being put into a medical examiner's van or my son's coffin being lowered into the ground . . . not so much.

"This isn't over, is it?" asks Kylie.

I want to lie to her, but I can't. "No. It's not. Whoever hired them could hire a dozen more like them. At least now the FBI is going to take this seriously, and I doubt we'll see anything like this again," I say hopefully.

"Yes. But the man who ordered this is still out there."

"He is. The men he hired, the Drako brothers, had an advantage in the FBI not taking them seriously. Now that it's clear someone's after you, I don't think he'll be coming directly for you anymore."

She pulls back and wipes the tears from her eyes. "Maybe not, but we're coming for him."

There is nothing idle about the way she says this. Kylie Connor has created two empires and has a force of will that's unmeasurable.

I don't doubt her, but I also don't want this to destroy her.

I've already lost too many people.

CONSOLE

I'm lying in bed in my motel room at the Mojave Super Six with half a beer on my nightstand and my mother on the loudspeaker of the phone resting on my chest.

"How did they take it when you called?" asks Mother after I give her the full story.

"Not well. Confusion, shock, denial. You know how it goes," I reply, relaying the calls I had to make to Benoit's and Paolo's families. "Paolo had an eleven-year-old son I didn't know about."

I didn't only lose a good person, I also took away a boy's father.

"I'm sorry, hon. So close to losing Jason. This has been a rough year for you."

"I've only made it worse," I reply.

There's a long pause. Finally, Mother responds, "It's not going to be one of those calls, is it? I thought we were past that. You want pity, someone to tell you that it's not your fault? Call a therapist. Or Kathy, whichever."

"Yeah, sorry," I tell her.

"You're not stupid. You're also not omniscient. You knew the risks. If it hadn't been you, then it probably would have been worse. But you'll never know. And you should have learned to live with that by now."

"I just think a younger me—" I start to say.

She cuts me off. "Was smarter than you now? I knew you when you were younger; you were way dumber than you are now. The marines, for crying out loud?"

She still likes to tell me that I made a dumb choice. She has nothing against the marines; she just felt it was the most backward way I could have gone about a career in intelligence.

I've tried to tell her that my goal wasn't to be a spy, but she doesn't believe me.

"I'm going to save you the trouble of making small talk with me and get right to the question you want to ask: What could you have done differently? Am I right?"

I sigh loudly. "Yes."

"I'll tell you what I've always told you. You play too fair. You have to fight dirty. The difference between us is that I know it's life and death. You think there's going to be some clean way to solve it. There isn't. There never has been."

"I do fight dirty," I argue.

"When it's too late. The moment you took that job, the gloves had to be off. Otherwise, you should never have taken it."

"If there was an opportunity, I would have—"

Again she cuts me off. "Bullshit. That cocky prick you ran into in Mexico? Does he still have all his fingernails?"

"He was just a pawn."

"Pawns can still kill. And you don't know *what* he is. Did you put people on her competitors? Did you have them watched?"

"No."

"Because you thought you could win by playing by the rules. How did that turn out? The body count might be the same, but at least you'd have more answers."

"Okay. What's your professional opinion?"

"Walk away. You're done. Let the FBI handle it. But we both know that you can't do that. You always have to be somebody's hero. What you don't realize is this isn't a game for heroes."

"Okay. Moving past that . . ."

"You need to find out who paid them and who's their person inside Wind Aero. It's that simple."

"What makes you think there's an inside person?"

"Because there always is. How did they know you were heading to the airport? They were up in the air before you pulled out of her driveway."

"They could have paid off a PI to watch," I suggest.

"Fine. But the gun parts that came from there? You've got a rat. There's no other way around it. Right now, you need to be putting the thumbscrews on staffers and finding out who talked."

"Sophia's flying back from Miami tonight with the rest of the team."

"Do you trust Kylie's lawyer not to throw you under the bus?" asks Mother.

"Morena? She's protective of Kylie. Me, I don't know."

"I looked her up. She's your type. Have you slept with her yet?"

I wish I could say this is the most awkward question my mother has ever asked me, but sadly, it's far from it.

"Uh . . ." I begin.

"That's a negative. I'm surprised she hasn't made a pass at you. I don't take her for a lesbian. Have you put on weight?"

"Not that I'm aware of. Can we change the topic?" I ask.

"This is your problem, Brad. You want to do things the polite way. If you two were hooking up, she'd be less likely to burn you when things get bad. And vice versa. It's a safety net. I'm surprised she didn't offer it to you."

"Let me write this down . . . *Sleep with lawyer.* Thanks, Mom. This is the kind of great advice that I call you for."

"I could tell you stories," she shoots back.

"Please don't. Anything else?"

"There's a side of you that makes me think you really are my son. It was that version of you that took out two assassins half your age. That's the man I raised. That's the man it will take to get the asshole behind this. You can't wait to get pissed off for that part of you to show up, Brad. He *always* has to be there under the surface. You understand?"

"I think so."

"If you can't, then you should just drop it. Otherwise, you're not going to make it through this."

UNLEASHED

"What the hell is *this*?" asks Morena as she storms into the conference room I've been using as an office.

She's standing in the doorway in the Lululemon shorts and top she wears to jog around the facility, clutching the letter of resignation that I drafted after talking to my mother.

"I think it's pretty clear," I reply.

"No. It's not." She slams the letter down and takes the seat across from me. "This job isn't done. I'm sorry that we lost some good people, but Kylie still needs you. This company needs you."

"I understand. But I don't think I'm the right person for the job right now."

She shakes her head. "No. I'm not buying it."

"I can't really say much more. Trust me, I care very deeply. I want to make it right," I explain.

Her eyes narrow and she studies me. "You're up to something? Aren't you?"

"I've just decided to move on."

"Men like you can't. It's in your DNA. You make a choice, act all stoic, and try to shut people out. Come on, Brad."

"Hypothetically, if I were up to something and it turned out bad, you'd want some kind of separation between me and this company," I hint.

"I don't need separation. Kylie doesn't either. Our people's blood is still on the ground. If you don't go to war, she will, and I'll be right behind her."

Morena's sincere. I don't know what "going to war" means for her and Kylie, but the claws are definitely out.

"We should talk about this somewhere else. The walls have ears," I say, pointing around us.

"We can go to my place."

"Fine. Let me get my things together."

"We can also get that other thing out of the way too," she says in a hushed voice.

"The other thing?"

Morena is sitting up at the end of the bed with a sheet wrapped around her body. Her hand is on my leg.

"So, what's next?" she asks.

I assume she means after we leave the bedroom.

"I'm going to pursue 'the Saboteur' while Sophia looks for 'the Rat,'" I tell her, using the names we've assigned to the people we're looking for.

"What can I do?"

"To be honest? Give Sophia room to do what she does. People are going to complain and come running to you. You need to assuage their concerns. If that doesn't work, you need to attack their sincerity and get them to back off. Remind them that people died."

"How hard is she going to interrogate people?" Morena asks.

"Don't worry, we'll save the car batteries and ball clamps as a last resort. That's a joke. She's going to go through files and look for any discrepancies, then push them. If someone says they got a 4.0 GPA and it was a 3.9 . . . that kind of thing."

"I don't know. I imagine everyone has something they're hiding."

"They do. That's the point. One of these people is hiding the fact that they sold out their colleagues and helped them get killed."

"You've done this kind of thing before, I take it?"

"There was a time when it was all I did. If there was a leak in an embassy, I was the outsider they brought in to scare everybody. Staffers would go through a more casual background check with a security officer, then they'd be told there was a problem with their answers and they'd be sent to a different room. They wouldn't know who I was or what agency I worked for. I'd do what Sophia will do—start with a tiny lie and then push from there.

"If they were clean, it was fine. If they were shady, I'd push them much harder. I found more than one mole that way. Half revealed themselves by crying. Others were stone-cold. One man confessed to killing his wife," I recall.

"Jesus," says Morena.

"We weren't even asking about that. It happened years before. He just broke."

"Try not to break our people," asks Morena.

"Don't worry. Sophia has a light touch. I'm the angry one."

"I wonder what you're like when you're angry," she muses.

There are two men in the morgue right now who saw that guy up close. And, to be honest, he hasn't left.

"What do we tell Kylie?" asks Morena.

"If she has a problem with us pressing her people, she can take it up with you. That's your job. You'll have to be the bad guy, even with her. If you're still game for all this . . ."

"I'm in. I trust you and Sophia know what you're doing."

"We don't. And that's the risk you're going to have to take."

"What about you? What are you going to do to find this saboteur?"

"I'm going to look for the weakest point and keep hitting it until something breaks."

SLEEPER

Sophia's pressure worked faster than I expected. I was still planning my next steps when I got an urgent call to meet her in the conference room of the empty hangar where employees had been told to go to be interviewed.

The walk in from the exterior door takes a while. You have to cross an entire bay that's mostly dark. The light from the window in the office door looks almost like a dark mirage from this distance.

Two security guards stand on either side of the lighted portal. The effect is that of approaching an execution chamber. Sophia might have taken this a little too far—or I'm getting too soft.

I nod to the guards and enter the office. Sophia's sitting on the edge of a desk with a raised eyebrow.

"What do we have?" I ask.

She shoves a folder into my hands. Inside are a photograph and résumé for a man named David Kotin. His title is "Facility Electrician" and his age is listed as sixty-five.

I glance at the photo and hold it up for Sophia to see. She nods. This guy is at least a decade older than sixty-five. He's healthy, but the expansion of sagging cartilage in his earlobes and nose tell a different story.

"What else about him?" I ask.

"His bio says he was born in Poland and emigrated in 1992. None of the companies checked out, and the Social Security number is for a man named David Antonov living in New Jersey."

"What does he do?"

"Changes the light bulbs, as far as I know. He's worked here since this place was founded. Apparently, they were sloppier back then about background screening."

"Apparently," I say, shaking my head.

"You haven't seen the best part."

"What's that?"

"Just go inside and talk to him," she says, motioning to the door to the adjoining conference room. "You'll see."

David Kotin is wearing a Wind Aerospace jumpsuit with the sleeves rolled up to the elbows of his crossed arms. He doesn't look amused as he watches me enter the room.

I place a Slavic-looking Donald Sutherland inside a light bulb on the gray worktable in the Time Traveller's shop.

I extend my hand to shake his as I sit down. "I'm Brad Trasker."

"David Kotin," he replies in an accent normally heard on the outskirts of Saint Petersburg.

I don't hide my grin. I flip open the folder. "Poland? Right?"

Kotin says nothing.

"Yeah. Accents are tricky. Let me guess: you were born in Poland, but your family were war refugees from Russia who homeschooled you. The accent stuck, and you were made fun of by other children and couldn't wait to get away from all the conflict to America. Does that sound about right?"

I've placed sleeper agents and I've hunted them down. I know more explanations for weak backstories than a Hollywood writer.

The problem with Kotin's is that it's thinner than nail polish. Sophia only had to look at his résumé and listen to him talk to know it was bullshit.

How did he get this far for so long?

I can understand why someone with an Eastern European accent wouldn't raise alarms here. Half the tech industry is powered by people born outside America. What I can't understand is how he didn't get noticed by the FBI, IRS, or Homeland Security at some point.

Our side has plenty of sleeper agents, but they have more plausible biographies. This one falls apart when you look at it.

"Are you a freelancer?" I ask.

"I'm full-time."

"There's that Saint Petersburg refinement I love. What I meant is, Did you come here as a sleeper, get recalled, and stay? Or are you still working for Moscow?"

"No offense, Mr. Trasker, but I think you've been chasing shadows for too long. You can't even see the light," he says in his deep voice.

"I saw the dead bodies of two people who worked here and another two men that were in the wrong place at the wrong time. All because somebody here has been put in a position of trust that they shouldn't have been."

"The loss of Mr. Paolo and Mr. Benoit saddens me more than you know," says Kotin.

I hold up the folder. "Then maybe you can express your sympathy by explaining this."

"And what should I explain?"

"We could start with your age. You look far older than someone who claims to be sixty-five. I assume that was the best you could do as far as a birth certificate. A forty-five-year-old man is vain enough to think that he'll pass as thirty-five, even if it raises questions later.

"But let's talk about Broward Vocational School. They have no record of you ever attending. Vincent Electrical doesn't appear to exist. The only real job we can prove you had is this one."

Kotin says nothing. He just watches me, waiting to see what I do next. I don't sense that he's afraid. I've seen this in men who've been interrogated before. Kotin has probably been in rooms like this and even spent time in jail.

He knows the real secret to making it through an interrogation—besides keeping your mouth shut. It's patience.

"You're clearly an intelligent man. So I won't bluff you or tell you something we both know isn't true. But after we're done here, I'm going to have the FBI come. You and I both know that means a trip straight from here to a jail cell. This morning will be the last time you'll have seen your house. Your pet that's waiting for you to come home is going to die never seeing you again. It's going to think you abandoned them.

"Best-case scenario, they deport you back to Russia. Maybe trade you for someone. Worst-case, you'll spend about twenty years in a federal prison and *then* get deported back to Russia—assuming it's still one country then.

"While you're sitting in prison, you're going to be worried about one thing. And that's whether the man you're working for will send someone after you. Our prisons run deep with Russian criminals. Nobody's out of reach.

"Unless you tell me who you're working for. Then I can make sure he doesn't reach in there and have you killed."

If you can't offer a Russian hope, offer them a chance at revenge.

Kotin stares at me. Not glaring, watching.

Outside I hear Sophia's raised voice, followed by another . . . Kylie's.

"I'm going in!" she declares.

The door opens and she bursts into the room.

Kotin looks up at her.

"What's going on?" she asks.

"Mr. Trasker and I were having a friendly conversation," Kotin replies.

"Ms. Connor," I say to her calmly, "we should talk outside."

"You don't have to tell him anything," Kylie tells Kotin.

"I think it's time for the truth. Don't you?" he replies to her. "Now is not the time to be hiding. We need to be attacking."

"Eto tvoye resheniye," she says in Russian.

TUTOR

Kylie, the man called David Kotin, and I are standing by her P-51 Mustang at the far end of the facility where Kylie keeps her personal planes parked. She wanted to talk things over—out of earshot but still within distance of what remains of our security team.

"Okay, who goes first?" I say after a long silence.

"I'm so sorry," she says to Kotin.

"There is nothing to apologize for," he replies.

"I can think of a few things," I tell them both. "Like the fact that we're in the middle of a Russian spy hunt and we have a man here with an accent thicker than winter ice on the Volga and a résumé that's as useless as a Politburo politician's promise."

"Brad, it's not what it looks like," says Kylie.

"Can someone please tell me what it *is?*"

"It's okay, Ms. Kylie," says Kotin.

"Are you sure?"

"Yes. All of it. Despite our first encounter, I trust Mr. Trasker to do the right thing," he assures her.

Kylie takes a deep breath. "Trasker, let me introduce you to Artem Tkachev."

The name takes me back almost forty years. "Artem Tkachev, the Russian scientist?"

"I prefer to think of myself as an engineer. But yes," he replies.

"But you're supposed to be dead. Back in 1986?"

"Good memory. That's when I became dead to the Soviet Union, thanks to your friends in the CIA," he says, enunciating each letter.

"Mr. Tkachev was smuggled out of Russia to work in the United States on advanced aircraft systems," says Kylie.

"My faith in communism was considerably diminished, and I decided to come to the decadent West for . . . well, the decadence," adds Tkachev. He points to the horizon. "I actually lived and worked about three hundred miles from here."

"Groom Lake?" I ask, using the official name for Area 51.

Tkachev shrugs. "Who is to say?"

"How did you end up as an electrician here?"

"Mr. Tkachev retired and moved to Riverside. He got bored and became a math tutor. I met him when I was twelve," Kylie tells me.

"Under the name your government gave me—David Antonov," says Tkachev.

"When he realized that I was into aviation he started tutoring me. One thing led to another, and I decided to create an aerospace company. Because Mr. Tkachev was living under an alias, and I knew there would be scrutiny, we hired him with the name of Kotin," she explains.

"Scrutiny from whom?" I ask.

"I'm still on a kill list," the older man says. "I'm sure nobody remembers what I look like, but I've decided to be cautious. That plus the circumstances of my death and rebirth in America are something your government would like to keep secret. I'm not the first one they did this for, nor the last."

I'm well aware of that. We've been running a sort of underground railroad for extremely high-value foreign assets since the start of the Cold War.

"So this explains the Sparrow and why it resembles the Night Owl," I say.

"Not quite. The general design, yes. But the Night Owl had numerous insurmountable flaws. We were never able to get the coating right, and hydrogen containment was a problem," explains Tkachev.

"I started asking him one day about hydrogen-powered jets, and he started throwing all kinds of complications at me. I filled notebook after notebook," says Kylie.

"But the general design?" I ask.

"I designed the fuselage. It's actually based on an earlier prototype your CIA knew about. But it was just an airframe. The resemblance was superficial, like the space shuttle and the Buran. The Night Owl was a nice idea, but a dead end. The materials didn't exist back then," he says with a shrug.

"When did you tell her who you were?" I ask.

"She figured it out and confronted me," he replies, cracking his first hint of a smile.

"I was in college and someone randomly sent me an old Russian magazine with an interview with Tkachev. There in the middle was his photograph. I knew he worked in aviation, so it was kind of hard for him to lie about it."

"Does anybody else know?" I ask.

"I've never told anyone. Not even Morena. Now it's you and Sophia," Kylie confides.

"Assuming you're telling us the truth, we'll have no problem keeping your secret," I say.

"Don't take him to the FBI," pleads Kylie.

"I won't." I turn to the old engineer. "I know the person who probably planned your escape. If he confirms it, then we're good." I pull out my phone and send a text to a seldom-used number:

If I came across Artem Tkachev in a super market in California, what should I ask him?

A moment later, I get a response:

Ask him what color were his slippers (polka dots). Also, he should look like Donald Sutherland.

"What color were your slippers?" I ask.

Tkachev laughs. "Polka dots. When they took me to the hospital for stomach pain, they were all out of men's slippers and had to give me a pair from the women's ward. Those were the ones I died in on the operating table. They were also the ones I wore on the submarine."

"Good enough for me. Thank you for your service." I offer him my hand.

Tkachev shakes it.

"Trasker, I'm sorry," says Kylie.

"No. It's fine. You did the right thing. Even when it was difficult. You have my respect and admiration."

"Would knowing this have—" she begins.

She's going to ask if the men who died protecting her would still be alive. "It wouldn't have changed a thing."

"Okay. What can I do to help?"

"You need to leave that to me now."

"I know you think I was only saying I was ready to do anything to get the person behind this because of adrenaline and nerves back at the airport. But I'm not kidding," she insists.

"I know. But this is different," I reply.

"Mr. Tkachev, would you excuse us?" asks Kylie.

"Good luck," he says to me with a shrug.

"Meet me back at that Cessna in thirty minutes," Kylie tells me.

"Do we really think the runway's safe?" I ask.

"It'll be safe enough. I need to think, and I do that best in the air."

WINDSWEPT

Kylie doesn't do much talking for the first forty minutes of the flight as we fly north. I can see why she likes to come up here. The tapestry of mountains, desert, and irrigated farms below us is beautiful. It stretches to the horizon in every direction. From up here, the world seems quiet and filled with possibility.

"You know we both have something in common," Kylie says as she takes us into a turn.

"What's that?" I ask over the intercom connecting our two headsets.

"We're the products of single-parent households. We were both raised by our mothers."

"This is true."

"But I think the difference is, I take after my father. From what I understand, you're a lot like your mother. Was your dad ever around to have an influence?"

"Not really. We're acquainted, but I'm kind of an inconvenience for him," I reply.

"That's too bad. He should be proud," says Kylie.

"Maybe. Maybe not. He's more diplomatic. I'm more tactical," I observe. "I've had more conversations with you than him by now."

"His loss. Hold on, we're going to land down there." She points to a field.

It's a wide, bald patch of dirt with no outstanding features.

"I'm not an expert on aviation, but there's no runway down there," I reply.

"It only takes a little imagination," she says as she drops us lower.

Kylie makes another circle, reducing speed, and lands us on a narrow strip of road that ends abruptly.

She powers down the engine. "Come on," she says.

I climb out, and she leads us to sit on large rocks next to each other.

"Isn't it an amazing feeling to have been a hundred miles away a half hour ago and now be somewhere completely different? I wanted that my whole life. The ability to go anywhere. The freedom."

"The freedom to visit exotic locales like this barren piece of nowhere," I observe wryly.

Kylie stares at me. "I'm sorry? You're not impressed by Connor Ranch?"

"This is yours?"

"All thirty acres. My father left it to me. He wanted to build a real ranch here. He'd have needed more than thirty acres, but it was a start. At least it would have been."

"He died young," I say.

"It wasn't that. He tried to make it work. The problem is the other ranchers here didn't want it to. They wanted the land because it connected two bigger parcels. Dad was able to get it because the old woman who owned it thought he was a polite young man. I may have helped convince her too. I was cute back then," she explains.

"What happened?"

"Dad didn't realize that Westerns were real. First, they cut off his road access, then they stopped his water. He tried to protest, but he wasn't connected out here and couldn't afford an attorney. The land wasn't worth much. Only to the rancher that wanted it. Then Dad died." Kylie sighs.

"Your mother refused to sell it?"

"It wasn't her call. The deed was in my name. Dad knew I loved his dream. Not the actual ranching part, but the idea of *having* a dream. They offered to buy it. I refused. They made a few threats. I got a friend to pretend they were a reporter from the *LA Times* to call them up. They backed off," she explains.

"And here we are," I say.

"Well, sort of. There's a part two to this story. I never forgave them for stopping my dad's dream." She points west. "A rancher had cattle a few miles that way. He'd cut our fence and let them wander over here to graze. Asshole move.

"I wanted to get back at him. So I patched up the fence and went to the cattle auction and bought five of the meanest bulls I could find and paid a couple of ranch hands to let them loose here.

"When the rancher came back a week later and cut my fence, he didn't realize I had the bulls. They went through the cut in the fence to *his* pasture and knocked up half the prize, purebred heifers he'd been planning to breed that season. Instead of pedigreed cattle, he got angry little half-breeds," she says with a wicked grin.

"This *is* a Western."

"Well, the end of it was I bought the guy's farmland. I now own five thousand acres. I let it sit fallow for a few years to kill everything that he'd grown, then had it farmed. It's still a money loser, but it's worth it. I kept this part like it is so I wouldn't forget."

This woman runs deep. "Remind me to never cross you," I say with a grin.

"You're not the one who crossed me. I brought you here to tell you that I'm in, all the way. I know you think I've just been saying that to sound tough, but I mean it. What the ranchers did was nothing compared to the man who had our friends killed. It's not about me or my work, it's about making sure he's punished. I'm willing to give up everything to get back at him. I wouldn't be able to look in the mirror otherwise."

"Everything is a lot," I remind her.

"It's not as if it doesn't hold value. I want us to find out who did it and hit them hard. I want to set the bulls loose and then turn everything they have into dust."

"Laws will be broken," I warn.

"I'm fine with that. As long as there are no more innocent bystanders, I'm good with anything. People already believe the worst about me. Losing people is the only thing that matters now," she says. "And I'm done doing that."

I study the determination in her face. I know she's still in shock from the airport, but I also know that a young girl with revenge in her heart who grows up to be a woman who never lets it go will not be deterred.

"It's going to take money and a reckless disregard for the law. And we're going to have to stay clear of our FBI friends," I warn her again.

"Where were they when we needed them?"

"Fair point. I want you to keep thinking about a motive that we haven't seen yet. I'm going to push on the one remaining loose end we have."

"What's that?" she asks.

"It's a who. A man I met in Mexico."

NETWORK

Part of my job is doing favors—off-the-books things you do so later on you can cash them in. If it was small and only took a few hours of my time and didn't jeopardize my own work, I did what I could. More often than not it was for people who were corrupt, but useful.

A man we'll call Vincente Vallardo was a colonel in the military of a South American country we'll call Notamala. Like every other person who worked for that government, he was a crook.

To be fair, let's divide corrupt officials into two camps: those who are outright crooks and those who are forced to adapt to a corrupt system.

I don't know which one I would be if I were born in a different country, but I'm pretty sure I'd be accepting soft bribes or kickbacks if I wanted a life in public service. It's just the way things are down there. It's not good, and that corruption is what holds such countries back, but there's no easy prescription. When I show up with suitcases full of cash to get a politician to support an American-aligned initiative, I know I'm not really *helping*. But that's the way it is.

I was in Notamala helping set up a communications and planning group that would work with different law-enforcement and military units to gather intel about terrorist groups that were coordinating with the narcos.

Consider for a moment that the cartels were paying off both the terrorist groups *and* the military I was sent to assist, which was combating the same terrorist groups. It was a big, stupid circle.

Vallardo was corrupt, but he was also our guy. He didn't love the way things worked down there and sometimes envied his brother, who had immigrated to America and now is an administrator for a school district. Vallardo was also furiously patriotic about Notamala and ran a unit that was highly effective at going after terrorist groups.

Vallardo also had enemies. When his name was covered favorably in the papers, others weren't happy. People talked about his political ambitions.

The colonel would have been useful to us, so I had a green light to help him if there was a chance we could collect on our kindness down the road.

One night I was sitting in my apartment in the capital and I got a call from Vallardo.

"Mr. Trasker?" he asked. I wasn't undercover, so he knew the name most people know me by.

"Colonel? What can I do for you?"

"When last we spoke, you told me to call you if I needed a favor. I'm afraid that time has come. It's a very large ask. But it is vital to all of our interests."

"What do you need?"

"Fifty thousand dollars US," he replied.

This wasn't the first time I'd had someone flat-out ask for an open-ended bribe. Smaller ones are easy. You know they'll keep working for you, because that drip of money incentivizes them to do so.

"That's a lot of money. What is it for?" I asked.

"I don't want to say. But I promise you I will be grateful."

I thought it over, texted my supervisor, then called Vallardo back.

"We can do it. When and where?"

"Well, that's the tricky part. I also need you to deliver it tonight," he replied.

"Tonight?"

"Tonight. No later than ten p.m."

I had an instinct about him and agreed—even when he told me where it needed to be "delivered."

❧

At precisely 11:00 p.m. that night, Captain Diamado, head of the capital city police and a friend of Vallardo, accompanied by television news crews, raided the home of Senator Montecito, Vallardo's sharpest critic.

Vallardo had heard that Montecito was about to make a public accusation and launch an investigation of Vallardo, strip him of his rank, and send him to prison.

Vallardo decided to strike first, but he needed an ally who had no clear connection to what was going on with the local politics.

The $50,000 was the "proof" Vallardo needed to back up the claim made by one of Montecito's former staffers about his corruption.

Montecito was dirty. Everyone in the game was. I didn't feel bad for what I did, and that favor ended up being a winning lottery ticket. Vallardo prevailed and pledged to end corruption. The public loved him. He's no longer Colonel Vallardo. Today, he's *President* Vallardo.

❧

"Hello?" says Vallardo as he answers his unlisted mobile phone.

"I'm calling to see if our friend Montecito enjoyed his present," I ask.

There's a long pause followed by a deep laugh. "I think you mean *Professor* Montecito now. He's teaching the students at the university. That is a better fit for him."

"That's good to hear."

"And what about you? I haven't seen your name come up for quite some time."

"I was retired," I respond.

"Was?" he asks.

"Yes. Now I'm not. I need a favor. I promise you I will be grateful."

VIP

Wagner, dressed in a designer blazer with a white open-collared shirt to accentuate his tan, strolls into the lobby of the Palacio Hotel and flashes a confident grin at the receptionists behind the dark marble desk.

He flew here on a private jet and is on top of the world. The luxury Land Rover that picked him up from the airport hasn't even been released yet in the United States.

He glances around the lobby, spots the short man in a business suit wearing a thick mustache, and greets him.

"José! Nice to meet you in person," says Wagner.

José shakes his hand and the two men sit.

Wagner waits for José to say something, but the man doesn't.

"I looked over your situation, and I think we can help. My firm's ready to dive right in," says Wagner.

Silence.

Wagner is confused. He'd corresponded with José in English via Telegram.

"*¿Lo entiendes?*" asks Wagner.

Well, technically Wagner didn't correspond with José, who claimed to be a fixer for Vallardo's political rival.

Wagner trusted the conversation was authentic, because the Telegram account it came from was verified by a friend of his, and when the initial text came to him, the device ID confirmed it was from the phone of José Resito, an attorney known to act as an intermediary between cartels and politicians.

What Wagner doesn't know is that Resito was apprehended weeks ago and is being held secretly by Notamala anticorruption police, who have full control of his electronic devices.

José is actually Commander Diamado, former captain of the capital city police, now commander of the country's version of the FBI under President Vallardo.

Diamado, playing Resito, stands and walks away. Wagner is baffled and stares at the man as he exits the hotel. He takes out his phone to text someone.

I let him sit there, a little off-balance, for a moment longer, then stand and walk over.

Wagner glances up from his phone and gives me a half smile of recognition.

"Trasker. Odd meeting you here," he replies, trying not to look like he's been caught off guard.

"Meeting friends?" I ask as I sit.

"Always," he replies. "Is this business or social?"

"That's really up to you. I think you'd rather this be social. You don't want to see me get down to business."

"Right, right. I've seen that side of you. Apparently so did those gentlemen in Mojave at the airport. I'm sorry to hear what happened to your team. That's got to be rough. I can't imagine what it was like calling their families."

Wagner is allowing himself to be voluble because he still doesn't know what's going on. He checks his watch and glances at the exit. Right now he's asking himself if he should just leave.

"I need to know who you're working for," I tell him.

"Oh, is that it? I already told you: I don't know. That's the way it's played now. I tried to explain this before, Trasker. Hell, I warned you something was going to happen if you didn't back off."

"You were smart enough to check on who was paying for you to come down here. I'm pretty sure you have an idea who you're working for," I respond.

"I'm sorry. Can't help you," says Wagner.

I see his thumb move on his phone. I snatch it away from him. When he leans over the coffee table, I pull a gun from my pocket and level it at his stomach.

"Last time you showed me a button you can press that would 'erase' me. This is *my* button. Sit down."

Wagner takes his seat and glares at me. He's trying to figure out if I'd pull the trigger or not, knowing full well I've already done it twice this week.

"You're going to regret this," he says.

"You're going to be grateful. When I give the word, José and his friends are going to take you to a tiny little cell just like the one you had Watkins put into. And just like Watkins, I'm the one that gets you out. Or not." I shrug.

"People know I'm here," he warns.

"I would hope so, especially when they find out that you were trying to smuggle twenty million dollars' worth of cocaine back to the US on the plane you chartered."

"I didn't charter that plane," he says smugly.

"It's under your name. You flew here on it."

A sigh. "I really don't know what you think I could possibly know."

"We'll have time to figure that out. When I believe you, that's when you go free."

"Fuck you," he says.

I wave to Commander Diamado at the front door. He and two armed men escort Wagner away.

❦

I meet Wagner in his cell two days later. He's dressed in a dirty jumpsuit and has a lost look on his face. Two days in a jail down here is like two months in a US jail.

When they put him in the cell, he was convinced I was going to show up a few hours later. I didn't.

I wanted him to think about his prospects and what it would be like to never leave the prison. I put him through the same torture that he subjected Watkins to.

The next day he waited for me to show up. He tried to bribe the guard for access to a phone. He offered more bribes. Reality was settling in.

Finally, I visited him.

"How long do you think you can keep me here?" asks Wagner defiantly from the other side of the interrogation table.

"If I had my choice, forever. The world would be a much better place, I suspect."

"When I'm out, you're going to regret this. So will your friends who helped arrange this," says Wagner.

"Did you see the empty field across the street from here when they brought you in? That's a prison cemetery. There are no markers. Only graves. I'd be careful about vowing revenge."

"This is dirty."

"*Now* you have a conscience?"

Wagner is trying to keep up his front, but I can see the look in his eyes. They're bloodshot. He's freaking out inside.

"I need a name," I tell him.

"Let me out and I'll give you one," he says in a lowered voice.

"No. You give me the name. I check it out, and *then* I let you out."

Wagner stares at me, trying to figure out an angle. "How long do you think your friends will keep me here? Do you really think you have that much pull?"

Andrew Mayne

"Longer than you can handle. So far, they've been giving you the luxury treatment. It can get a lot worse. Nobody has even put a hand on you yet."

Wagner thinks about the implications of what I said. I don't want to take it that far . . . but I will.

"I'll give you the name of the man who brought me on. He's the middleman connected to whoever you're after," he says at last.

"So much for your layers and layers of anonymity."

"Some people are sloppy. Some are careful. This guy made a few mistakes when he contacted me. Even sent me the wrong text message."

"Who is he?"

"He goes by Avionco. I don't know his real name. It's just a handle. He trades in defense secrets, mostly aviation. Some people say he's the one that sold the F-35 blueprints to the Chinese. He's got people in all the facilities around you. Private, government, all of them."

"How do I get his attention?"

RECYCLER

Zach Matok pulls up to the Aviation Salvage scrapyard in a beat-up pickup truck. He's not Avionco or the man who hired him. Matok is merely a minor link in the chain.

"Chris?" Zach asks me through his rolled-down window.

"Yep," I reply.

I've got a goatee, aviator glasses, and a baseball cap on. I also match the description of a machinist who works at a machine shop in Palmdale that does contract work on stealth planes.

According to my Facebook posts, I spend a lot of time in Vegas and love high-stakes poker. I'm also living in a crappy apartment that suggests my love of the game isn't based on any skill I possess.

"You said you had a gearbox?" he asks.

"In there. I'll show it to you."

Matok parks his truck and we walk through the gate of the scrapyard. He waves at the manager, a woman in her sixties sitting inside a small mobile unit with a scale out front.

Aviation Salvage works like most other salvage yards. People give them their old parts in exchange for hauling them away for a fee.

Some of the scrap is useful. You can find pistons, flight controls, and a million other parts that would cost you tens of thousands of dollars to purchase new.

Resourceful aerospace entrepreneurs have even found rocket engines in yards like this and put them into orbit. There's treasure to be found—if you know where to look. Sometimes the treasures are even planted. A machinist working at an aircraft parts manufacturer can swap out a high-quality part for a low-quality one they made at home and then smuggle the good one out of the secure facility from means as simple as tossing it into a recycling bin or sending it off to be tested by a bogus company.

I texted a number connected to Avionco from a phone number that traced back to a Chris that worked at Precision Instruments in Palmdale.

Avionco never responded. However, Zach Matok did.

He texted to me as "Chris:" I'm looking for a gearbox.

Chris responded back: I know where to find one. What's the finder's fee?

Matok: If it fits my Cessna, $9k.

Chris: Not worth it. thx.

Matok: What's ur price?

Chris: $100k. Bitcoin.

Matok: LOL. Not happening. Good luck.

Chris: Counter?

Matok: $20k if I like it. More next time.

Chris: Deal.

"This way," I say, leading Matok through the scrapyard.

He's in his midtwenties and has a scruffy beard and dark hair under his F1 baseball cap. His real name is Kevin MacLaughtery according to his cell phone transmission.

We walk past airplane wings, propellers, engine blocks, and row after row of airline seats deteriorating in the desert sun.

"Over here," I say, pointing to a pile of scrap metal that was dropped off last night.

I start to sort through pieces of aluminum and old actuators until I find the flat metal panel with air holes cut through it.

The metal has a dark-blue sheen and is extremely lightweight. It's not the alloy Kevin is looking for, but it would take a chemist to know the difference. What matters is the shape—it's the exact dimensions of a thrust diverter for a top-secret stealth aircraft.

I hand it over for him to inspect.

He eyes the machining, then takes out a pair of calipers to measure different points. A few microns off and he would know this didn't come from a precision machine shop.

"I'll give you ten," he says.

"You said twenty."

"I said twenty if I like it. I don't know if I do or not. What I do know is that I don't know *you*, that's for sure."

"You gotta help me out," I say with a hint of desperation.

"We can do fifteen, but I'll need a list of what else you have besides the baffle."

"I can tell you right now."

MacLaughtery almost drops the part as he reaches his hand up to shush me. He's paranoid. In the event that I'm wired, he needs plausible deniability.

"Just text the other number. I'll send the bitcoin to your wallet for this," he explains.

"When?"

"After you sign this," he says, pulling a sheet of paper from his back pocket.

"What is it?" I ask.

"Just a procedure. I need you to state that you were paid a finder's fee and verify that you promised nothing was stolen. Like what they have you sign at some pawnshops. Same thing," he explains.

Clever. If "Chris" decided to go to the feds or got caught, MacLaughtery has a document from me claiming it wasn't stolen property. This would complicate a legal case.

I use the pen he gives me to sign it. AXWELL AVIONICS is written across the side. I hand the document back and offer the pen.

He waves it off. "I got a million of them. They went out of business years ago."

He takes out his phone and taps on the screen.

"Check your wallet," he tells me.

I open my crypto wallet and see that $15,000 worth of bitcoin has been added.

"Thank you."

"If this doesn't check out, there's going to be a problem. Understand, Chris?"

"Yes," I say meekly.

"Okay. I hope you brought cash. You need to give Alice twenty bucks for this at the gate."

TRIANGULATE

In the back office of the empty hangar where Sophia conducted her security screenings, she, Morena, and Kylie are staring at a laptop screen showing the location of the part I sold MacLaughtery.

Though it looked innocuous, Kylie milled the piece of alloy in such a way that we could fit a tracking device thinner than a credit card into the material.

MacLaughtery was cautious and went on and off the highway, taking surface roads to make sure he wasn't being followed, but the intermittent ping of the hidden device made that pointless.

He's been driving for over an hour in a direction away from his home in California City. I've been following from a long distance, letting Kylie guide me so I don't get spotted.

Getting to Avionco was going to be a challenge. He's evaded arrest for decades. Clearly, he has some insight on how to not get caught.

Using an intermediary like MacLaughtery is one part of the solution. Another is knowing how to spot a fed from a mile away.

Taking the meeting with me was risky, but Avionco felt comfortable enough that if the FBI took MacLaughtery it wouldn't point back to him. Either he has a high amount of trust in the man or there's some kind of firewall that has enabled him to do business like this for so long.

"Looks like he's headed to Santa Clarita," says Sophia as she follows his progress.

An hour later I pull into an upscale residential neighborhood and go down a street opposite of the one MacLaughtery turned onto.

Children ride bicycles under warm streetlights, and couples walk their dogs in the nice evening breeze.

"What do you have?" I ask.

Sophia's voice answers through my car speakers. "He's been stopped for three minutes. We're getting the address now. The approximate address," she corrects herself. "It's hard to triangulate precisely."

"What's the plan?" asks Morena.

"Kick open his door and pistol-whip him until he begs to tell me everything," I reply.

"No, seriously," she responds.

"Did that sound like a joke?"

In my rearview mirror I see MacLaughtery's truck coming back the way it came. He pulls out of the neighborhood and drives away.

"Do you have an address?" I ask.

"I think so. It's 2224 Beachwood," says Sophia.

"Good enough for me," I reply.

I turn around and head down the street I saw MacLaughtery pull out of.

I bring my SUV to a stop four houses down from 2224 Beachwood and put in my earpiece.

The houses are all two stories and have large yards. Each one had to cost two million or more.

"Nice neighborhood. Do we have a name?" I ask.

"Not yet. The home is in a trust. I'm trying to find out who owns it," says Sophia.

I feel the adrenaline kick in. "I'm going to knock and find out."

"I just need a few more minutes," she says quickly.

"If he x-rays that device or even puts it next to an RF meter, the jig is up. Not to mention the fact that Wagner has been missing for three days. If Avionco was in contact with him, he might be jittery. We need to move now."

"Just give me a minute," says Sophia.

A stocky, bald man in a dress shirt and slacks emerges from the house and walks toward a BMW parked in the driveway.

"He's on the move," I call out.

I get out of my vehicle, draw my gun, and move briskly down the sidewalk and up his driveway.

He's messing with the controls on the display when I grab the door handle and pull it open.

"Out of the car," I tell him as I put the muzzle of my gun to his temple.

He looks at me, eyes wide open, and raises his hands and gets out.

"Anybody home?" I ask.

"No . . . no . . . I mean," he stammers.

"I'll take that as a no."

I put a hand on his shoulder and the gun into his back, then shove him toward the front door.

"Unlock it," I command.

He fumbles with his keys and opens the door.

I push him into the living room.

"Fingers folded behind your head and sit down."

I guide him to the couch. He takes a seat and stares at me. He's angrier now than frightened.

"I know who you are," he says.

"Congratulations."

"Brad?" Sophia calls out over my earpiece.

"What's your name?" I ask.

He's silent for a moment, then he starts to laugh. "You have no idea how stupid you look."

"Brad!" Sophia yells.

"What?" I reply.

"I got a name. Karl Hassad," she tells me. "He works for Homeland Security!"

Jesus.

"From the look on your face, I can assume your friends just told you who I am. Maybe lower your weapon and we can talk, Mr. Trasker?"

I don't lower the gun. I'm still processing what's happening.

"The man you followed thinks I'm an arms dealer. I've been running him for over a year. That is, unless he saw you. In that case you've ruined one of the most complicated cases I've ever worked on," explains Hassad.

"You're DHS?"

"Yes. Put the gun down," he says calmly. "I know you've been under some stress. Put it away and we'll talk. I won't mention this to Broadhurst or Morrel, okay?"

I point my weapon at the ground.

"May I lower my hands now? Maybe you should put that away and we can talk."

"Everything okay?" asks Sophia.

"It's fine," I reply.

He lets out a sigh and relaxes. "I can't say that I've ever had a gun pointed at my head. You do live up to your reputation. Have a seat and let's talk." Hassad gestures toward the chair behind me.

I keep standing but bring my gun to my side.

"How about a beer?" he asks.

"Yeah, that would be good."

Hassad smiles and stands. "One second."

As he turns, I bring my pistol around fast and hit him in the temple so hard that he's unconscious before he hits the carpet.

"Brad? Everything okay?" asks Sophia.

"Yeah. I need to go dark for a few hours."

SHALLOW

I pull Hassad from the back of my SUV by the crook of his elbow and throw him to the ground. I yank the pillowcase off his head, and he looks up at me with anger. I've taped his mouth and bound his wrists with a zip tie.

I yank the tape off his mouth, and a trail of slobber glimmers in the moonlight as I toss it to the ground.

Hassad looks at the gully I've brought him to and realizes he has no idea where the hell we are. Neither do I. I drove for an hour until I reached the exact center of nowhere.

"You're goddamn insane, Trasker. You're going to go to jail for a long time. We're way past interfering with an investigation now. This is fucking kidnapping!"

In the distance, a coyote calls out.

"How long are we going to keep this up?" I reply.

"Keep what up?"

"Seriously?" I sit on my tailgate and cross my arms.

"Seriously what? Call my office. Speak to my supervisor," he pleads.

"I'm sure he'll tell me that you've been doing undercover work with industrial espionage," I reply. "That's why it makes sense."

"It makes sense? What the fuck are you talking about?"

"This Avionco that nobody could find. Always a step ahead. Hell, I bet you're the one they tasked with finding him."

"What you're suggesting is absurd."

"No. It's predictable. I know two things about you, your name and that you work for DHS, but I actually know everything about you. You were assigned this job because you were the only one in your field office that knew about aviation. That makes me think you're former air force and worked in procurement. Am I close?"

He sighs. "Yeah, I was in the air force. And you're out of your mind."

"Nobody around you understood what you knew and the value of the secrets you were supposed to protect. Here you are in a government job when there are people you know in the civilian sector making ten times as much. Fuck them? Right?"

"You're delusional."

"Sure. Your little lie back at the house was convincing until I thought about it. The house was too expensive. The furniture looked too new and unused. I bet your neighbors think you work out of town most of the time. Really, you live elsewhere."

"Of course I do, dumbass. That house is where I meet suspects and informants!" he yells.

"Right. Then why is it under your name?"

He's gone to considerable effort to conceal who owns the house. But that was to protect him from internal affairs.

"This is the way it's going to play out," I continue. "You're going to tell me who set all of this up, and then I'm going to drop you off with the FBI. If you don't tell me, then I'm still going to hand you over. Now we both know they'll talk to you, maybe hear me out. Then they'll let you go while they conduct an investigation with the DHS. And then it's a matter of time before they realize everything you've done. You'll be spending life in prison if you don't run.

"But I think you will. You've probably put away a fortune. By the time they realize what you are, you'll be gone. Which may sound like an okay plan, but there's a problem. Either I'm going to hunt you down and kill you or the man you're working for will.

"So here's my counteroffer: tell me who hired you and let me go after him. If you run, maybe I don't care at that point. At least he won't be hiring hit squads from every corner of the world to kill men who look like you."

"You're insane" is all Hassad says.

"Karl. You know by now that's not true. You know I'm going to do what I said, because there's no threat there. It's the logical choice for me. You need to think about the logical choice for you."

Hassad sits up. "I'll tell you about him. But I'm not going to talk about me."

I think he's worried I might be recording this. I'm not. It wouldn't be admissible and would incriminate me.

"Talk," I tell him.

"He's untouchable. His name is Sydney Strier, but people know him as the Spire. On paper, he's a hedge-fund investor, but what he really does is place large bets—like loaning money to multinationals to take over countries. He moves money for the CIA and sets up banks in third-world countries so the US can influence local politics."

I've heard Strier's name come up before, but almost always attached to building a well in Africa or fighting disease in Southeast Asia.

"How come he's been able to go on for so long?" I ask.

"Because he doesn't interfere with US interests. He gives China and Russia a middle finger and helps Israel with Iran. He's the CIA's wet dream of a billionaire," says Hassad.

"Why Wind Aerospace?"

"Project Velocity," he replies.

"What's that?"

Hassad shakes his head. "You really are clueless. It's a Pentagon initiative to move all of our supply systems to drone aircraft. Need fifty tons of artillery delivered to the Ukraine? Use drones. Need to keep a marine unit in an Afghan valley resupplied? Drones. And not just drones but next-generation drones. Hydrogen-powered ones that can be fueled by electricity anywhere. They think it's the future. I think it's a headache. But they'll spend trillions to learn why."

"Why go after Wind Aerospace?" I ask.

"Strier has a sizable piece of four of the top five companies in this space. He doesn't have a piece of Wind Aerospace, and they're already years ahead. The Pentagon is going to do a request for proposals, and Connor's the only one who stands a chance of landing one.

"She's smart. She didn't just design the damned plane, she designed the support system to keep them moving. It's the same reason why people are driving Teslas instead of Toyotas. Musk figured out the charging infrastructure was critical. Kylie is doing that for autonomous aviation. She'll become a trillionaire if Strier doesn't have a say.

"His biggest problem is that Connor's so far ahead. He can push one of his companies that's close, but not one that's years behind. If she gets the government contracts, the billions he's been putting into competitors won't be worth anything. So he decided to take Wind Aerospace and her out of the running."

"You've become extremely chatty since we first met," I tell him.

"Fuck Strier. I wanted a part of it and he brushed me off. And this is the last time I'm going to tell anyone about this," says Hassad.

"Not even Broadhurst and Morrel?"

"If I say his name, Strier will hire someone like you to come after me. One of you is enough."

"How do I get to him?"

"He'll see you coming a mile away and have you removed from the face of the earth," Hassad tells me matter-of-factly.

"The last person to tell me that has now found himself removed from the face of the earth."

"Wagner? Good riddance. He was Strier's puppet anyway. Except Wagner was too stupid to realize that." Hassad rolls his eyes. "Useless."

"What about Wind Aerospace? Who do you have on the inside?"

Hassad grins. "I'm out, man. I told you about Strier. That was the deal."

"I could beat it out of you . . ."

"Yeah, but if you bring me in like that, I'll have an easier job of convincing them this was all a setup by you."

SALUTE

Kylie is sitting between Morena and me in a Kentucky church pew as the friends and family of Benoit file in for his memorial. The church is already half-full. I see a lot of people his age he probably went to high school with.

Kylie dabs a tissue on the corner of her eye as she watches Benoit's mother and father somberly welcome guests.

We paid them our condolences earlier at their house. Morena discreetly asked them if it would be a distraction if Kylie attended. Benoit's mother said it would not and even asked if she would say a few words.

It's an incredible amount of pressure to put on someone. But it's nothing like the loss of a child. This I understand.

I have a hard time looking at Benoit's coffin. The fact that it's sealed only makes it impossible for me not to think about Jason.

"Tell me about Strier," asks Kylie. I hear grit in her voice.

"Hassad was right," I tell her.

Hassad has gone missing. I told Morrel and Broadhurst this would happen, but they didn't get it. The moment he left the FBI office on his own two feet, he was gone.

They're now realizing they let the mastermind behind the biggest intellectual property theft in history slip away. After I deal with Strier, I might take care of that problem for them.

"Strier's connected at a level I'm not able to penetrate. He funds political action committees that swing pivotal races. He's created an entire funnel of attorneys to the US Attorney's Office. Then there's all of the ex-military brass he pays to do bullshit consulting," I explain.

"Project Velocity is real. My Pentagon contact told me there was going to be a request for proposals in a few months," says Kylie.

"That's good."

"I don't know if we're going to bid on it. I'm not too excited about delivering bombs around the world."

"It turned out all right for Boeing," I reply.

"Maybe. All I care about right now is getting Strier. I know it won't make me feel better about this. But it will be something."

It'll be something.

"He knows something is coming. After I turned Hassad over to the FBI, he had to start wondering how much Hassad told me. If Strier is who we think he is, he'll be coming at us from a completely different angle. No more Russian hit men. No half-assed fixers. It'll probably be people from our own government."

"This is insane," says Morena.

"This is the game. That's why we need to move fast. It'll take him a little while to put together whatever he's planning if he wants to do it through legitimate channels."

"How do you think he'll go about it?" asks Morena.

"I don't know. That's what worries me. He knows I'll either try to find a way to send him to prison or put a bullet in his head."

I'm downplaying my level of anxiety. I have two security teams outside, plus a van with a receiver listening for bursts on the frequencies that federal agents use.

I wouldn't put it past Strier to get the FBI office in Pittsburgh or somewhere to connect me to a crime they can use as an excuse to extradite me to some country where he has a lot of pull.

Morena has attorneys ready on speed dial if that happens. And Bianca has a press release ready to issue.

I won't go down without a fight.

But Strier knows that as well.

The real way to go after me is through Kylie. He tried killing her, but there are other ways to hurt her. Instead of me getting picked up with false charges, it could be her mother and stepfather.

That's my true concern. I can handle pain, lots of it, when it's directed at me, but not when it's aimed at the people near me.

Everyone finishes taking their seats, and the reverend steps up to the podium next to the large portrait of Benoit.

Despite all my mental tricks, every time I remember the moment Benoit was killed, I see the bullet going through Jason's head instead.

The helpless way his head fell slack to the side, blood pouring through the exit wound.

Every detail is right except for the face. It's Jason every time.

I like to talk tough about putting bullets through people's heads. I've even done it in self-defense, but never in cold blood.

Looking at Benoit/Jason, I realize there might be a first time . . . when I meet with Strier.

"You okay?" asks Kylie.

I realize I'm squeezing her hand.

"Yeah. Thinking about Jason," I reply, realizing I've never mentioned him to her.

I know by now that she had a pretty good idea why I was at that college the night we met. But she's never brought the topic up. I suspect she's known that it always lies below the surface.

When she told me about her father, it might have been her giving me a chance to open up about myself. She said we were alike. I think what she meant was that we were still going through mirror images of loss. With Kylie, her father. With me, my only child.

"I want you to tell me about him when you have a chance," she whispers.

"I will. You'd have liked him. He was nothing like me."

INTRIGUE

Sydney Strier, a.k.a. the Spire, is the man in his late sixties sitting by himself at a table at the Chef's Table, a high-end Manhattan bistro known for its thirty-dollar pastrami-on-rye sandwiches and lobster grilled cheese.

It's the kind of place you go to when you have too much money, crave comfort food, but wouldn't want to be caught dead in anything resembling a diner.

Strier eats here every Tuesday and Friday. Tuesday by himself, Friday usually with a friend from the athletic club or some journalist to whom he'll dish off-the-record commentary.

I slide into the booth on his left.

Strier glances up at me from his Cobb salad for a moment, then returns to pecking away at it. "The grilled cheese is overrated. You'll like the hamburger. The beef comes from a farm upstate. The cold weather gives it more taste, if you ask me."

He casually turns the screen of his phone facedown.

"Thank you," I reply. "I'll have to try it."

"It's already been ordered for you, Mr. Trasker. I've also requested takeout for your men in the two SUVs conspicuously parked at either end of the block. I ordered a salad for the woman. Sophia, right?" he says, barely making eye contact.

I was expecting the unexpected . . . but not this.

"I can tell by your silence I preempted your monologue. Please proceed. I'm curious to hear what you're going to say. And we know it's going to just be talk, because otherwise you wouldn't have brought witnesses to an assassination."

"I wouldn't be so sure."

"I would," he says sharply, his gray eyes boring into mine. "That's why you're you and men like me pull the strings of the people who pull your strings. I don't think two steps ahead, I *created the fucking game*." He emphasizes each word by jabbing his finger in my direction.

An older waitress steps over to the table and drops the menus while Strier is still emoting.

"Would you fucking mind?" he growls at her.

She apologizes and backs away.

He redirects his ire at me. "You came here to say something. Let's hear it."

I need to stall. So I begin, "How much is enough for you? I understand a little greed, but to the point that you start killing innocent people? Do you even know what a conscience *is*?"

"Amusing. How many people did the weapons you smuggled into the Sudan kill? How many bullets that you helped procure ended up in the bodies of child soldiers? That's not counting the people you've killed directly. I looked up that number, by the way. Is 'conscience' just a word you throw around to distract from your own lack of one?"

"So it's just about money," I respond.

"You're still not getting it. That half-wit Wagner sort of saw it. But he was an idiot. As was Hassad. If you feel like you toppled a couple of criminal masterminds, let me disabuse you of that illusion. They were useful because they were stupid. As are you. Any man that is willing to lose his life for a cause he doesn't understand, let alone can't control, is an idiot."

"What is it, then?" I ask.

"I'll indulge you, Mr. Trasker, in recognition of your efforts, foolhardy as they may be. The Russians found themselves outmatched and unprepared because the Ukrainians were able to get access to strategic weapons early on in the conflict. Meanwhile, China looks across the Taiwan Strait with envy, knowing that they don't have the technical advantage to prevent the United States from deterring an invasion. A few thousand next-generation missiles would make all the difference. But they don't have them. Nor will they until the United States has a countermeasure.

"The Iranians keep spinning their centrifuges but struggle to build a nuclear bomb. This is something we accomplished in just thirty-six months almost a century ago without even an instruction manual. I'm the reason they still haven't accomplished that. *I'm* the reason the only global wars we've experienced have been cold ones.

"It's not easy. New technology disrupts. The atomic bomb ended world wars. The cruise missile gave the most advanced powers the ability to project force in any corner of the world—at the price of being disconnected from how best to use it.

"Your employer, Ms. Connor, is trying to create something she doesn't have the maturity to understand or wield responsibly. She doesn't know who the warmongers are and which ones are the pacifists. In the wrong hands, in our *own side's* wrong hands, it could cause a very dangerous imbalance.

"I acted with urgency. Perhaps too much. But I made my choice carefully and with calculation. More than you did when you decided to confront me here."

The waitress returns with a take-out box. "Will there be anything else?" she asks as she sets it down.

"Please give that to Mr. Trasker. He has a long flight ahead," Strier tells her.

The waitress slides the box over to me and leaves us.

I push the box away. "I'm good. It's only five hours."

Strier shakes his head and laughs. "No. Your next flight will be much longer than that, I'm afraid. Once you step outside, some gentlemen from the US Marshals Service are going to meet you. They are to escort you to the airport, where two Interpol agents with an extradition order are going to take you on a flight to Argentina.

"There you will face charges for the torture and murder of Antonio Miralles—a man last seen getting into your car by five eyewitnesses from the US embassy. All telling the truth by the way, none coerced."

Damn it . . .

Miralles did get into my car. I took him to a safe house, questioned him, then told him not to go anywhere. He snuck out, presumably to see his mistress. His body was found two days later. His head a week after that, when it was mailed to the newspapers with the word *"Rata"* scrawled on a piece of paper in his mouth.

It was a political killing. We knew that. The local police knew it. But the left-wing press claimed it was a CIA killing to diminish the influence of the US-backed right wing.

I left the country and never looked back.

Unfortunately for me, Strier did look.

He went looking for an expedient way to get rid of me, and somebody talked—someone in a position of power. Someone I worked for at some point.

I look at the door to the kitchen.

Strier smiles. "You could try leaving through the back door. Of course, you'd have to keep going. This extradition will follow you everywhere."

I contemplate making my exit but suspect it's just a mindfuck.

"I'll give you an easy out," he offers. "Name a number, and if I think it's reasonable, I'll put that into your bank account and you walk out the front door and the extradition order gets rescinded.

"Last. Just to turn the screws tighter . . . If you're thinking that a recording of this conversation is going to help you, that would be folly.

I've chosen my words carefully and have been saying whatever I can to save my life from the trained killer who has a gun pointed at me under the table."

He looks past my shoulder. I glance back and see two US Marshal SUVs pull up to the sidewalk. Four officers get out.

"Your escorts are here," says Strier, smug over how he's turned the tables.

I could call my team or make a run for it, but that would lead to a gun battle between people who have no business shooting at each other in the middle of the most crowded city in America.

I get up quietly and walk out, holding my hands above my head.

GREEN BUBBLES

Spire: I need Trasker handled. Now.

Noncom: Give me a minute to make a call.

Spire: ASAP. We need to shut him down. His team just took off from CA.

Noncom: I see their flight number. How badly do you want him?

Spire: Top priority. And fast. We need to get him out of the country and shut him down.

Noncom: Okay. Use the Argentinian thing?

Spire: Yes.

Noncom: I'll have a judge issue the docs. We can use the Marshals and Interpol. Route to Argentina?

Spire: Yes but then notify Kosgrad. Let him handle it. He'll want Trasker after what he did to his favorite pets.

Noncom: On it.

TRANSPORT

"So, how's your day been?" I ask the marshal sitting next to me in the SUV as we race through Manhattan, the flashing blue light and siren triggering when someone doesn't move fast enough to get out of our way.

Two minutes ago, he had a gun to the back of my head as his colleagues searched my body while I was facedown on pavement that smelled like you'd expect New York pavement to smell.

The most embarrassing part wasn't the gawkers; it was how little most New Yorkers cared as they strolled past me.

Sophia and our security team came running up once they saw me. I shouted for them to stand down.

"Are you a comedian?" asks the marshal.

"That depends. You know the guy back there, the one that made the call to his connected friends that led to us meeting? Sociopath. He hired hit men to kill my boss. I thought you should know."

"Hey, Cormac," he shouts to a man in the front seat. "Did they tell you if this guy needed any kind of medication?"

"We'll check with the Interpol agents. We might be able to get a doctor at the airport to tranquilize him."

"Let me guess: They told you I was crazy?"

"'Snapped' is the word I heard. 'Dangerous' too. But you seem like a well-behaved guy. Let's keep it that way."

I realize there is literally nothing I can say or do to convince them to stop the car and let me out. I'm also certain that Strier isn't bluffing.

When we get to the airport, I'm fairly positive I'll be handed over to an Interpol agent, who will then take me on board an airplane, handcuff me to a seat in the back, and escort me to Argentina, where I'll be met either by Argentinian authorities or hit men who will take me to the middle of nowhere and kill me.

Strier knows what I'm capable of. They won't send men I can overpower. This will be a trained group of killers.

Strier has every angle covered. He's been at this longer than I've been alive and accumulated way more favors than I could in a thousand lifetimes.

I played my biggest card with Vallardo to get to Wagner and ultimately Strier. And that got me here.

I think the expression is, *You played yourself.*

"I really don't want to get on that airplane," I tell the marshal.

"That's unfortunate."

"I'm just telling you as a professional courtesy. There's a high chance that I'm going to put up so much resistance that you'll have to injure me to the point that I'll have to go to the hospital."

"That's fine with us," says Cormac from the front. "There's a hospital at the airport. You're still getting on the plane."

Before I left government service, this situation wouldn't have bothered me. I knew that the people I worked for would make a call and I'd go free.

It was in less friendly countries I had to worry. That's how I got the scars on my back. But even then I knew there were people trying to apply pressure to free me.

Now those people are the ones helping Strier send me away, never to be seen again.

He's determined to eliminate me. My bigger concern is what he'll try to do to Kylie, Sophia, and Morena. The people close to me who will make the most noise when I'm gone.

Will he make them an offer? Stay quiet and Trasker lives?

That would be the prudent move. It might be what an intermediary is telling them right now.

I hope that's the case. I don't want him trying to do to them a version of what he's done to me.

His creativity and resources have no limit. And that scares me.

I can outthink creative people with limited resources or resourceful people with no creativity. But not this.

As Strier said, it's not a game where you have to be two steps ahead. You have to be writing the rules of the game.

Strier is an elite with a vast network of other powerful elites. They snap their fingers and people like me do their bidding.

The only way through them is to see how they look at the world and then find a way to short-circuit it.

Assuming they don't see that coming as well.

I see the freeway signs for the airport.

"Excited, buddy? You're going to have a long trip," says the marshal next to me.

I turn to him. "When do you want to stop being the puppet and control your own strings?"

Cormac calls out from the front seat. "We just got the order to have him tranqued."

"Thank God. But we should do it after the handoff. I don't want to deal with lugging him around," says the marshal next to me.

"If you promise to behave, we'll put you in a wheelchair so we don't have to drag you. Sound good?" asks Cormac.

"I'll behave."

The SUV pulls up to the international terminal and Cormac climbs out.

There's a tall man in a dark suit waiting by the entrance who starts walking over to us. He's escorted by two airport security officers.

This must be the Interpol agent.

"I'll tell them to get a wheelchair," says Cormac.

Three minutes later I'm sitting in a wheelchair with my hands in a new set of cuffs, being pushed by an airport security officer and flanked by Inspector Lavois from Interpol and another airport security officer.

The two officers' job is to see me safely onto the plane and secured to my seat next to Lavois.

Lavois's job is to see me all the way to Argentina, have local police sign a document, and then fly back to wherever—likely being one of the last people to see me alive.

A security guard waves a wand around me and then I'm wheeled through the security gate and past the line of people wondering why the man in the wheelchair is handcuffed.

On the other side, an older woman with a doctor's bag is waiting with a huge orderly.

"Looks like nighty night for you," says Lavois in a Belgian accent.

"I have to use the bathroom really bad," I say to the doctor.

"Is there one we can take him to? I also need to give him the injection in a place that I don't think the passengers want to see," says the doctor in a Brooklyn accent.

"This way," says one of the security officers.

They wheel me to a family bathroom.

"Do you want us inside?" asks the officer pushing my chair.

"I think the inspector and Ricardo should be able to handle him. Right?" the doctor says, looking at me.

"Yes," I sigh.

I'm pushed inside and watch in the mirror as the doctor sets her medical kit on the counter and pulls out a bottle and a syringe.

Lavois lowers his head to whisper to me so only I can hear. "You know, I worry every time I go under if I'll ever wake up. Maybe for you it would be better if you didn't."

His words would carry more threat if it weren't for the fact that the doctor prepping the syringe behind him is my mother.

MEDICAL INTERVENTION

Mom jabs the syringe into Lavois's neck. He's falling before he realizes what happened. Savoy catches him and gently lowers him to the floor.

Savoy takes a suit from a backpack and sets it on the counter. Mother removes Lavois's gun and credentials, then takes off his jacket. She finds his keys in a pocket and removes my handcuffs.

"Wear this," she says, handing me a polo shirt from her bag. "You look good in blue."

There's a loud knock on the door.

Mom opens it a crack and asks, "Everything okay?"

"We just got a call about a problem in the other end of the terminal. Are you going to be all right with the prisoner?" asks the airport security officer.

"We gave him a tranquilizer before putting him on the toilet. We'll be fine. It might be a while," she says.

"Your flight boards in twenty minutes," reminds the security officer.

"*Oui*, I have it under control," I say in my best Belgian accent.

"Okay. You can reach us on the radio if you need anything."

Mother shuts the door and turns to me. "What part of Belgium was that? If they'd been Stasi, we'd be dead by now."

"If they were Stasi, that would mean we were time travelers and could get ourselves out of this mess," I fire back.

"Time is something we don't have. We have to get Savoy and our sleeping beauty on the plane. He then needs to check in from Lavois's phone."

I glance at the phone she set on the counter. "Damn it. Security code."

"We could find the number and use a relay to fake it," she says.

"No. If it's not from this one or a clone, Strier will know."

Mom kneels down and slaps Lavois, hard. "You're having a medical emergency. We need to use your phone! What's the passcode?"

He blinks and mumbles, *"Sieben sieben drei."*

"Got that?" asks Mother.

I type it into his phone and the lock screen vanishes.

"You got that, Savoy?" I ask as I scroll through the messages.

"Uh, what language was that?" he replies.

"German. Seven seven three is the passcode." I point to a name. "See Mr. S in the chat? Right before you take off, you need to text him, 'We're taking off. Mr. T is very asleep.' The airplane captain will want to see your credentials."

Mother is leaning over Lavois's passport with a surgical knife and a roll of clear tape, switching its photo to Savoy's. "This should be good enough. I'll come with you to the Jetway and do the talking. You'll need to give him another injection in four hours to keep him sedated."

"There's a stopover in Bogotá, Colombia," I tell Savoy. "You'll have to use a wheelchair to get him off the airplane to avoid questions. Take him to a stall and then use the ticket we'll send you. We want you on the next flight back to the United States."

I can tell from the look on Savoy's face that this is overwhelming.

"You'll be fine. I'd tell you to keep him here, but the captain has already been told you're coming. Okay?"

"Yeah. Fuck these guys," replies Savoy.

"How are we on time?" I ask.

"Strier is probably at his office getting ready to go home. We'll have to take a car back and not the helicopter," she explains.

"Everyone else is good?" I ask.

"Strier's people are watching them. They're pretending not to notice."

"It's going to be tight," I say.

"It always is," Mom agrees.

FOLLOW-THROUGH

Spire: What's the status?

Noncom: Trasker is on plane and on his way. Confirmed with pilot via air traffic control.

Spire: Make sure Argentinians are ready w/ ambulance for his medical emergency on arrival. They'll need to say he's being treated at an undisclosed hospital because of his condition. I want a hand off to Kosgrad as quickly as possible. He needs to keep Trasker alive until told otherwise.

Noncom: Understood. Extradition judge down here is on board. What about Lyon?

Spire: Interpol is fine. Small hit set for UK and Euro press.

Noncom: His people have been making calls to different agencies. His lawyers too.

Spire: Izler with DHS is handling the agency part. We're about to get a search order for the law firms docs for an unrelated matter. That should disrupt them.

Noncom: What about unofficial channels they may go through?

Spire: Discredit KC. Get an ambulance and a deep suicide crew to her house. Do we have the video her bf made with that actress?

Noncom: Yes.

Spire: Can you use it?

Noncom: Yes. Use her face to make a deepfake. It'll be obvious after 24hours, but plausible.

Spire: Have that ready.

Noncom: Okay. This is hitting hard.

Spire: Fuck them. We'll slowly wind down the rest when there's less attention.

KILL SHOT

The doorman to 1 Atlantic Tower grabs the nickel-plated knob and pulls the door open for me as I get out of the SUV.

I step inside the lobby, and the man with the thin mustache glances down at his screen and taps a button. The security guard, standing against a white marble wall with hundreds of yellow roses artfully sticking out, looks at me, then returns his gaze to the street outside.

"Mr. Cavendish?" says the desk clerk.

"That's me," I reply.

"Elevator six on your left. That will take you to the penthouse. I'll let him know you're coming," he says, picking up the phone.

My pulse speeds up as he touches a button on the phone.

He taps his fingers while waiting for someone to pick up, then waves me on. "Please go ahead."

"Thank you," I reply and walk to the bank of elevators. The nape of my neck is burning.

We were able to get into Strier's guest-reservation system, but was that enough? Does he know I'm coming?

What happens when I step off the elevator? Will he have men ready to kill me?

Strier sees every angle . . . almost.

When I approached him at the restaurant, I had a suspicion about a weakness.

He appeared to confirm it for me . . . but that could be another layer of deceit.

He's a puppet master who gets to see the stage and the audience, but there's one point of view he doesn't have. You only get it from experience. It's why men like him make the same mistakes over and over and people like me pay for them.

Strier doesn't know what it's like to see the world through the eyes of a puppet.

The elevator doors open into the foyer of the penthouse. Glass walls stretch twenty feet from floor to ceiling, overlooking a view of the tops of skyscrapers emerging from a cloudy mist.

Strier has his back turned. He's on the balcony talking into his phone, drinking from a whiskey glass as he stares out at the skyline.

I walk through the living room and through the glass door.

"Great talking to you, Alice. Ask Frank when he wants to go fishing again. I have a new lodge in New Zealand on a trout stream that's out of this world."

Strier doesn't see me until I lean against the railing across from him.

A flash of confusion crosses his face.

Did somebody fuck up? he's wondering. *Was Trasker* supposed *to be here?*

His thumb moves toward the screen of his phone.

"Drop it or I toss you over the side of the building," I warn him.

Strier cautiously places the phone on the ledge as he studies me, trying to calculate whether I'm bluffing.

"You don't make it out of this building alive," he says.

"The moment I see someone come through that doorway, you're dead. So we'll be even."

Strier turns away from me and faces the concrete-and-metal structures that fade away into the fog. No doubt wishing he had someone on a nearby balcony ready to take a kill shot.

Strier's confidence came from his ability to throw an infinite number of people and resources at a problem.

For every person on my security team in Manhattan, he had five more people watching. Strier walked around unworried because he could control everything. That sense of control is his weakness.

"Who is your inside man?" I ask.

"I genuinely don't know. You should have asked Hassad before he got away."

"I'm sure our paths will cross."

Strier laughs. "He's not going to be crossing paths with anyone. Neither will you. You should walk away. Killing me will only make it worse. You'll be a fugitive in this country and your friends accomplices. It's a dead end for you. But you can't see that."

"There's one little detail *you're* not seeing."

"Indulge me," he says as he crosses his arms.

"I can kill you and get away with it. You gave me an alibi. As far as anyone knows, I'm still on that plane to Argentina. You used your connections to put me there. I can't be here and there at the same time."

He shrugs. "There may be a few questions when the wrong person shows up in Buenos Aires and my contacts realize that. Either way, the Interpol order will still stand. You're in a bit of a bind."

I take my gun from my hidden holster and set it on the railing and take out my phone. I tap on the screen for a moment, keeping a watch on him, then set it down.

Ten seconds later, his phone buzzes. Strier glances toward it.

"Don't touch. That's probably the Chinese embassy saying they can have a car to you in an hour unless you can make it there yourself."

The phone buzzes again.

"A slower response. That's your Russian contact, offering asylum too," I tell him.

Strier rolls his eyes. "This is absurd. So what? You faked my number and texted the station chiefs at their embassies? This is rookie psyops.

Are you going to drug me and put me in a car like in some Tom Cruise movie?"

"I think you're going to want to get into one of those cars when you hear the next part." I hold up the phone in my hand. "This isn't my phone. *It's yours.* We've had it for the last several hours, unlocked and decrypted. While we've been talking, your data's been uploaded—including your text messages with your inside man at Interpol. I don't think anyone is going to try to enforce my extradition after they see that.

"As far as the rest, you'll just have to wait and see. Leak by leak, you're going to be destroyed. It doesn't matter what influence you had when you woke up this morning. Nobody is going to lift a finger to help you, because they don't know if their name is going to be the next one to get blasted across the news. It'll be a miracle if you're still alive by tomorrow. If you decide to jump, you might get lucky and land on me when I exit the building . . . if you time it right."

Strier's face goes pale as he puts it all together. "The waitress at the restaurant . . ." he mumbles.

I don't give him the satisfaction of an answer and instead leave him alone on the balcony.

AFTERBURN

"Was it suicide?" Kylie asks me as I walk across the tarmac with her and Morena toward the new Sparrow prototype.

The aircraft gleams in the Mojave sun, looking like an unearthly twin of the one that was lost.

"Hard to say. It was indirect suicide at the very least. You can only hold so many debts before people decide the less risky choice is to just kill you. But don't underestimate the personal shame. Strier was used to having people kiss his ass, from presidents to other billionaires. Finding yourself in a tiny cell is a huge update."

"Yeah, but what do you think?"

"My guess is that someone made it easy for someone else to pull it off."

I walk over to the Sparrow and stand under the wingtip, admiring the way the smooth curves fold into sharp edges.

"Are you going ahead with the Pentagon request?" I ask.

"I've thought about it. I'm not sure if I want to become a defense contractor. But is it arrogant to say I'm even more worried about who might get the contract in our place? Strausman is a good guy, but he's got a board of directors to answer to . . ."

"Plus the fact that sixty percent of his company is actually owned by Strier-controlled entities," Morena points out.

"Well, he's dead," says Kylie.

"I wouldn't be too comfortable with the people rushing in to fill the void he created. We only know who his direct connections were. A lot of other people were involved but not implicated. I think it would be a good idea if you did it. I'd feel safer," I tell her.

"Yeah. We'll see. I want to take it step-by-step and not wake up one day hating myself."

"Understandable," I say.

"And you should stick around," she tells me.

"We'll see. We'll see."

We still haven't found the mole or moles. Sophia has gone through an entire screening of all employees and even brought in an outside polygraph expert to look for discrepancies. We've uncovered some petty theft, a handful of affairs, and much more drug use than Sophia and I were expecting. But so far, no suspect.

I've decided to sit down with each person myself. It's time-consuming, but I hope that if I meet them all face-to-face, I'll see something.

EXIT INTERVIEW

Artem Tkachev sits across from me in the conference room, his arms folded as he looks at me with pity. He's my last interview, and he knows it hasn't been going well.

"You have my sympathy. I almost wish I was the spy you are looking for," he says.

I loosen the collar on my sweat-stained dress shirt and lean back in my chair, staring up at the ceiling.

"I know it's not you. Hell, if there's anyone I'm convinced completely about, it's you." I point to the stacks of boxes containing personnel files. "Everyone else is the problem. I keep looking for that little crack that could have been wedged open. The personality traits of someone who's primed to turn on their employer."

The biggest such trait is narcissism. It doesn't always look like that on the surface, but it lies beneath the surface.

Meanwhile, people have confessed some pretty crazy things to me. Two of them I advised to get lawyers.

I've been looking for either a real version of my "Chris" persona—someone with an opportunity to cheat who chose that route because of financial pressure—or someone who imagines themselves as a mastermind watching everyone stumble around them.

That's what Robert Hanssen was. On the surface, he was a dedicated FBI counterintelligence agent tasked with finding spies. In reality, he was a double agent supplying information to the Russians. Not because he liked their politics, but to prove that he could. It was an addiction for him. His financial gains should have been noteworthy, but they weren't hugely ostentatious because it wasn't about the money.

Hassad, on the other hand, built an entire industrial espionage ring because it made him money. A lot of money. We're still finding bank accounts and crypto wallets attached to the missing DHS traitor.

Besides the home in Santa Clarita, he had a mansion in Las Vegas that he shared with two strippers. He was living the good life until I pistol-whipped him in his living room.

FBI agents Morrel and Broadhurst have also gone through the backgrounds of everyone here and even checked the bank records of extra-suspicious people. They came up empty as well.

"What is the current theory?" asks Tkachev.

I picked him to interview last because I like the guy and really just wanted to get his take on things. He's the one person I know who actually did steal industrial secrets—in his case, from Russia and for justifiable reasons.

"Broadhurst says that we may have had a temporary data leak. That could have compromised other things like our communications systems. Maybe. I know they had a huge data loss when I was here."

"That was rather scary," says Tkachev. "People here were afraid that we'd lost years of work. Thankfully it had all been backed up remotely."

"Yeah. All it takes is one USB thumb drive loaded with spyware and you can own a system."

With an unwitting insider, it would actually be easier than what we had to go through to get access to Strier's phone.

That required my mother watching his key presses as he unlocked it, and then some clever sleight of hand to switch it out on the restaurant table.

I was convinced he would know what was up when he looked up to yell at her.

He didn't. He was too engaged in one-upping me to even see her. She was hardly even a distraction.

And that was his weakness.

"I pull the strings of the people who pull your strings," I say out loud.

"What's that? It sounds like something my superiors would have said," Tkachev observes.

"Close to it. Strier said it to me. But it's why he didn't see my mother coming or what we were going to do next. If all you know are strings, you're helpless without puppets. He was always at the top and never in the trenches. One by one, all his many skills failed him. He didn't see something obvious in front of him."

"And that was his downfall," says Tkachev.

"But it's mine too. I don't see our spy because I'm like Strier in some way."

"Well, in hindsight I'm sure Strier regrets not paying more attention. You at least still have time to adapt. The past is the past, but there's still opportunity," he tells me.

"Perhaps." My mind starts to wander. I feel the imaginary copy of *The Time Machine* in my pocket.

"Would you excuse me? I'm going to walk over to the other hangar to look at something," I explain as I get up.

MIND PALACE

Walking through a memory palace isn't anything like what I've seen in movies and television. It might be because I'm doing it all wrong, or the people who write those visual stories feel the need to make it overly elaborate.

In my case, it starts with opening a book and revisiting the setting in the first few pages.

I can do this while lying still in bed or driving. Either way, it's not like I jump into some dynamic environment filled with bustling crowds and loud noises.

It's quiet. I see only what I direct my attention at. This means I have to look at how one thing is connected to something else and pay attention to the empty spaces in between. They're not really empty; I just have to remember the details.

Technically, the memory technique I use is a form of the method of loci. It's assigning things to physical spaces. I use locations in books because they're easy for me to remember and store away for later.

The most famous practitioner of the method of loci was Simonides of Ceos—a Greek poet and orator known for his encyclopedic recall.

Simonides was once called upon to do an oration at a banquet but got called outside to speak to a messenger. While he was on the street, the building he'd been in collapsed.

As horribly mangled bodies were pulled from the wreckage, rescuers and family members were at a loss at determining the identities of the bodies. In a society where funeral rites can vary from family to family, this presented an existential crisis on top of the tragedy.

Thankfully for the family members, the lone survivor, Simonides, had used the method of loci to remember the seating position of everyone at the banquet. He was then able to name each victim by the location of their body in the rubble.

I'm no Simonides. I squirrel away little bits of information that stand out and people who are of interest to me. While the process gives me a better recall of events and locations than I would have otherwise, I'm not some kind of prodigy who can turn back a VHS tape in his head and play back moments of my life.

I have to walk around, recall details, and try hard not to invent anything. If you push your mind too much, it will fill in the gaps with false information. This is how gaslighting works and how false confessions and accusations are forced.

In the Soviet Union they had a near 100 percent conviction rate because everyone confessed. The party leaders assumed this was proof of their superior ideology; the reality was that it was a system designed to convince the innocent of their guilt by using their own mind as an interrogator. People became convinced they did things they couldn't have.

A form of this happened in the United States when therapists and law-enforcement officers convinced of satanic influence guided young children into describing impossible demonic rituals they had become convinced they'd been subjected to. They even coerced adults into admitting guilt for things they had no recollection of prior to interrogation.

Memory is tricky. In my experience, most of the hypnotherapists I've met who practice memory recall are either charlatans or delusional.

When I step into the pages I've hidden my memories in, I constantly remind myself that not everything I see is true or even what I actually experienced.

Using my memory palace, I survey the hangar's interior and try to place everything where it was that night the Sparrow exploded. Photos and videos of the event are available, but I want to remember it for myself and then check against the visual record to get a baseline of how much I remember.

I see the high-top tables appear. Did they have blue or gray coverings? The ones in my memory palace are blue, but I don't remember that much blue.

Gray and blue?

I take out my phone and check a photo.

Yes. Blue and gray alternating table covers.

I see the DJ booth and the three separate bars.

I walk by the space on the west side of the hangar where the longest bar was located.

Did any faces stand out?

None especially.

Did I see anything that looked odd or suspicious beforehand?

No.

There were little things I noticed and even random objects I took from tables, like a napkin with an email address tossed aside by a woman in a green dress who was not as impressed by the man talking to her as he was by himself.

There was a book of matches, which seemed out of place in the smoke-free hangar. But nothing to raise a red flag.

What else?

I reach into my empty pocket and take out the mental image of a pen I found.

There was writing on it . . .

What did it say?

Axwell Avionics.

A strobe light flashes in my mind. Hassad's man, Kevin MacLaughtery, a.k.a. Zach Matok, handed me a pen with Axwell Avionics written on the side when he wanted a signature on the document declaring the scrapped alloy piece wasn't stolen.

Were those pens in wide circulation? I don't know.

It would be a pretty dumb thing to hand out something like that to everyone he did business with.

Or would it?

Part of the brilliance of Hassad's operation was that it didn't trace back to him. And MacLaughtery had a legitimate reason behind every purchase he made.

If someone said they'd met with MacLaughtery, the pen would be inconsequential proof. MacLaughtery's strategy wasn't to run from any alleged connection but to prove that as far as he knew, the purchases were legitimate.

The only person the pen could incriminate was the person who sold the stolen technology to MacLaughtery to begin with. That is, if they even realized it was a crime.

The pen I found was carelessly left on a table. Perhaps all it indicates is that someone met with MacLaughtery and got a pen.

In my latest round of interviews, I asked about Hassad and MacLaughtery.

Several people knew MacLaughtery's alias—he was someone they'd seen around. None of them had ever been approached by him to do anything illegal. None knew who Hassad was.

I walk around the hangar, trying to see if there are any more clues to be found in my memory.

Although I have interviewed all the employees at Wind Aerospace, I haven't had a chance to talk to the other half of the audience who were guests that night.

Being a guest didn't mean that a person had access to the kind of information that was used to destroy the Sparrow. At most it suggested some relationship, either personal or professional, to what was going on. I'm walking in circles now. I should be wandering through *The Time Machine*, recalling the items I placed inside there.

Okay.

I set myself in the Time Traveller's study. What do I see? Who do I see? What gives me an emotional reaction?

I remember seeing Lopez, one of the security team members, talking to the bartender. I made note of this and placed him in a tiny bar by the fireplace.

There were other people there too. I recall a couple having an inaudible argument. I remember this because I can see the cartoon bubbles of angry words.

Where was everyone when the Sparrow exploded? I remember who was closest to me a few minutes before. But they weren't anywhere near afterward.

In retrospect, that timing seems . . . suspicious.

OVERSTEP

He sits down across from me in a booth in a little diner at the far end of a stretch of highway in a small town twenty miles from Mojave Spaceport.

He gives me a friendly grin as I shake his hand. He's trying to hide his fear.

"How's it going, Brad? This place a regular for you?"

"I thought I'd try something new."

Actually, I didn't want to have this conversation at Wind Aerospace or his home.

"Well, it's great to have a chance to talk to you."

"I'm actually surprised you came," I tell him.

"Surprised, why? Did you think I was too busy?" There's a slight hesitation in his voice.

"Because this conversation is going to be unpleasant."

"Why? What happened? Is Kylie okay?" he asks anxiously.

"This is how it works. You give me honest and direct answers. If I believe you're telling me the truth, you'll be alive tomorrow. If I don't, you won't make it to midnight." I sit back and watch his reaction.

He looks to the waitress at the far end of the diner. I paid her to keep this section empty.

Will he scream to her for help?

I shake my head. "Perhaps I haven't made a suitable impression upon you. This is a no-win situation."

"I don't understand," he stammers.

"Did you know they were going to blow up the Sparrow and try to kill Kylie?"

"I have no idea—" he begins.

I've lost my patience. I grab his wrist and squeeze it hard as I pull him over the table until his face is inches from mine.

"Feel the piece of metal against your kneecap? That's my Glock. It's got a six-pound trigger pull. Right now, I have ninety ounces of pressure on it. When I get to ninety-six, your knee is going to be splattered over the back of the booth and I'm going to pay the bill and walk away while you bleed to death."

"Honest to God, Brad," he whines.

I can see the tears in his eyes. I can smell his fear.

"Ninety-one ounces . . ."

"I don't know anything," he sobs.

"Ninety-two ounces."

His chest heaves as he starts to hyperventilate. "I didn't know. I didn't know."

"Then why did you leave the viewing area?"

"I didn't. I was near you! We talked. Remember?"

"I remember you not being there when the explosion happened. I remember Kylie's mother being all the way at the back of the hangar after you said something to her."

"That's not what happened," insists Evan Fimley, Kylie's stepfather.

"Ninety-three ounces."

"I didn't know. I had a bad feeling. That's all."

I shake my head.

"They wanted specs. I had no idea what they were going to do with them. It was nothing!"

"You saved yourself."

"I just . . . Fuck it." He breaks eye contact and looks out the window. "I don't have to talk to you. This is fucking theater."

"Ninety-four ounces."

Something comes over Fimley now. The fear is replaced with rage. "Fine, you fucker. I didn't know. But I didn't fucking care! Do you know how many times I offered to help that little bitch? Do you know how many times she shot me down? Her fucking lackeys laughing at me behind their backs because they think I'm some kind of has-been? Fuck them! Fuck all of you! I wish that tank had been full and that overbuilt piece of shit she copied from the Russians killed *all* you assholes. I didn't know, but I prayed it would happen," he snarls.

"The keycards Kylie kept losing? The computer problems?"

"That arrogant bitch leaves her laptop open at our house. Anyone could fucking do whatever they wanted."

"I guess she thought she was safe there."

"I guess fucking not."

"Last question. The airport. That was you?"

"What airport?"

"Ninety-five ounces."

"I don't know what you're talking about. I had nothing to do with that. You know I didn't have access to her schedule after your Nazis took over."

"Earlier that night Kylie's mother texted you and said she was going over to Kylie's house to say goodbye. A minute later you texted someone, 'Tonight.' Who was that?"

"I don't know," Fimley whines.

"Ninety-six ounces."

He opens his mouth to say, "You're so fucking full of . . ."

Bang!

I can feel the warm blood from his shattered knee spray over my hand.

Fimley lets out a scream, finally getting the waitress's attention. I get up from the table and wipe the blood from my hand, then drop the soaked napkin onto the paper placemat.

Fimley is in shock, face drained of color. He's whimpering, but that will stop when he loses consciousness.

I toss the gun on the seat and walk out of the diner.

Flashing blue lights fill the parking lot as a sheriff's deputy pulls up to the scene in his cruiser. A stocky young man gets out and runs up to me.

"Did it happen?" he asks.

"It happened," I reply.

"What a dumb son of a bitch. Pulling a gun on you."

In the distance, an ambulance siren wails. I'm not sure if it's going to make it in time.

I don't care.

Pulling the trigger was easy. The hardest thing I'll have to do tonight is tell Kylie that it was her own stepfather who betrayed her.

Then I'll have to tell her mother.

I should have suspected Evan when it first went to hell. It had to be someone close.

I picked up Kylie's distance from him as a personality clash. Normal stepdaughter stuff. But she knew she didn't trust him.

She was afraid to say anything because she wanted to keep her mother happy.

It was in front of me, but I chose to ignore it, hesitant to scrutinize the distance between them because I was afraid it might feel too familiar.

It would have been better if I had put a bullet in Evan Fimley's head, but even I don't have that kind of pull around here.

DARK CHANNEL

The barren branch doesn't realize that it has no leaves, yet it bends and swings in the desert wind as if it did. I watch the hypnotic sway of the tree's sparse limbs backlit by the bright white lights of the emergency room entrance and wonder if I went too far.

The rational part of me says that I let my emotions get the better of me. The other part . . . let's be honest . . . the father in me, says I didn't go far enough.

What flashed before my eyes the moment I pulled the trigger wasn't what Evan Fimley almost did to Kylie. It was what he casually threw away.

He used Kylie and her mother for his personal gain. Part of it was financial, part of it was revenge for making him feel like a small man.

Fimley had been a would-be entrepreneur his whole life. From half-baked internet businesses in the 1990s to crypto speculation, he was always trying to scheme his way to success.

He didn't see Kylie as a mentee, someone to whom he could offer the gift of life balance. She was an opportunity. Fimley was willing to sell her out little by little until he was complicit in her attempted assassination.

Maybe it started with selling minor bits of information. Even an honest person can get caught up in "consulting" as a side job and find themselves revealing trade secrets to competitors or, even worse, speaking in front of a classroom in Beijing filled with CCP-connected industrialists.

But at some point, you have to realize you went too far.

Evan Fimley passed that point a long time ago. From hacking Kylie's computer when she visited her mother to sending her whereabouts to Strier.

Telling Kylie about what he did was next on my list before the FBI came to speak to him. I didn't really process the order of events in my head and now find myself sitting in the parking lot trying to figure out the right words to explain why I shot her stepfather.

I shot him because of my anger for what he could have had and what I'd lost.

Whatever fortune he might have made is nothing compared to the relationship he could have had with his stepdaughter.

I shot him because I was jealous.

I'm jarred by the sound of tapping on my window and see Kylie standing there.

A rare sense of panic washes over me as I feel like I've been caught in some embarrassing act.

She walks around the SUV, opens the door, and drops into the passenger seat.

I stare at the swaying branch, unable to make eye contact.

She stares straight ahead too. I can see the clench in her jaw she gets when she's trying to process something emotionally.

"Evan just told us quite the story," she replies. "He says you shot him in the leg in cold blood."

I respect her enough to tell the truth. I also trust her to do the right thing with it, whatever that may be.

I start to speak. "I—"

She cuts me off. "Don't tell me. If I'm on the stand in a civil suit or a criminal case, I don't want to have to lie. I will. But I'd rather not. So let's keep it simple."

I nod hesitantly.

"I'm guessing he was our mole. I'm never going to forgive myself for being so stupid."

"It's not that—"

She cuts me off again. "I'm still talking. You have your burdens. I have mine. I still see Benoit's face when I go to sleep at night. The other bodies under tarps. Not that it will make me feel any better, but did Evan have anything to do with the shootout at the airport?"

For some reason, the words are hard to say. I take a slow breath. "Evan texted your mom to find out when we were leaving. He passed that on to Strier's people."

Her jaw clenches even tighter. I see her eyes start to well up.

"Did he hate me that much?"

"It wasn't about you. He never really saw you. You were just part of a scheme. Your mother too."

"I should have—"

It's my turn to cut her off. "Don't go there. You can't live your life worried that the people closest to you might betray you at any moment. You have to be vulnerable sometimes. Even if it means . . ."

"You should have aimed a foot higher," she says. "Right now, my mother is in there doting over him. Over that asshole."

"I'll tell her."

"No. I'll do that. After I do—if I can't keep her away from him—he won't make it through the night."

"I can see that he doesn't," I offer out of nowhere, feeling a surge of ice in my veins.

She shakes her head, taking me at my word. "No. It's not worth it. Will there be a problem over what happened?"

"One of the men who died in the control tower had a wife who was a deputy. The sheriff and I have an understanding."

"Good. That's one less complication."

"And I'm sorry for it."

"Shut up. The only direction is forward. The only way I'm going to ever feel anything other than regret is if we clean this up."

"I think Evan's kneecap was the last loose end."

Kylie stares at me intensely. "You don't see it. Or rather you're avoiding it."

"Is there someone else?"

"Someone or something. That network Strier, Wagner, and the Drakos used for commerce? Dark Channel? I've been looking into it. It's used for everything from drugs and assassination to sex trafficking. The Russians were paying mercenaries to kill Ukrainian citizens with it. That's how Strier paid for the hit on our people," she explains.

"It's decentralized. Law enforcement around the world have been trying to shut it down. They haven't had any success," I tell her.

"All I know is some asshole is collecting eight percent blood money on every transaction. Maybe it's time he gets shut down."

"Things will get messy."

"Things got messy. I told you I was serious about going to war. I'm not going to stop until we get every bastard that had something to do with the deaths of our people. Are you in?"

"And here I was thinking you were going to fire me for shooting your stepfather."

"Fuck him," she snaps.

"This isn't the way to deal with loss."

"If I wanted a shrink, I'd hire one. I hired you because I know exactly what you are. Are you with me on this?"

There's a fire in her eyes I've never seen before. But I recognize it. It's the burning rage I glimpse in the mirror every day.

I should be guiding her toward closure. I should tell her to move on with her life.

But that's not who she is.

It's not who I am.

"I'm in," I reply. "When do you want to start?"

"Tonight. After I tell my mother she has to divorce that asshole."

LOST WORLD

"Long time no see," says my ex-wife via video call.

"I know. It's been a while."

"It's been quite eventful for you. I can't watch the news without seeing you come up," she says.

"Yeah. I used to keep a lower profile. So much for that. How's Mark?"

"Watching football in the other room with Rachel."

Her husband has a daughter from a previous marriage. He dotes on her nonstop, as does Kathy. I wish Kylie had had that kind of relationship with her stepfather.

"Tell him I said hello."

"What did you want to talk about?" she asks.

"At some point about Jason. But I'm not ready for that. I want to ask a favor. I want to know if you still have something that belonged to him."

"What's that?"

"An old paperback book. Sir Arthur Conan Doyle's *The Lost World*."

"I still have some of the books he left behind when he went to college. I'll look for it."

"Thank you. It would mean a lot."

There are a lot of memories in that book. Some of them real good ones.

ABOUT THE AUTHOR

Andrew Mayne is the Amazon Charts and *Wall Street Journal* bestselling author of *The Girl Beneath the Sea, Black Coral, Sea Storm,* and *Sea Castle* in his Underwater Investigation Unit series; *The Naturalist, Looking Glass, Murder Theory,* and *Dark Pattern* in the Theo Cray series; and *Angel Killer, Name of the Devil,* and the Edgar Award–nominated *Black Fall* in his Jessica Blackwood series. He was the star of A&E's *Don't Trust Andrew Mayne* and swam with great white sharks using an underwater stealth suit he designed for the Shark Week special *Andrew Mayne: Ghost Diver.* He currently works on creative applications for artificial intelligence and as the science communicator for OpenAI, the creators of ChatGPT.

Printed in Great Britain
by Amazon

33959935R00179